MURDER IN MARIPOSA BAY

A Bella Kowalski Mystery
set on California's Central Coast

Sue McGinty

—2013—

This is a work of fiction. The characters and story live only in the writer's imagination. Any errors are mine alone.

Butterfly image used under license from www.Istock.com

ISBN: 1482707837

ISBN-13: 9781482707830

Acknowledgements

For Novel Idea—you are so much more than a critique group.

Thanks to Beverly McGinty, Alice Way, Barbara Wolcott and Diane Broyles for reading early drafts and making spot-on suggestions. Thanks also to Carroll McKibbin, who found the words when I couldn't.

A special flourish of the writer's quill to my FBI friend—what you told me in Vegas about wearing a wire did not stay in Vegas. Instead, it found its way into Bella's story.

The cover opens a window into the heart of the book. Thanks to Pat Siemer for stunning photos on short notice, and to Liam Heckman for crafting them into a work of art. Also to Joe Laurenzi, Manager, Los Osos Library, for the author photo.

As always, a tip of this writer's hat to Jerry Douglas Smith, 2013-2014 Poet Laureate of San Luis Obispo County.

Couldn't have done it without you all!

Prolog

Sunday, April 11th, 2010, midmorning

The man once known as Steve Pizniak stood by the campground office, Camel pinched between thumb and index finger, job app tucked into jacket pocket. His gaze slid to a guy in a nearby lawn chair. Pizniak sucked in a puff and exhaled, squinting through the smoky haze.

Oh, Christ. It can't be.

He shoved the cigarette into the corner of his mouth and tugged down the bill of his Detroit Tigers cap—the one thing he'd kept from his past—and chanced another look. The guy was older and heavier now (*hell, weren't we all?*) but he had the same world-weary eyes. He was reading a newspaper folded to highlight the lead story, a local sewer issue that had dragged on since the Reagan administration.

A dagger of fear plunged into Pizniak's gut. There had to be a connection between this guy and the Cadillac Escalade that had been following him. Had his past caught up with him—here in this remote place on California's Central Coast? They promised a few strokes of the computer would give him a new life. Just goes to show—you can't trust those bastards.

Now he'd have to quit his job at the Inn, then he and his wife would do another disappearing act to god-knows-where. He'd told her his story, though he wasn't supposed to, and she'd go along with the new plan.

Pizniak yanked the application for campground handyman from his pocket, ripped it in two and deposited it in the recycle bin, then ground his cigarette into the dirt with his boot heel. He started to tug the cap even lower over his eyes, then thought better of it and stuffed it in the trash under a paper bag. Head down, eyes averted, he hurried to his pickup.

Because his eyes were focused elsewhere, the man once known as Steve Pizniak didn't notice the Escalade parked near the restroom, didn't observe the man behind the wheel put a cell phone to his ear, didn't hear the call that would end his life.

1

Sunday, April 11th, early evening

Who would have thought an event that turned our world upside down would begin with a rite gone wrong?

Each year around our anniversary, my husband and I make a date with each other that we call, "Mike and Bella's Romantic Sleepover." First, we camp at the Mariposa Bay State Park for one night. Making love in a sleeping bag with people a stones-throw away may be exciting, but it's hard on fifty-year-old hips. So, the next evening, hoping our neighbors don't have itchy fingers, we stow our gear and bikes in the tent, drive our old Subaru down the road that parallels the park, check into the Mariposa Inn and indulge in a wildly extravagant dinner. Dessert is a romantic tryst in one of Inn's luxurious rooms.

Except this year we decided to walk. Bad idea.

For the past day and a half, the weather had been spring-perfect, the kiss of sun on our faces and arms, a light breeze blowing in from the bay. We spent most of our time in lawn chairs, where Mike finally caught up with his newspaper reading. I alternately napped and devoured a Louise Penny mystery novel.

Now all that had changed; bone-numbing Central Coast drizzle clung to my skinny frame like plastic wrap to a wet chicken.

The damp spot between my shoulder blades from my backpack did not bode well for the dress and heels nestled inside next to the champagne. "Mike, I don't think this is such a good idea after all."

"Don't forget this hare-brained hike was your idea, Bella." My husband gave me the grin I fell in love with, the one that lightened his gray eyes and erased the pale worry lines from his sun-browned face.

The grin remained, but his eyes darkened with concern, a reminder that this year we especially needed the break. My mother, suffering from cancer, had moved here from Detroit so I could care for her. It was either move her here or head back to Detroit, impossible with my job as obituary editor at the *Central Coast Chronicle* and Mike's septic service business. Mom and I hoped to use this time to mend our strained relationship.

Having Mom here had been hard on all of us. She is often difficult, rarely seeing the bright side of any issue. Although, God love her, she now had good reason for her bad attitude.

Mike and I definitely needed time alone. And what better place to spend a goodly portion of it than tucked into one of the Inn's super-king-sized beds?

A car horn blasted. "Watch out!" Mike said, almost shoving me into the gully that bordered the narrow road. A hulking SUV bore down on us like a charging bull. The black Escalade barely slowed as it swerved onto the bank on the bay-side of the road. All I saw were a pair of hands on the wheel. The vehicle disappeared into the night.

My husband raised his middle finger. "*Dupek*!"

While Mike continued to comment in Polish on the driver's anatomy, I did a mental forehead-smack. A couple of any age, but especially in their fifties, one of whom wore thick glasses (me), and the other of whom has a heart condition, had no business walking a narrow winding road in fog soup.

I charged ahead of him, calling over my shoulder. "Let's walk single file."

"Whatever you say, Sister," he taunted. I used to be a nun, so when he wants to remind me not to be bossy, he calls me "Sister." Most people assume nuns are bossy and often they're right.

Even though I've been "out" for years, I still struggle with the complexities of the husband-wife relationship. But a smart-alec comeback was far from my mind at the moment. I just wanted to get to our destination in one piece. If I'd been bossy, too bad.

We trudged along for what seemed like an eternity. At least there were no more Escalades. No more anything. Or anyone.

Mike caught up to me. "Almost there," he said, slightly out of breath.

"Well thank goodness for…" Movement caught my eye, no more than a shadow in the eucalyptus grove known as the Wandering Nun, which borders the south end of the Inn. Locals claim that a black-clad woman, flame-colored hair covered by her dark veil, patrols the grove's narrow path, protecting this sanctuary of the Great Blue Heron. So pervasive is the legend that the Inn has named their restaurant after her.

I shivered as though someone had walked on my grave.

* * * * *

Steve Pizniak flicked the ash off his cigarette onto the path. He needed to get back to his present job at the Inn's reception desk. He heard voices from the road and peered through the trees. *Oh, no.* The guy he recognized at the campground this morning, accompanied by a woman, heading that way. He briefly considered not finishing his shift. Impossible. Management paid him in cash and tomorrow was payday. He needed get-out-of-town money.

* * * * *

Hearing another disturbance in the grove, I stopped and turned. "Mike?"

"What?"

I pointed toward the sound. "Something's in there. Do you suppose it's the Wandering Nun?"

"If so, she's a smoker. See that red glow through the trees?"

Minutes later we approached the Mariposa Inn with its signature butterfly sign swaying in the evening breeze. The hotel itself consisted of a group of 1970's two-story modern buildings painted sandy beige. White trim on the stairways and around windows and doors gave the place a faux Cape Cod look. Typical California eclectic, yet somehow it worked.

Upon entering the parking lot I glanced at the gardens, noting signs of neglect. The Inn had always prided itself on showcase grounds and employed a host of gardeners to keep them that way. Even the staunch English lavender seemed a bit down in the mouth, as did the Australian fern. I glanced up. Outside lighting imparted a gray cast to the buildings' white trim.

Perhaps the rumors were true; the Inn was in financial trouble.

"Might as well enjoy this while we can," Mike remarked, obviously thinking the same thing.

"If this is our last hurrah, so be it." I grabbed his arm. "Come on, let's register. I'm freezing. The hot tub is calling my name." We always book room 221, which features an in-room hot tub and a fireplace. It has no view of the bay, but so what? There's a gorgeous vista of the bay and open ocean from our windmill home in Los Lobos, a mile to the south.

A separate building announcing "Reception" housed the check-in area, restaurant and bar. Here the California modern motif became more apparent in the generous use of fieldstone and glass. We passed the circular fountain in the courtyard. Green slime floated in the water.

Pale yellow wallpaper and lots of brass gave the reception area a cheery look, even if the brass did need an application of spit and polish. The foyer was so dimly lit Mike muttered, "What are they trying to do, save electricity?"

"Shh, they'll hear us." I needn't have bothered; no welcoming body with a cheery smile stood behind the reception desk. Mike gave a sigh of exasperation and punched the bell on the counter.

"One moment." A man in his mid-fifties materialized from an adjacent room. He stood before us, separated by the counter. "Do you have a reservation?" he inquired, hands poised over the computer keyboard. He smelled smoky.

Mike froze. "Steve?" he began, as though recognizing him. The clerk's dark eyes flickered and he put a finger to his lips. The briefest of gestures, but I caught it.

"Sorry, my mistake," Mike muttered. He turned and walked away, head down.

What was that all about?

I'd find out later. Right now, nothing was going to deter me from that hot tub. I stepped forward. "Room 221. Kowalski. Mike and Bella." The man nodded, fixing all his attention on the monitor. My husband continued to study his shoes as though waiting for them to sprout wings and fly him away.

Sounds of tapping keys filled the silence. Mike's behavior was not unusual, I decided. He's often abrupt with strangers, part of the ex-cop persona.

I felt a tug on my sleeve as I fished for my credit card. Ignoring the clerk, Mike peeled me over to a table that held a silver urn. I caught a glimpse of myself in its reflection, recoiling at brownish circles almost the same color as my eyes showing beneath my specs. I needed a good night's sleep in a real bed.

Mike put his free hand on the pot. "I don't think this a good idea, Bella. Coffee's not even hot. Christ, they used to set out free wine and cheese at Happy Hour."

I glanced over my shoulder. Head still down, the man waited for us to finish our conversation. He was about Mike's age and build, with thinning hair and shadowy jowls.

I turned back to my husband. "Do you know that guy?"

"Um, I thought so, but I was mistaken. Let's cancel."

Cancel? Again, I thought about the hot tub, the fireplace and the king-sized bed waiting in our room. I thought about the split of champagne in my backpack. I thought about the empty parking lot, which meant lots of privacy. With Mom in the house, we hadn't had much of that lately.

So desperate were we to get away that we'd considered a drive up the coast to Punto Solitario and a funky old motel we passed on a recent day trip. The place had been almost deserted, just what we were looking for. Because of Mom's illness, we had to postpone those plans, staying close by in case she needed us in a hurry.

I grabbed the front of Mike's jacket with both hands and gave him what I hoped was my best seductive look. "Think about it, our own private hotel, and much better than Punto Solitario. Go admire the wallpaper or something. I'll pay for the room."

Not giving him a chance to argue, I pulled a credit card from my wallet and marched toward the counter.

* * * * *

"There you go, Ma'am." The desk clerk returned my card. "Have a pleasant stay," he said, avoiding my eyes.

"Thanks." I half-turned and pointed across the lobby toward the shuttered doors of The Wandering Nun restaurant. "What time do they open? We're so looking forward to dinner there."

The man shrugged. "Restaurant's closed."

"*Permanently*?"

He shrugged again, a "who knows?" gesture.

2

Monday, April 12th, the witching hour

I sat up in bed, checked the bedside clock, yanked the down comforter up to my neck and took a deep breath to calm my pounding heart. What is there about sudden sounds in the night? *There it was again. The sound of an engine.*

In a time-honored ritual of wives everywhere, I shook my husband. "What's that noise?" He groaned and turned over. *Hopeless.* Stopping only to throw on the complimentary bathrobe, I stumbled to the door and cracked it open, chilled by a sharp wind. Nevertheless, curiosity drove me outside onto the small portico. I peered around the corner and back to the left.

It couldn't be. A black Escalade sat with its door open in front of the reception building. A tall dark figure darted from the Wandering Nun grove, slid into the car and slammed the door. The SUV shot from the parking lot and melted into the darkness. As it passed beneath me, I recognized a California license plate; without specs, I couldn't read the number. An icy band tightened around my chest.

I hurried inside and bolted the door.

* * * * *

Sometime later, Mike slipped into my side of bed and spooned himself behind me. "You awake?"

I'd half-heard him fumbling around the room for the last few minutes. "I am now," I said, snugging myself into him, hoping to warm him back to sleep. "Did you hear that car earlier?"

"What car?" he asked, but I felt his body tense. He'd heard it all right.

"The one that roared out of the parking lot. You sat up in bed."

"That doesn't mean I was awake." I heard him smother a yawn.

"Your eyes were open."

"Sure you weren't dreaming?" he asked.

Was I? Too much thinking for so early. I settled into Mike and the covers. "Maybe I *was* dreaming. Let's sleep some more, enjoy this room as long as possible. I'm so glad the management is taking care of the rooms and the amenities, even if they've let the outside go to hell."

"Except they no longer provide in-room coffee." Mike uttered the sigh of a man who is not himself without his first cup. "Let's walk down to the lobby and see if they finally got around to plugging in the pot."

"No qualms about facing the desk clerk?" I asked half in jest.

"Probably crawled back to his cave," Mike muttered, but his body tensed once again.

Last evening, we'd walked in our dress clothes, with me in high heels and cursing every step, back on the park road to the nearby Bayside Café. Here we'd dined lavishly (for us) on bay scallops in béchamel sauce and a liter of house Chardonnay. Afterwards the earlier encounter with the clerk hadn't tamped down Mike's Wandering Nun fantasies and I'd happily complied.

"I can make you a cup of instant with hot tap water."

"I'd rather drink boiled oil," he groused.

Finally I had to address the elephant in our bed. "What's with you and that desk clerk? You started to call him something that sounded like 'Steve.'"

"Did I?" He shifted his weight. "He looks like someone I once arrested. No big deal. It was years ago and if it is the same guy, he didn't recognize me."

"Mike, he did. You know he did."

* * * * *

In a skinning wind that ripped through the trees, we fought our way down the steps to the parking lot and hurried to the reception building. Across the road the sun was just peeking over the hills beyond the golf course. We stepped inside the dimly lit foyer. Mike sniffed and grabbed my arm. "Bella, stop. Right now."

"Why?" I asked and then it hit me; an odor, metallic but sweet.

Blood.

"Let's get out of here!" he said. "Could be a robbery in progress."

Too late. I'd already shaken off his arm, crossed the room and peered over the reception counter. Blood slickened the floor behind the counter. It spattered the wall. Left tracks to the entrance. I dashed to the door.

"Stay inside!" he warned, contradicting himself.

"No way. There's someone hurt out there."

"Or a bad guy," he said. Again, too late. I'd already pushed the glass door open. Bloody footprints led to the footpath through the eucalyptus groove. I stepped toward it; Mike blocked my way. "Stay back."

"No way."

I followed the blood spots several hundred yards through the grove to a small beach below the Natural History Museum. Then I saw him. The clerk lay on his back, sightless eyes staring at the rising sun, his shirt a bloody swamp.

"Jesus H. Christ!" Mike, his face milky gray, stared at the body. Without warning, he grabbed my arm and pulled me toward the parking lot.

"Stop that. You're hurting me."

His eyes were a fury. "Listen to me. Walk back to the campsite, take down the tent. Go home."

"But—"

"Will you *listen*? Leave a bike by the bathroom. I'll ride home later."

"That's crazy talk. We need to call 911."

"I'll do it later. Trust me."

I took two steps and stopped dead. I wasn't going anywhere. I pulled my cell phone from my pocket and thrust it at him. "Trust has nothing to do with it, Mike. Now do you want to call, or should I?"

*****

The Wandering Nun braced herself with one hand against the tree, gaping at the drops of blood on the beach. She knew there was a body beyond, just out of sight. She'd seen and heard the couple arguing over it, their shrill voices disturbing the morning stillness. They were gone now and the quiet had returned, but it wouldn't last.

Her birds were in mortal danger. The couple would bring people with vehicles and equipment and lights to violate the sanctity of their grove and frighten them away.

Her eye fell on a wicked looking knife half-buried in the dirt. She picked up the bloody thing with two fingers and studied it briefly. Maybe the strangers would leave her and the birds alone if the murder weapon was never found. She could make that happen. She grabbed it by the blade, drew her arm back and hurled the loathsome thing into the bay, drawing strength from desperation.

3

Monday, April 12th, early morning

Mariposa Bay PD Detective Frank Ironwood was in his late forties, all starch and officialdom from the neck down. From the neck up, his shaved head, close-together slate eyes and pit-bull jaw made him look like a thug. He took a seat opposite us at a table in the closed restaurant where our preliminary interview would be conducted, away from the media's all-seeing eyes.

His mirror image, partner and presumed brother, Detective Rick Ironwood, had gone to sniff out coffee. Since the Inn was within city limits, the Mariposa Bay PD, rather than the Tolosa Sheriff's Department, had jurisdiction over the crime.

I forced myself to concentrate on the "now" of my surroundings and not worry about what was to come. Mike, being a law enforcement professional, seemed to be doing a good job of covering his nervousness. Though he was a bit pale.

The restaurant remained an impressive sight despite its present air of neglect. The showpiece bar of rich, hand-carved mahogany featured a brass rail and fittings, both now somewhat tarnished. Bar stools covered in burgundy leather matched raised, tufted banquettes that flanked both walls at right angles to the bar. Light from three chandeliers cascaded like crystal rain from the ceiling. A scene straight from the 1890's.

An enormous painting hanging over the bar dwarfed the room's other charms. Titled "The Wandering Nun" after the local legend, it depicts the profile of a black-clad young woman, wisps of red hair escaping beneath her veil. She stands on a path beneath a towering arch of eucalypti, close to the beach where Mike and I found the body. Darkness shrouds the trees, but the woman is bathed in a halo of light. A Great Blue Heron, ignoring the roosting habits of birds, watches the woman from a low hanging branch. The area is a sacred spot for bird lovers.

A French door leading to the patio had been left open and wind gusted through, blowing in leaves and dust to mingle with the faded cabbage rose pattern of the carpet.

"Want me to shut that?" Mike asked.

"No, leave it," I said. "Please." Perhaps fresh air would purge the stench of death from my nose.

I imagined the scene outside: official vehicles, radios squawking and lights flashing, littering the parking area like abandoned Tonka toys. The fire department, Search and Rescue. No need; the man was dead. And of course, media everywhere.

From his jacket pocket Detective Ironwood extracted a crumpled pad and stubby pencil, both standard issue for detectives. That I knew for a fact. In the past three years Mike and I have been involved in several other murder investigations.

Did the good detective realize that Mike was more shaken up than an ex-cop should be, given that he'd spent years dealing with violent death? My roiling gut told me there was more than a casual past connection between my husband and the dead man. I'd heard the Inn manager, who'd arrived with the first response vehicle, tell the detectives that the dead man's name was Joe Milosch. Mike had started to call him "Steve." Would he tell that to the detectives?

Rick Ironwood, Detective Frank's lookalike except for a nasty V-shaped scar on his square chin, joined the table. The two men exchanged a terse nod—coffee was on the way. "Are you the one who actually found the body?" Detective Frank asked Mike, who flinched.

"No, I did," I interjected. Technically, that was true. I was several steps ahead of him at the murder site.

An especially sharp gust of wind swept a bunch of old newspapers from bar to floor. Without a word Detective Rick rose and shut the door. The wind caught it just right and it closed with a bang. Mike jumped.

"Sorry about that," Ironwood mumbled. The two detectives exchanged another nod; they had noted his skittishness.

Detective Frank licked the tip of his pencil, poised it above the notebook and gave me a penetrating look. "Well then, if you found the body, I'd like to hear about it."

With Mike adding small points and both detectives occasionally asking for clarification, I spent the next ten minutes relating what we'd witnessed: how the clerk who the manager identified as Joe Milosch had checked us in, how there'd been no sign of him when we'd walked to the nearby Bayside Café for dinner. Also the engine noise I'd heard from our room around two AM, how I'd stepped onto the portico and witnessed the Escalade, driven by a tall man, disappearing into the darkness. In my nervousness, I forgot to tell them of our previous Escalade encounter on the park road. Guess Mike forgot too.

Sometime in the narrative I'd been vaguely aware of an employee appearing with a large pot, paper cups and other accouterments. The smell of brewing coffee fought with acid boiling in my stomach resulting in profound nausea. Even Mike, who in typical cop fashion could drink coffee through a major gun battle, looked wan. I wondered why he didn't tell them he recognized the dead man.

At least the detectives hadn't interviewed us separately. That would have been so much worse for not knowing what Mike might say.

Detective Rick cleared his throat. "Sir, didn't you find it odd that there were no other guests in the hotel besides yourselves?"

I could see from Mike's expression that the question surprised him.

"The Inn's rumored to be in financial diff—" I said.

"I asked your husband, Ma'am," he said, his eyes still on Mike.

My interruption apparently gave Mike think-time. "Um, not really, Not long ago, we stayed at an all-but abandoned motel at Punto Solitario up the coast."

I glanced sideways at him. We never actually stayed there.

"Abandoned? You broke *in*?" The detective apparently didn't hear the qualifier "all-but."

Mike backpedaled. "No, nothing like that."

"Name of the motel?" he deadpanned.

Mike didn't expect that. "Uh—Bella, what was the name of that place?"

"Beats me," I said, unable to think of a quick lie. The motel name would be easy for them to check. So would the registration records.

"Why stay in a seedy place like that?" Detective Rick interjected.

"For the adventure," I piped up with as Mike said, "For romance, of course."

The detectives exchanged bemused glances. I felt myself flush.

Thankfully Detective Frank decided it was time to move on. He studied his notes, looked at me and nodded. "We don't know yet whether the vehicle you heard and the stabbing were related."

Unsure if I was supposed to comment, I didn't.

The detective now addressed my husband. "Did you hear the vehicle as well?"

Mike shook his head and managed a tight smile, the first since we'd discovered the body. "Afraid not." He ran a hand through a thatch of crew cut grown whiter since his heart attack. "I had too much wine at dinner. Slept through everything."

I knew better. After I crawled back into bed, he only pretended to be asleep. It's almost impossible to fake the deep, even breathing of a sleeping person. I know. I'd tried it often enough myself to discourage his advances when things were tense between us.

Detective Frank's eyes narrowed. "You don't know Milosch? Have never seen him around?"

"I've never seen him in my life," Mike declared.

My heart gave a sickening lurch at the lie.

At that moment, the door that led to the reception area opened. A tall, attractive woman in a red designer suit and three-inch heels appeared. She tossed back her mane of dark hair, a gesture I'd seen her do often on TV. "Heard there was coffee in here," said Alena Lupino, anchor at KFAX News.

My heart skipped a beat and then another as her dark eyes raked over the detectives and moved to Mike and me. Any reporter worth her badge could figure out we were witnesses.

Mike stared at her with a "this can't be happening" expression, then dove under the table as though he'd dropped something.

4

Monday, April 12th, midmorning

"Ma?" I called from the front hall. "Debby?" No answer. The caregiver and Mom must have gone shopping. Good. Mike and I needed time alone to discuss the morning's horrific events. "You going to work today?" I asked him as a way to open the conversation.

This man with the work ethic of a Puritan patriarch looked at me as though the word was an alien concept. "Actually, I'm going back to bed."

Back to bed?

He raised a warning hand. My husband seldom napped. And never in bed, though he sometimes falls asleep in his recliner. He'd never admit it, claiming instead to be resting his eyes.

"Okay, suit yourself. I'm going to take a shower and go to work." Officially I had the day off, but perhaps giving Mike some space would help him recover his equilibrium and we could rationally discuss this morning's events.

"Do me a favor," he said. "Take your shower in the other bathroom?" He pointed toward the one between the kitchen and laundry room.

"Sure," I said, waving him toward our bedroom. "Get some sleep."

"Get your clothes while I'm still awake," he said.

"I have some on the dryer. Go!" And he did.

Left alone, I decided on a bracing cup of Irish Breakfast tea before my shower. I put the kettle on and stared idly out the kitchen window while waiting for it to boil. *What was this?*

Mom and a strange woman faced each other in lawn chairs by my kitchen garden, deep in an animated conversation. Mom's laughter tinkled through the glass.

The kettle shrieked; I ignored it, stepping outside. "Hey, Mom, who's your friend?" I gave a curt nod toward a diminutive brunette in her mid-fifties.

Mom evaded my question, saying instead: "Bella? Back so early? I've been so worried about you two." She turned to the woman. "Imagine, at their ages, sleeping on the ground." My mother is an expert at offering criticism in the guise of concern.

The woman nodded in a noncommittal way. "And who might you be?" I asked.

She struggled to her feet as Mom said, "This is Rosa. Debby can't come for a few weeks."

Swell. "And how did you find us, Rosa?"

"Debby and I are friends from the church," she said in excellent, though slightly accented, English.

Okay, a promising start. "Ma, can we have a private word inside?"

She hesitated, her round little face troubled. "Isn't it rude to leave Rosa out here by herself?"

"Ma. Inside. Now."

"Of course, dear." With no indication that she'd overheard our rude exchange, Rosa grabbed Mom's walker and placed it in front of her.

I gestured for Mom to go ahead of me. As she made her careful way toward the kitchen door, I reflected that she looked better than anyone had a right to look after months of intensive chemo and radiation.

The wig helped. Mom was not without funds and I'd urged her to invest in a good one. The fluffy Betty White style framed her face and lifted her spirits, if not to the actress's level of intensity, at least to some semblance her former feisty self.

"Okay," I said, once we were inside. "I've got a million questions, starting with two: "When did all this happen?" and "Why didn't you call me?"

She stared at me, blue eyes wide, cupid's bow mouth quivering. "I didn't want to bother you, dear. You both drive yourselves so hard I figured you needed as much time alone as possible."

There she goes again, I thought, my blood pressure shooting the moon.

"Debby's husband called her from the hospital. He broke his leg in two places while trimming their trees, though what a man that age was doing on a ladder, I can't imagine."

"Just the facts, Ma'am." I often channel Sergeant Friday from "Dragnet" to marshal her wandering thoughts.

"Well, Debby called Rosa, and one of Rosa's grandsons brought her right over. He must be unemployed to be home midday like that. She has six, and I can't imagine how they can find jobs in this economy."

"Wait!" I raised my hand like a traffic cop. "Wait just a minute. You took this woman in with no references?"

"Of course not, dear. I *told* you, Debby and Rosa both go to Saint Pat's. I had her stand on the porch while I telephoned Father Rodriguez. Of course he vouched for her. She's in the Altar Society."

She squared her shoulders and raised herself to her full height of just under five feet. "Besides, may I remind you that I'm paying for my own care, and I'll make my own decisions about it, thank you very much."

I know when I'm licked. Or maybe not. "Okay, okay," I said, needing to have the last word. "Rosa stays. For now. But I have some questions for her. Why don't you fix us all a nice cup of tea while I do that?"

* * * * *

Rosa and I sat in the shade of my garden's lone apple tree and had a pleasant conversation. She was obviously a woman of breeding and education. With comeliness and a quiet air of capability, she told me she was a Cuban émigré who'd fled Castro's regime thirty years before, after her husband was assassinated for speaking against the government.

She explained that she needed a ride to our house today because her car was being repaired. Normally she would drive, and take Mom for chemo treatments when needed. Because she lived with her son and daughter-in-law and their boys, three of whom attended the local junior college, she was willing to spend the night if necessary. This in itself was big plus. Debby always had to get home to the man she referred to as "The Hub," a phrase I associate more with car wheels than spouses.

5

Monday, April 12th, noon

"First a murder and now this!" Margaret Cavalier, managing editor of the *Central Coast Chronicle,* held aloft an obituary that had appeared in both yesterday's paper and today's. It identified one Percival Fillmore, whose photo showed him to be a very old man indeed, to have been born on April 10th, 2010, and died the same day.

"Like maybe he had that disease that ages a person prematurely?" I asked. She met my feeble attempt at humor with a sharp look. I gripped the doorjamb of her office, exhausted and so not in the mood for a chewing out.

"We *do* have a copy editor to catch such things," I pointed out.

She snatched off oversized purple-rimmed glasses, allowing them to dangle on a matching cord against her queen-sized chest. "We both know Chastity's not going to make it unless she pays less attention to the text on her cell and more to the text in front of her." She shook the paper so hard it rattled. "But this happened on your watch."

I spread my hands, palms down, the gesture acknowledging the truth of her statement, but also saying, "Enough already." When Margaret first arrived from the formerly venerable, currently beleaguered, *Detroit Free Press,* we got along famously. Most of the time we still did, except when she vented her considerable temper on something gone wrong. Like now. More than the situation warranted, I thought.

She adjusted one of the clippies that held back an avalanche of yellow-streaked gray hair, narrowing her dark eyes to pinpricks. "What are you doing here?" she asked, looking down her Roman nose at me. "I thought you were off until tomorrow."

"Uh, Mike got an emergency call from some guy with septic tank problems. I figured that if he had to work, I might as well come in and catch up on some things." In reality, he was at home, building a wall around himself.

She nodded, mind obviously elsewhere. She perched her glasses on the end of her nose and studied the obit as though the words would change themselves, leaving me time to ruminate.

Earlier, after the preliminary interview, with another scheduled for Wednesday, Mike and I had been assured that we would be identified as only "unnamed witnesses." Whether the detectives could make that stick after news anchor Alena Lupino stumbled upon us seemed highly speculative. We could only hope for the best and see how the situation played out. If Margaret, with her reporter's nose for news, found that I'd been personally involved, she'd press for details, the better to scoop other media.

In the time she'd been managing editor, I'd learned she'd act like a terrorist until saying her piece, and then she was fine. In that sense she was like her predecessor Amy Goodheart. Amy left under a cloud when an investigative reporting assignment went horribly wrong and almost cost me my job. After that, I decided I lacked the fire in the belly for hard-core journalism. I was just fine with writing obituaries.

"You know," Margaret said, finally cracking a smile, "the old guy dying on his one-day birthday is pretty funny, and I'm surprised we haven't heard from the family."

"Me too. Could they sue us for making a laughing stock of their loved one?"

Good one, Bella.

She didn't hear me, or chose not to. "Know any good copy editors? Seems like in this economy there should be plenty out there looking for jobs."

"I don't." I shook my head, thoughts still on Amy. I never thought I'd miss her but I did, in all her spangled excess, propelling her *zaftig* self across the room on four-inch heels, leaving a trail of Obsession perfume and mortally wounded reporters in her wake.

Margaret, an inveterate smoker, always reeked of tobacco. Clad in an un-ironed white shirt, rolled at the sleeves, baggy dark trousers and black lace-up oxfords, she made a different fashion statement, a strange mixture of sixties counter-culture and girls' softball coach.

The phone rang. She turned, picked up the receiver and said, "Detective Ironwood, what's goin' on?" She listened for a few moments, then made a shooing motion for me to leave the office. I stared at my favorite stain on the ceiling tile, pretending to ignore her.

As she talked with the detective, she turned her back, keeping her voice low. I heard a "snap, snap" sound. Toying with her Zippo lighter again, an annoying stress related habit.

I wondered which Ironwood called, not that it made much difference. Sweat beaded on my upper lip. Despite needing to hear her end of the conversation, I wanted to leave, take myself home, crawl in bed and pull the covers over my head. But my husband was there, doing just exactly that. There wasn't room for two of us in the marriage bed right now.

Had to be some reasonable explanation for his behavior, but what? He and I have what some consider a "troubled" relationship; despite that, we love each other deeply and can't imagine a life apart. But this latest incident was over the top. Way over.

"Thanks Rick, keep us in the loop."

So, she was on a first-name basis with law enforcement.

Margaret put the phone down, pocketed the lighter and swiveled her chair to face me, replacing the snapping of the lighter with finger-drumming on the desk. "Now where were we?"

"Um, you asked about finding copy editors."

She shrugged. "Well, keep your ears open. Chastity's history."

Wow, that was cold.

The managing editor returned to her computer screen and began tapping keys. I'd been dismissed.

Head down, staring at a hole in the sock peeking out of my Birkenstocks, I took two steps and collided with news anchor Alena Lupino. Our second meeting today. Probably not a coincidence.

"Whoa." She put her hands on my shoulders, her dark almond eyes lingering on my face a tad too long. Here to rat me out? No, she'd want to keep that scoop for herself.

"Alena, you're early." Margaret shot from the chair and smoothed down her shirt with more-than-necessary zeal. "Where's lunch?"

"How about the Tolosa Inn since you've never been there?"

"Sounds good," Margaret answered. "We can share a piece of that sinful Black Forest cake I've heard about."

Alena's eyes traveled up the other woman's body, bottom to boobs. Again she flipped her long dark hair off her face, her signature gesture. "Not that you need that extra thousand calories, my dear."

Margaret's face fell at the insult, revealing an insecurity that surprised me. She attempted recovery. "My friend is such a kidder," she said, turning to me and swiping her fingers as if to shoo away a fly.

I almost swooned with relief. The two women had a lunch date. But wait. Had Alena recognized me as a newspaper employee this morning? If so, she would almost certainly try to pump Margaret, hence the "impromptu" invitation. My gut tightened.

Torn between the need to stay and protect my interests and the desire to escape, I succumbed to the latter. Walking backwards, I was almost out the door when Margaret said, "Bella, do you and Alena know each other?"

"Don't think so." I continued to inch back.

Alena wasn't about to let me escape easily. She sashayed over and took my hand in hers, giving me an appraising glance. Up close she showed every one of her forty-something years: fine lines around the eyes, parentheses bracketing too-red lips, a slightly sagging neck. But height, an expensive haircut held in place with lots of product, and good clothes were on her side. Her well-cut red wool suit with its mandarin collar and snug fit, the black silk tee, made me acutely conscious of my levis and sweatshirt. Every day was Casual Friday at the *Central Coast Chronicle.*

Alena continued to hold my hand, shaking it a little."Bella, why don't you join us?"

I repossessed my hand. "Oh, I couldn't. You see I've got—"

"Lots to catch up on." Margaret finished for me.

"I insist," Alena said. "My treat."

6

Monday, April 12th, lunchtime

The hostess at The Horseshoe Cafe showed us to a small bistro table, offered menus and hastily withdrew. The room buzzed with conversation and the clatter of silverware. The ornate coffee shop, one of two restaurants inside the famous Tolosa Inn, had a sort of Bonanza meets Bordello theme. A café-in-the-round, it repeated the family's signature pink motif with the addition of copper accents that should have clashed—but didn't—with the shiny red leather stools of the horseshoe-shaped coffee bar.

The owners, the Falcone family, had made kitsch cool.

I fidgeted on a small chair, trying to get butt-comfortable. The two sat opposite me, chatting away with no sign of their earlier animosity.

A busy server brought drinks and rolls and took orders. I still had that "hot seat" feeling. I added sugar to my steaming tea and stirred, wishing I could disappear into the eddying whirls.

Despite my mind's unease, my mouth watered in response to the aromas of upscale, down-home food: sizzling ranch beef, rib-sticking chowder, and of course, warm pastry. I opened the menu, huge and trimmed in pink. Yikes! Twelve bucks for a hamburger. Good thing Alena was paying.

I peered over the top of the menu at the two women, heads bent toward each other. A strange friendship, the glamorous Alena and plain-wrap Margaret. At least she had one friend. Up to now it seemed as though she had no life other than her job.

"Alena, where did you work before coming here?" I asked, attempting small talk to cover my nervousness.

"I was the anchor at WXYZ-TV in Detroit."

"Really. Did you know Margaret there?"

"I did," Alena answered, watching her friend slather a roll in butter, her mouth a red rose of disapproval. "By coincidence we found ourselves working on the Central Coast," she added, though I didn't ask.

This whole thing stank like mackerel stew. Alena had asked me here for one reason only: to grill me about finding Joe Milosch's body. She wanted Margaret as a witness, but why?

"Bella and her husband stayed at the Mariposa Bay campground last night." Margaret turned to me. "You must have been close to the murder scene."

I was wrong. She wasn't just Alena's witness, she was her straight man.

"Do tell?" Alena eyeballed me over the top of her of iced tea, and took a reflective sip. "See anything?"

"Actually," I said, thinking fast, "we changed our plans and drove up the coast to Punto Solitario instead. We stayed at the motel there." Scarlet cheeks, I'm sure, belied my words. Gulping hot tea to hide my discomfort resulted only in a burnt tongue.

Alena arched an agile eyebrow. "Really? I know that motel. It's a dump. Why drive all the way up there when you can get a room with a gorgeous view right here?"

"Oh, we just wanted to get out of town," I said. "And we needed more privacy than a campground offers." I batted my eyes to hint at a night of wild lovemaking.

A new server approached, an attractive older woman with a radiant complexion. I smiled at her, grateful that she'd saved me from falling off a conversational cliff. A young man hefting an enormous tray followed. The woman wore a stylish dark suit with a pink scarf knotted at the neck. She selected a plate from the tray and set a hamburger the size of the Superdome before me. "There you go," she said in a down-home manner.

"New job, Fifi?" Alena asked.

Our server was none other than Philippa, aka Fifi, owner of the Tolosa Inn and Mom-in-Chief of the Falcone family. The Falcones were one of two prominent Tolosa business families. I'd dealt with the other, the Mercados, several years ago when their daughter, Connie, was brutally murdered.

"Alena," Mrs. Falcone said, setting a catch-of-the-day in front of the news anchor, "good seeing you. I didn't realize you were here." She pushed up huge spectacles slipping down her rather prominent nose. Reddish curls piled in a precarious topknot threatened imminent escape.

"Short of help?" Margaret asked, peering at a Caesar salad that would feed all of Rome.

"Just for today," Fifi said. "Annie Carter, one of our servers, called in with a family emergency. She won't be in for the rest of the week, and we already have two others out with colds."

She straightened up, working a kink out of her spine with a knuckle. "Poor Annie, I feel for her. Seems like the original bad luck kid. She's a smart one, an English major type, but she has a disability that makes serving difficult for her. And now this family emergency…" She let her voice trail off as though she'd said too much.

"English major?" I repeated, hoping to catch Margaret's ear.

"Oops. Gotta go." Mrs. Falcone hurried off in response to a customer's signal.

I leaned across the table. "You heard her, Margaret. Maybe we could hire this Annie as a copy editor."

Her voice took on a hard edge. "Why would I hire someone who can't show up when she's needed?"

"Mrs. Falcone said it was a family emergency."

Margaret harrumphed as though a family emergency should not deter an employee from her appointed task. For a moment she reminded me of her predecessor, the hard-driving Amy.

We left more than half our lunches and declared ourselves too full for Black Forest, or any other species, of cake. Mrs. Falcone brought the check; Alena ignored it.

Margaret rose to her feet. "I need to pee."

Alena smiled. "First time here, check out the men's room. It's a hoot."

"I'd better make sure it's empty first."

"Hey, don't let that stop you. And don't try to smoke in there."

Alena waved her off and turned back to me, allowing an uncomfortable silence to build. Had Margaret left as part of a plan for Alena to get me alone? Why hadn't I gone with her? Maybe it wasn't too late. I jumped up. "I have to go too."

"Sit down, Bella." She grasped the edge of the table and leaned toward me. "I recognized you from this morning. You and your husband found the body."

"I can't imagine what you're talking about," I said, looking around. Where was divine intervention when you needed it? "We were a fifty miles from there."

"Bullshit." She leaned further across the table and cupped a hand over her mouth. "I also know what an obituary editor makes and I know your husband's septic service business will be in the toilet when the wastewater plant is built." Her dark eyes flashed. "I can see to it that the station makes it worth your while to give me an exclusive."

"You're wrong, Alena, that wasn't us in the restaurant." *Oops.*

The incriminating word "restaurant" hung between us like a noose. If I were indeed miles away, I wouldn't know where the interview with the police took place.

She didn't seem to notice and I took that as my cue to assume the high ground. "Offering us money for an interview is against journalistic ethics."

She cocked an eyebrow. "And you and I know it's done all the time."

Margaret reappeared sooner than expected. Maybe there was something to this divine intervention business after all. "What are you two gabbing about?"

Alena ignored her question. Instead, she of the twenty-eight dollar catch-of-the-day aimed a scarlet fingernail at the check. "Shall we split this three ways?"

"I thought you were treating," I said.

7

Monday, April 12th, early evening

I drove west on Los Lobos Road, relieved to escape the office, tickled to have called Alena's bluff on the check, dreading what I'd find at home. Mike needed to open up. Perhaps after getting some rest, he would. He told me he'd arrested the dead man in Chicago and that made sense. But what about Alena Lupino? Perhaps he knew her in Detroit.

Strange. Alena and Margaret from Detroit, Mike and the dead man from Chicago. The Central Coast was certainly attracting its share of Midwesterners lately.

Perhaps I was making too much of this. He might be familiar with her from a KFAX billboard or one of their "coming up at eleven" spots.

Being a world-class procrastinator when it comes to difficult domestic conversations, I decided to stop at the Los Lobos Library and pick up the selection for next month's book discussion. Our head librarian, Kathy Tanner, had placed it on the Holds shelf for me.

I turned right onto Community Drive, swinging a wide left into the library parking lot across from the tennis courts. Beyond was Saint Patrick's church, safe once again in the hands of Father Rodriguez.

That hadn't been the case two years ago and I briefly recalled the drama that started at the Community Center. It involved a fundraiser for the homeless, overseen by the former Saint Pat's pastor. Things got out of hand and the resulting scandal and fall-out led to multiple murders that rocked this small community to its core. It came hard on the heels of the execution-style slaying of Connie Mercado, part-owner of the land where the wastewater treatment plant was to be built. After her death, the county assumed responsibility for the project and selected a new site east of town.

That, however, had not made the project any less controversial among the Los Lobos citizenry. Now the county had a new proposal, and the promise of money from the much-maligned federal government. The brouhaha brewed anew.

I parked the old Subaru facing west under a tree canopy, turned off the ignition and waited for the engine to quit bucking.

One thing at a time, Bella, one thing at a time. What was it Dad used to say? "When you don't feel normal, do normal things." *I'm trying Dad, I'm trying.*

A man in his mid-forties sat behind Kathy Tanner's desk. He had smooth caramel skin and viewed the world through luminous green eyes.

"Where's Kathy?" I blurted in surprise.

"On extended leave," he said, pronouncing "extended" with a long "e." A British accent, but with a softer cadence. "I'm taking her place temporarily."

"You're a long way from home," I said. "Australia?"

He smiled, displaying even, white teeth. A handsome man. "New Zealand. South Island."

That explained the accent. "Is Kathy all right?" I asked the man, who with a muted necktie and ironed shirt, looked a bit too buttoned down to be a librarian, especially in laidback Los Lobos.

He offered a small smile. "I'm sure she's fine. A personal matter. I'm Neal Grale."

As in 'Holy?" I asked.

"As in G-r-a-l-e," he said, holding out his hand, his smile widening to crinkle the corners of his eyes. "And who might you be?"

"Bella Kowalski," I said, taking his cool hand in mine. He had about him a woodsy aroma, as though he spent a lot of time outdoors.

"Kowalski?" He cocked his head to the side. "I believe your husband was in earlier."

Mike in the library? That would be a first. "I doubt it. My husband prefers magazines to books and he buys them on the newsstand."

"My mistake, I'm sure," said Mr. Grale. "I had a lovely chat with someone who had a similar name. Now what can I do for you?"

After I explained about the book discussion selection, he pointed me toward the Holds shelf and returned to his computer keyboard. The library staff seemed to be interacting with him in a comfortable way. The whole thing with him replacing Kathy seemed a bit strange, maybe because it was so sudden.

I hoped her "personal matter" didn't concern Martin, her son, Tolosa County's first African-American sheriff's deputy. He'd briefly been a person of interest in the murder that took place at the Polar Bear Dip in Cuyamaca Beach two years ago.

A bad apple in the department had targeted him because of his race. A call to Kathy was in order for this evening.

After grabbing the assigned book from the Holds shelf, I glanced at Mr. Grale. He continued to watch me as though *I* were a person of interest.

"Come on Bella," I chided myself. "You're being paranoid."

Once again I reminded myself of my dad's advice, that doing normal things would make the world seem right, even if it wasn't. I always read more when I'm under stress, escapist literature that I can blow through in an evening that would otherwise be devoted to worrisome thoughts. As I examined books on the New Releases shelf, I again felt eyes on my back. I turned quickly and, sure enough, caught Mr. Grale watching me.

My quick move had flustered him. He rose, grabbed some papers and ducked behind the checkout counter and out the back door to the trailer office, which stood close to the row of trees I'd parked under.

I checked out my one book and hurried to the lot, surprised to see that darkness had fallen in the short time I'd been in the library. I could see Neal Grale watching me, silhouetted in the trailer's open door. I had the strangest feeling about him, and I couldn't decide if it was good or bad.

* * * * *

Monday, April 12th, early evening

The phone rang as I hurried up the steps of our windmill home. It quit, then began again. I jammed the key in the lock, threw open the door and ran down the hall to the kitchen. Just as I reached the message center, the call went to voice mail. *Darn.*

I dialed our voice mail number, keyed password, was informed password was incorrect, keyed again. Whatever happened to the old answering machines that displayed your messages and didn't require a password, to say nothing of a monthly fee?

I finally accessed my messages only to find four hang-ups. The house felt empty, cold as Tut's tomb. "Mike?" I called, "Mike?" And then, "Mom?" "Rosa?"And finally, "Sam? Are you here?" No human affirmation, no answering patter of paws or rattling of collar links from our Golden Labrador.

Heading for the thermostat in the front hall to kick up the heat, I heard the phone again. This time I lunged for it. "Hello."

Hesitation. "Is...is Mike there?"

A young man's voice. "Chris, is that you?" I asked, worried that my nephew working as a caterer in the Bay Area might be in trouble. His impulse control was not always the greatest.

"Uh, no," the young man said. "Is Mike there?"

"Who is this?"

Click.

I stared at the mute phone. A man, young, wanting Mike. If it was Little Mike, his employee, why not say so? Or...did this call, and the earlier hang-ups, have something to do with this morning's murder?

I turned the thermostat up to seventy-five and checked on Mom. She had turned in early.

Hearing a disturbance at the back door, I hurried to the kitchen to see Sam struggling through the huge doggie-door we'd installed so he could come and go freely. "Hey, Sam, did you finally hear me? You don't know how good it is to see you."

He limped toward me, eyes alight and tail awag. *I thought you'd never get home, Bella.*

My heart contracted as I reached down and stroked the silky head. Not only was Sam pretty deaf, he now suffered from the hip dysplasia common to most older members of his breed.

Footsteps sounded overhead. Mike was here after all, in the second floor study we called his "East Wing." I had a West Wing counterpart; mine was on the top floor of the adjacent windmill. Here we found the space our marriage required.

Sam and I stood at the foot of the spiral staircase, looking up. First I saw slippered feet, then sweat pants, then a slightly bulged midsection. Finally the whole man appeared. He looked drawn and tired, gave me a crooked smile and patted Sam's head. The dog almost dissolved with pleasure.

"Mike," I said, "we have to talk." Difficult words.

He nodded, put his arm around me and pulled me close. I felt him shiver. "This is hard, but you have a right to know."

A right to know? I drew back. What did that mean?

"Come." We have two places where we discuss problems, the kitchen table, and for more serious ones, our king-sized bed. I took his hand and led him there now. He leaned back against the pillows, shivering still. I dragged the comforter off the floor, pulled it over him and crawled under it, sidling close to him. "Okay, now tell me."

* * * * *

He began slowly and seemingly off-point, telling me about life in the Chicago PD before the accident that killed his wife Grace and son Ethan. I gave him time and when he faltered, I reminded him gently, "And Joe Milosch?"

Mike worried a loose thread on the comforter. "I knew him in Chicago. He was a bad cop—"

"Really?" Somehow that surprised me.

"Yup. Drugs, prostitution, kickbacks, the whole enchilada."

"Your partner?"

He shook his head. "No. Well, not exactly. He worked in another precinct, but sometimes we collaborated on things. I knew him as Steve Pizniak."

Of course. He whispered "Steve" when we first saw the desk clerk.

"Pizniak," I said. "Strange name."

A grim smile. "Polish, like me. He had a reputation as a loner and a rogue cop. The brass looked the other way at his misdeeds because of his impressive arrest record."

"And now he's known as Joe Milosch." *Was known.*

He turned away; I pressed on. "Any idea how he landed out here, working as a hotel clerk, and stabbed by someone driving a black Escalade?"

"We don't know that the guy you saw pulling out of the parking lot did the killing."

"That's not the point, Mike."

"I know."

"Are we in danger?"

"Not likely. Unless…" His voice trailed off.

"Unless what?"

"Unless Pizniak was into something shady out here."

"That seems like a big leap on your part," I said, studying my husband's face, knowing every line, every hollow, every imperfection. They say eyes mirror the soul and now I sought his. He focused on the dresser across the room. *What else does he know? What isn't he telling me?*

"Why did you act so squirrely about calling 911 after we found the body? That's so not like you."

He ran tense fingers through his cropped hair. "I lost it Bella, just lost it. I had this crazy idea I could go back to the hotel and erase our reservation."

His answer raised the tiny hairs on my neck. "Why would you want to do that?"

He sighed deeply. "If Pizniak is tied up with a rogue cop out here, I didn't want the guy to learn about us. It was a crazy idea. Forget it."

Not likely, Mike.

"You should at least tell Ryan Scully what you know."

"No way."

"*What?* He's your buddy, and he gets you investigative work at the sheriff's office. You owe it to yourself, and him. I'm sure he can offer good insight."

"Some buddy," he scoffed. "The sheriff's office hasn't offered me any work for over a year. Has Ryan gone to bat for me? Not on your life."

What he said was true. He had worked a cold case involving the murder of a member of a prominent winery family a year and a half ago, and only a few minor cases since then. It seemed strange to me; Mike acted like he didn't care. Until now.

I tried to grab his hand and he wrenched it away. "Here, I'll show you something." He pushed the comforter back and, with a grunt, rose and crossed the room to the dresser. He fumbled in the top drawer, finally holding up a yellowed news clipping. "Read this."

The story from the *Chicago Sun-Times*, dated February, 1996, showed a photo of Detective Steve Pizniak in handcuffs. Arrested for selling drugs and money laundering, he'd been suspended.

"Was he convicted?"

"Oh God, yes. Probably still serving time." He stared at the ceiling for a moment, then apparently realized what he'd said. "Uh, guess not."

"You need to tell law enforcement what you know. If you don't, couldn't that make you an accessory?"

An exaggerated sigh. "Bella, let me handle this in my own way. You're just going to have to trust me." We remained under the comforter staring at the ceiling for a long time. At last I got up and started dinner.

8

Monday, April 12th, early evening

I unwrapped a package of pork chops, thinking that in all the times I'd been in Mike's dresser drawers, putting away folded socks and underwear, refolding those I'd folded after he rummaged through them, just plain snooping, I'd never seen that clipping. Which begged the question: Had he kept it somewhere else and put it in the drawer recently? So he could pull it out and offer an explanation for his recognition of Joe Milosch, aka Steve Pizniak?

I'd had a day filled with many unanswered questions; I needed to have success with one that should be easy to answer. Like, why Kathy Tanner had gone on leave.

I slapped Cajun seasoning on the chops and while they sizzled, dialed the librarian's home number. It went immediately to voice mail. Okay, plan B. Call her son.

"Tanner."

"Martin, it's Bella Kowalski."

"Hey, Bella, what can I do for you?"

"I just wondered if your mom is okay. Her temporary replacement said she's on leave."

He laughed. "She doesn't want everyone to know, but I'm sure it's okay to tell you. She's having what she calls 'a nip and tuck.'"

"Nip and tuck?"

"A facelift."

"Oh," I said, not knowing what else to add except, "give her my best."

"Will do, Bella. Gotta go."

I stared at the silent phone. One question answered, many more to go.

* * * * *

Monday, April 12th, late evening

"Mike said I needed to trust him," I said to the portrait of Emily Divina hanging on the wall of my study. Glass of wine in paw, I'd retreated there after a dinner Mike and I hardly touched.

Our windmill home has its own ghost. The woman whose portrait I stared at, Emily Divina, killed herself by jumping from the widow's walk outside my window when her lover failed to return from the sea. In a jealous snit, her miller husband turned her portrait to the wall. At least that's the story we heard when we moved here. Mike and I turned Emily to again face the world.

Since then Emily and I have been through a lot together. She's my touchstone when things get rough. They'd been plenty rough in the last few years: several murders in our area and a personal crisis that culminated in Mike's heart attack. This after he asked me to trust him in a personal matter, and that trust was violated.

I swirled wine in my glass. "Would you trust him, Emily?"

Her familiar countenance stared back at me, dark hair parted in the middle and swept back over her ears, a scrimshaw broach at the neck of her pleated shirtwaist, the thin, straight-arrow mouth. All this was overshadowed by her dark eyes, which managed to reflect, not only sadness, but some latent passion destined to end in tragedy. My husband's gray eyes have taken on the same sadness in the past few years.

"Em, I just can't trust him on this. But what should I do? Confide in Detective Scully?"

Emily did nothing, said nothing, but her presence made me feel less alone.

"Nope, can't do that. It would drive a huge wedge between us. Dear God, I'm not a fool. So why do I love this imperfect man?"

Emily continued to stare straight ahead. "I mean, I'm not perfect either. But I don't lie. Well maybe a time or two, but those weren't trust-busting issues." I thought for a moment. "You know, I've always heard when you don't know what to do, do nothing."

Emily did nothing, and we left it at that.

* * * * *

I came downstairs and back into the house to see a note tacked on the refrigerator. "Dear Bella," it said. "Need to go out for a while. Back soon. Don't wait up. Love, M."

I set the note on the counter. Had the young man who wanted to speak to Mike called back as I talked to Emily? If so, was the matter so urgent that it required a late meeting?

9

Tuesday, April 13th, early morning

Mike left for work as usual, saying nothing of last evening's conversation about Joe Milosch. Not unusual. My husband is the progeny of plains-hardened ancestors who don't express feelings. When I asked about the phone call and his subsequent departure, he claimed there was a problem with a customer's septic tank. Logical, but unlikely. My gut told me his meeting resulted from a call by the young man.

One final event in a day full of strange events.

I finished the breakfast dishes and opened the refrigerator, seeking dinner inspiration: milk, a hard wedge of cheese, dried up chops from last night's dinner.

I missed Chris, my nephew, who'd done most of the cooking when he stayed with us after his parents kicked him out. Now he worked as a chef for a catering company in the Bay Area, for experience, he said, until he felt ready to apply to a five-star restaurant. Misplaced confidence, perhaps, but at least the kid had a plan for his life.

Suddenly needing to hear Mike's voice, I grabbed my cell phone. "Hey you, what do you want for dinner?"

"Um," he said, sounding surprised to hear from me, "anything. Since we had pork last night, how about something fresh and vegetarian from the Farmers Market?"

"Good idea," I said, glancing at the stove clock. I could do that; today was a late day at the paper. I would bike there for some much needed exercise.

On my way out the door, I eyed my bike helmet hanging on a hook over the bench that held things we didn't want to forget: keys, sunglasses and the like. Chris had piled the bench with everything from skateboards to Skittles when he was with us. Now it looked a little lonely.

I grabbed the helmet, then changed my mind. My freshly shampooed hair wasn't completely dry. Wearing a helmet would result in hat-hair for the rest of the day. Better to let my short graying locks, what we used to call euphemistically a "pixie cut," fluff in the wind.

* * * * *

I turned left onto Los Lobos Road, then made another quick left toward the Farmers Market. The organizers had recently moved the event from its customary spot on Monday afternoon to Tuesday morning, which worked great for me.

As I biked along, dappled sun and a gentle breeze alternately warmed and cooled my face. On my left, the bay sparkled in the morning light. Being outside and communing with nature was so healing to the soul. My soul needed it.

A quick glance over my shoulder revealed another cyclist half a block behind. Probably a hot-shot in silver spandex whose dirt I'd soon be eating. Passing under a copse of trees I felt a leaf fall onto the back of my head. I put my hand up to brush it away and felt a distinct nip on my knuckle. A rustling about my shoulders almost me made me lose control of the bike. The intruder was a small black bird. I probably came too close to her nest.

My pulse raced. I'm terrified of birds, even canaries. The attacker's beady yellow eyes surveyed me before she flew off. Not for long. She circled, preparing for a second attack. Why hadn't I worn my helmet? I raised my hand to fend her off; an outstretched wing touched my bare arm. I recoiled in horror and the bike wobbled. I concentrated on keeping it and myself upright, hoping the bird would tire of the game. *No such luck.*

Again she circled. My whole body froze.

Without warning a bright blue object shot through the air—straight at the bird. Not a direct hit, but close. She disappeared into the trees.

I hopped off my bike on shaking pins and walked back to the object on the ground. A backpack. A young cyclist, the one who'd been behind me I now realized, picked it up, dusted it off, and adjusted the straps on his shoulders. I gulped several deep breaths to slow my racing pulse.

"You okay?"

I ran my hands through my hair to check for bird droppings. "I…I guess."

The young man grinned, reminding me of someone, I wasn't sure who. Probably that teen idol from the Central Coast, the one with the shaggy haircut and big eyes girls are gaga over.

"Want me to ride with you for a bit?"

"No thanks," I said, "I'm just heading toward the Farmers Market. I'll be fine now."

He shrugged. "If you say so."

Pumping hard, I sped off. I looked over my shoulder. The young man stood in the road, staring after me.

* * * * *

The market teemed with early shoppers milling around white-tented booths. Los Lobos has many retirees and a thriving work-at-home and arts population, both of whom set their own hours. Several young couples shared stroller duties, parent and child bonding at the open air market.

I parked my bike and began, as I always do, with the produce stands at the Second Street entrance. As usual, everything looked fresh and tempting, but I'd survey it all before making my first purchase.

Across the street sat Making Whoopi, a popular watering hole. The sounds of music and laughter, to say nothing of the distinctive smell of beer wafting through the open door, spoke of patrons already hard at it. *Mental note to Bella. Have Mike take me there some Saturday night.*

Mike… Just the thought of this new secret from his past that, like the angry bird, had come winging into our lives, gouged a fresh wound in my heart. *One day at a time, Bella. One day at a time.*

I sauntered by the stands, pausing when something interested me, spring peas at one, the tangy aroma of strawberries at another, making a note to return if I didn't find something better.

The sun sat high in the sky and warmed, not only my face, but my shoulders and arms as well. Suddenly I felt eyes on my back. *Come on Bella, get a grip. That bird didn't follow you.*

I shook off the feeling and continued browsing, jotting notes on a small pad: free-range brown eggs at Stall 9, organic greens at 15, fresh herbs at 18. I couldn't buy too much with only my bike basket to carry purchases.

As I reached for some early tomatoes, I again felt eyes on me. I whirled around and, sure enough, the young man with the blue backpack stood behind a woman in the crowd. He gave me a self-conscious little wave and ambled off.

Did he follow me here? And if so, why?

I made short work of my marketing and selected a more direct and well-trafficked route home. As I huffed and puffed my way up the hill, I saw the young man loading his bicycle into an old green van.

* * * * *

Tuesday, April 13th, lunch hour

Margaret waylaid me outside my cubicle. "Happened again," she announced, waving the obituary page. "That's twice in two days."

Sure enough, the date of a woman's funeral was listed as three months *before* her death five days ago.

"I made that correction. It's not my fault if Chastity didn't apply the change. Here, I'll show you." I booted up my computer, pulled up the corrected copy and showed it to her on my oversized monitor.

She shook her head. "Doesn't matter. As obituary editor, you're responsible for what goes to print."

"How can you say that?" I thundered, aware other cubicles had grown quiet as people listened. I was about to say more when I realized she spoke the truth. "So what do we do about it?"

"I want you to find someone to take her place."

"Why me?"

"Because I don't have time."

"*You* could use a headhunter," I said, emphasizing "you."

"They're expensive, and our budget won't allow it."

"A Craig's List ad? A want-ad in our own paper?"

"No, you get nothing but spam on Craig's List and those blockheads in HR can't tell shit from Shinola. They'll send me the dregs and let the good ones go." She paused. "You know, I was just thinking…"

"Always a dangerous practice," I muttered.

"What?"

"Nothing."

She paused as though processing what I'd said, then shrugged and continued: "Fifi Falcone said one of her servers was an English major. Go on over and check her out. You can expense your lunch."

I stared at her. I'd suggested that very thing just yesterday and she shot me down. Go figure.

* * * * *

Fifi Falcone stood behind the cash register just inside the ornate entrance. She picked up a menu. "One for lunch?" In response to my nod, she offered a smile that managed to be practiced and warm at the same time. "Right this way."

She showed me to a corner table and pulled out a chair facing the room. As she handed me a menu, her eyes met mine. "Weren't you here yesterday with Alena Lupino and the other lady?"

"That's true," I said, deciding to tell it straight. "I'm from the *Chronicle* and I came to talk to your server. The one you said was more of an English major type."

Her brown eyes twinkled. "That will be our secret if you don't mind. You're in luck. Annie will be your server today."

A young man appeared with ice water, then Annie arrived, notepad in hand. She walked with a noticeable limp. Poor kid, being on her feet all day must be tough.

"May I tell you about our specials?" Annie asked, trying for perky and falling short. I remembered Mrs. Falcone saying something about a family crisis.

"No thanks, I've decided on the catch of the day." I could expense it after all.

"Good choice. Halibut. Fresh caught." She scribbled a few strokes on the pad. Beanpole thin, she looked as though she could use one of Mrs. Falcone's hearty meals. Her hair, a deep, golden blonde, was done up in a bun. The few escaping tendrils that framed her thin face gave her a sweetly old-fashioned look.

"Um," I said, "do you have a moment?"

Her eyes registered shock, and something else—fear perhaps. "Not really."

"Your boss said it would be okay."

"Are you a cop?"

A cop? I forced a smile to put her at ease. "I'm from the *Chronicle*. The obituary editor actually."

"No," she said. "I don't want an announcement." Tears glistened in her eyes.

A death in the family? Better not to ask directly.

"It's not about that," I said, without knowing what "that" meant. "I'm here on behalf of my boss. Knowing your background, she'd like you to apply for a copy editor position."

She turned toward Mrs. Falcone. "But I couldn't leave…"

"She said it was fine." A pregnant pause. "I didn't mean that quite the way it sounded."

She gave me a little smile. "I know that." She spent a few moments rearranging my silver, obviously thinking. "I'd like to apply."

"Great." I handed her my card. "Let me know after you've talked to Human Resources and I'll make sure your application gets to our managing editor."

Was it my imagination or did she stand a little straighter?

10

Thursday, April 15th, early

After Mike left, I went back to bed. After our second interview yesterday, we'd spent another restless night. Thank goodness I didn't have to be at the paper until later. Mom was sleeping in as well. I stretched and yawned, catching sight of bright sunshine streaming through the window.

The day was too pretty to waste on escapist sleeping. I flew the few steps to the closet, peeled off my nightgown and stepped into an old pair of jeans puddled on the floor, the better to work in my prayer garden, an activity I always found healing.

I had just retrieved trowel and hand rake, knelt into the soft earth and begun to plant rosemary shoots, when a plain wrap sedan pulled into our driveway and began its wide swipe to our front door.

I shielded my eyes against the sun, trying to identify the vehicle's lone occupant. He came closer and I realized it was one of the Detectives Ironwood. As he stepped from the car, I studied his chin for a scar. Good. It was Frank, not quite as creepy as his brother Rick. What was this all about?

"Detective, good to see you." *Liar, liar.* "Why isn't your partner with you?" I wanted to ask, but didn't. "What brings you out on such a fine morning?"

"Is it?" He looked around as though he hadn't noticed. "Your husband at work?"

"Left half an hour ago. You can catch him at the shop."

Ironwood shook his gleaming head. Amazing, it didn't even have a five o'clock shadow. He must shave it daily. "I'm here to see you." He didn't ask if it was a good time. "Got coffee?"

"Uh, no, but I can make some."

He accepted without hesitation. We walked in awkward silence to the house, down the hall and into the kitchen, the longest walk in the world at that moment.

The detective seated himself at the table and gazed mutely out the window at my kitchen garden, the other less formal patch of land I putter in. I joined him with cups for both of us, offering a wide-eyed guileless look that I hoped would hide my nervousness.

"I want to review the events of the other day," he said without preamble.

"Detective Ironwood, I don't mind, but we went over this repeatedly at the murder scene Monday morning and then again yesterday."

A nod of acknowledgement. "True, but after another night's sleep you may remember things a bit differently."

I saw it now. He wanted to question me away from Mike. But for me to tell the detective that he recognized the murdered man could lead to disaster. My husband would become a suspect at worst— at best, it would look like I had a wifely ax to grind.

Through two cups of coffee that gave me heartburn, I repeated what I heard and saw early Monday morning. How the idling engine woke me from a deep sleep, how I moved onto the portico in time to see a tall dark figure emerge from the path, enter a black Escalade and bolt from the driveway. Acting on some instinct I couldn't explain, I again failed to mention our earlier encounter on the state park road. Thinking about it, I realized the first Escalade was driven by a shorter man.

"Did you get the license plate number?" he asked, narrowing his eyes.

Acid boiled in my throat. "No, I told you, I didn't have my glasses on."

"I see." Ironwood drained the dregs of his second cup as though caffeine were his lifeblood. I didn't fare so well; my stomach rebelled and my knees knocked together. I can drink tea from dawn to dusk, coffee not at all. Add to that the stress of these questions…

Detective Frank interrupted my reverie. "Okay, tell me again what you saw in the grove near the beach." He took no notes.

Tamping down my growing irritation, I repeated how we'd walked into the lobby looking for coffee and saw blood tracked on the floor, puddled behind the counter and spattered on the wall. How we followed the trail to the beach where we found Joe Milosch's body face up on the sand. I didn't mention that Mike at first refused to call law enforcement.

"The victim was stabbed as you know," he said. "Did you by any chance find anything that could have been used as a weapon?"

They hadn't found it? "No, of course not."

"You're sure?" he pressed. I nodded like a good girl. "Did you see anyone lurking, or smell anything out of the ordinary?"

"No one. And just the smell of blood in the hotel. I couldn't get it out of my nose for hours."

"Okay, you and your husband have been very consistent in your stories."

Did that mean *too* consistent, as though we'd rehearsed? "You interviewed him as well?"

He ignored the question. "Almost done. Let's go back to when you first woke up and heard the sound of the car engine. Was your husband asleep next to you?"

"Of course. Where else would he be? I tried to wake him, but he rolled over and moved to the other side of the bed. The beds at the Inn are enormous," I added unnecessarily, and felt myself redden.

The detective remained impassive. "And after you came back inside?"

"He was awake and sitting up in bed."

"His appearance?"

"Scared," I said without thinking.

*****

He left before I could explain or equivocate. Of course Mike looked scared; he'd just been jolted awake. Several times I started to phone the detective with this mundane observation and each time ended up putting the phone down.

His sudden appearance left me with several questions of my own. Did the Brothers Ironwood feel our stories were a bit too tidy? And why was Detective Frank so interested in Mike's reactions? Did he know, or suspect, that Mike knew the murdered man? The missing weapon also presented a conundrum. Why did he think I knew anything about it?

11

Saturday/Sunday, April 17th, 18th

Somehow Mike, Mom and I got through the weekend, with her sleeping more than ever. This gave me a new worry about the toll the treatments were taking on her body.

I wore myself out weeding, digging and fertilizing both my prayer and kitchen gardens, activities that worked wonders on my nerves.

Mike spent lots of time in his upstairs study, doing who-knows-what, except that it involved a lot of overhead pacing. Later, I overheard him turn down a phone invitation to play racquetball with Ryan Scully, a first.

I hated to see him rebuff people who cared for him at a time when he needed all the support he could get. My husband does not always act in his own best interests.

* * * * *

Monday, April 19th, early morning

I arrived at my desk to see Annie Carter occupying the cubicle opposite me. "Welcome," I said. "That was quick."

She looked up from filling out a form and smiled. "I'm working the early shift for a few days until I learn the ropes." I nodded. Copy editors generally start work shortly before the day staff goes home.

"I wanted to give Mrs. Falcone two weeks notice, but she said I could leave right away," she continued. The smile widened a bit as she gestured toward her bad leg. "I wasn't a very good waitress anyway."

Today her blonde hair fell into ringlets as though set in the rag curlers my English grandmother favored. That and her green argyle sweater, matching plaid skirt and buckled oxfords gave her the look of a 1940's school girl.

I walked across the aisle and placed my hand on her thin shoulder. She flinched at my touch. "Not to worry. You did just fine and Mrs. Falcone thought so too. This job will be easier on you." She nodded, relaxing, but seeming to expect more.

"Um," I asked, "is your family crisis over?"

Tears sprang to her eyes. "It will never be over," she breathed, reaching for a tissue. "My husband died recently."

I remembered at the restaurant, when I told her I was the obituary editor, she said something about not wanting an announcement. She'd said something else too, something surprising. What was it? I couldn't remember. I tightened my grip on the shoulder of this young woman, who couldn't have been more than twenty-four or –five. "I'm so sorry. Was it sudden?"

"Yes," she said without hesitation or elaboration.

* * * * *

Monday, April 19th, late afternoon

The first thing I saw when I pulled into the driveway was Mike digging in the front yard. My heart sank like a stone in a well. Septic problems were the last thing we needed.

I shut the Subaru door, Sam's signal to emerge from one of his several hidey holes. Today proved no exception. "Hey, Sam, how are you, boy?" The tail answered for the dog, a wag of pure joy. We walked over to where Mike stood in a deep ditch tossing dirt over his shoulder.

"What on earth are you doing?" I asked, although it was obvious. "And where's Mom?"

"Napping." He squinted at me and wiped his sweaty brow with a dirty palm. The mark it left gave him the look of a painted warrior. "Thought I'd check out the tank before we hook up to the sewer system."

"That's at least a couple years away," I said, referring to the latest pronouncement in our ongoing sewer saga. The debate to sewer or not sewer had been raging among Los Lobos residents for an unbelievable number of years. Finally Tolosa County and the state water board had stepped in and proclaimed: "Thou shalt…Or else!"

"Why now?"

His eyes remained on this task. "I need to work off some stress."

"Now *that* I can understand." Sam, being a vocal as well as a sensitive canine, whined his approval. He always picked up on our stress signals.

We both became aware of a sedan making its way up the driveway. Sheriff's Detective Ryan Scully. *Oh swell.* Join the crowd, I thought, remembering Detective Frank's recent visit.

Mike swore softly. "Bella, I can't talk to him right now. Take him inside and make nice while I get myself together."

Get himself together? "He probably wants to play racquetball."

He looked at me and I looked at him, both knowing that wasn't the reason.

Ryan pulled to the side of the driveway closest to us. He unfolded himself from the car; first a foot and leg, then a belly smaller than when he and Mike first started playing, then the dark hair, big face and bright smile of a true Irishman.

I hurried to meet him, squeezing his plaid sport-jacketed arm. "Ryan, come on in and I'll make tea." He liked his late afternoon tea. As did I.

He shook his head. "It's Mike I want to talk to." Then he seemed to reconsider. "But a wee spot of yer fine tea would be lovely."

* * * * *

I left the men alone at the kitchen table with their tea. They probably figured I'd retreat to the living room or my study. Instead I remained just out of sight in the front hall where I could overhear.

Ryan didn't mince words. "This guy who was killed over in Mariposa Bay, this Joe Milosch, the fooker's got no past."

Silence then, "What do you mean?"

"When the Mariposa Bay PD checked, they found a false social security number and driver's license, a nonexistent address and no next-of-kin on the employment application."

I wondered how a sheriff's detective knew all this. Agencies are often reluctant to share information.

"The Mariposa Inn didn't check when they hired him?" Mike asked.

"Apparently not, according to Frank Ironwood."

"He talked to you about the case?" Mike sounded incredulous.

"We conferred colleague to colleague," Ryan allowed.

Interesting. Apparently Mike thought so too. "You're shittin' me. How did—"

The furnace kicked on, making it difficult to hear. I studied the nearby thermostat. Should I turn it down so the furnace would go off? Better not. The click the dial made when rotated would announce my presence as surely as a gunshot. I moved closer to the pocket door that separated kitchen from hall, hoping I wouldn't cast a shadow. Better, but not perfect.

"Could Milosch be illegal?" Mike asked.

"Possibly," Ryan answered, "though Ironwood said according to Inn personnel, he spoke with a Midwest accent."

I thought back to the night I'd talked to Joe Milosch when we checked in. Did he have an accent? I couldn't recall.

"No such thing as a Midwest accent," Mike said.

"Go on with ye," he countered, slipping into a hard-core brogue. "It's yerself you should listen to. Speak through yer nose, you do, with a broad A. Like, 'paasta.'" He did a pretty fair imitation.

"What about DNA?"

"Cremated," Ryan answered.

"The coroner released the body? To whom if there's no next of kin? How did *that* happen?"

"Beats me." Ryan took a noisy slurp. "Not my jurisdiction."

"Fingerprints?"

"Not on record," he said.

"Sixty-five million sets of prints in that database and none of them matched Milosch's?"

"That's what I'm trying to tell yer, Mike."

"What are you thinking?"

"Body released prematurely, prints wiped from the database. Witness protection, maybe."

"That means Feds," Mike said. "U.S. Marshal's Office, maybe the FBI as well."

"True," Ryan said, "but the Mariposa Bay PD doesn't want to go there yet."

"Jurisdiction, jurisdiction, jurisdiction."

"They don't want to, what do you Yanks say?, 'Jump the gun.' Maybe you could poke around, see what you find. If the chap's from the Midwest, you must have contacts there and you could..."

"Wait a minute," Mike said. "This stinks of a cover-up. Too hot for me to handle. Besides..." he hesitated, "I can't.

Of course you can't. We found the body. Had he told Ryan this? Apparently not, or they would not be having this conversation.

"Why can't ye?" Ryan asked. "We'd find some money to pay you. Try to find out more about the Ironwoods. They seem a bit, I dunno, hinky."

"Hinky?" Mike asked in a puzzled voice.

"You know, unreliable. Hinky. There was a scandal a few years ago involving Frank. But it came to naught. And get this, they still haven't found the weapon that killed Milosch, probably a hunting knife from the size of the stab wounds."

"Really?" Mike whistled.

"Achoo!" The sneeze surprised even me. *Maybe they didn't notice.*

"What was that?" Ryan asked. *Maybe they did.*

"The dog has allergies." *Good one Mike.*

"Tell me again why you can't take this job?" Ryan pressed anew.

Mike's voice rose a notch. "A lot of reasons, but mostly Bella complains when I take investigative work."

It was all I could do not to scream. I never complained about his moonlighting, the extra money came in handy. I hate it when someone makes me a patsy.

"Besides," Mike continued, "The business is having cash flow problems. I may have to lay off Little Mike and then I wouldn't have any spare time."

Wait a minute. I do the books and we can still afford to pay his assistant.

Which begged two questions: Was there something I didn't know about our business? And—why not just tell Ryan he had a conflict of interest in this case because we found the body? *A missing link here, a big fat one.*

Chair legs scraped on the tile floor, cups and spoons were picked up, a clatter as they were dumped in the sink. For me to wash, naturally. This normally wouldn't bother me, but I was already steaming.

I strode back into the kitchen. "Let me show you out, Detective Scully, while Mike here washes up the tea things."

Mike gave me a look that would stop a drone. "I'm on my way back outside. *I'll* show you out, Ryan."

* * * * *

I stood at the sink scrubbing a tea stained cup until the yellow rose adorning it squealed in pain. Who was this man I married? How dare he shut me out? And why did I feel compelled to wash his dishes?

"Not *my* fault," the rose seemed to say.

Tea things washed up and stowed, sink and stove scrubbed within an inch of their lives, I decided to give Mike a piece of my mind. And shove it down his throat if I needed to.

I realized there was something wrong even before I made it to the end of our front walk. Mike studied the large hole in the ground, speaking into his cell phone.

I ran to him and stared into it as well. In it lay bones, including a skull and what appeared to be a human pelvis.

* * * * *

Ryan returned immediately in response to Mike's call. They peered into the hole, scratched their heads and speculated about who it might be. Both thought from the color and texture that the bones had been there a long time. I told them I thought they belonged to Emily Divina, our resident ghost, who jumped to her death from the windmill when her fisherman-lover died at sea. The two men disagreed, insisting the pelvis, because of its size, had to be male.

Most likely Emily's husband Isaiah, the miller. If so, why was the old coot buried in the front yard, instead of the Los Lobos cemetery? And why hadn't he been found before now? Like when the hole was dug for the septic tank, probably in the 1940s?

In response to a call from Ryan, law enforcement experts who know about such things arrived. They also peered into the hole and scratched their heads, then did what experts do: took photos, wrote reports, unearthed more bones, and finally, removed the whole lot for further study.

Which left Mike and me alone with our problems.

* * * * *

The sun disappeared, the evening chilled, and still we remained side by side, gazing into the now-empty hole in our front yard. Finally I could stand the silence no longer. "Mike, you have to tell me what's going on."

"What do you mean, 'What's going on?' We found an old skeleton on our property, and now we'll have law enforcement sticking their noses in where they don't belong. I shouldn't have called Ryan."

"Why should that matter?" I asked. "Finding an old skeleton in our yard has nothing to do with us finding the body of Joe Milosch."

"I don't want the bastards hanging around here, sticking their noses into our business." He glared at me.

"I know why you don't want them, Mike. You're afraid they might find out what I already know." I held up three fingers. "One, you told Ryan that I objected to you taking on investigative work. You know that's a lie. Two, you also told him our business is in trouble and you might have to lay off Little Mike. Three, not only did you use me as an excuse, you have either lied, or been keeping things from me, about the murder."

"Aha, so you *were* listening."

"Of course I was listening!"

An exasperated sigh. "Look, I know I've told you this several times in the last few days, but you're going to have to trust me. The business is fine and I'm not going to lay off Little Mike. I just don't want to do this anymore."

"Do what?" I asked.

"Take investigative work."

That's not what he said a few days ago. "Mike?"

"Yes?"

"What happened in Chicago?"

Slowly, as if to a child: "I told you, Steve Pizniak was a crooked cop who, apparently, after he was released from prison, found his way to the Central Coast and got himself killed." He made a "enough already" motion.

I wasn't having it. "We've been together a long time. Don't insult my intelligence. There's more to this than you're telling me."

He turned away, silent as the grave.

12

Tuesday, April 20th, predawn

After several sleepless hours in bed next to a husband fighting his own sleep demons, and later on the living room sofa, I decided to seek out Emily Divina. It sounds strange and it is, but the company of our resident ghost offers me insight and comfort when I need it most.

With the startling clarity that often comes with sleeplessness, I resolved to set aside the problem of Mike's lack of candor and hope that time would give us both perspective. What better way than to concentrate on the puzzle of those bones found in our yard?

I shivered in my terrycloth robe as I crossed the enclosed breezeway (surely a contradiction in terms) to the old mill. I stood at the bottom of the stairs and flicked on the light. Or tried to. The darned thing was temperamental; it would glow for months on end, mysteriously go dark, then come on again for no reason, often in the middle of the night. I grabbed the flashlight I kept at the ready for the dark times and allowed it to lead me up the winding staircase.

Flicking off the beam, I pushed the door open, leaned over to turn on my desk lamp, then decided otherwise. A shard of light from the quarter moon filtered through the picture window, casting shadows on the furnishings and Emily's portrait on the wall.

"Hey Em, big day in the yard."

She didn't disagree.

"You know, we have to find some better way to communicate," I said, easing my tired bones onto the padded window seat Mike had built for me. I pulled the fisherman's knit afghan I made last year into my lap and spread it over my legs. The soft wool, smelling of linen water and Emily's presence did their magic; warmth flowed through me.

I stared up at her portrait on the opposite wall. At first I could make out only the outline of two dark masses, oak frame and her hair. As my eyes adjusted, her skin and blouse took on an eerie translucence.

"Nice blouse, Em, hope you like it. You're stuck wearing it for eternity." *Silence.*

"Come on, don't be sore. That was a joke."

More silence. Her obsidian eyes remained flat, as always staring straight ahead.

"Okay, be that way. Let's get down to brass tacks. Who's buried in the yard? Is it your husband?" *Silence.*

"Aha, don't want to talk, I don't blame you."

It probably wasn't unusual to bury people on their property in those days. I thought a moment. "Do you think the Los Lobos Historical Society would have more information?" *Silence.*

"Okay, I agree. Clara, the historian, told me the tale of you and your fisherman lover and your creepy husband." Clara LeBeau, *was* the Los Lobos Historical Society. Since her death no one had stepped forward to take her place. I was likely the only person who knew Emily's story. Or was I? It seemed like such a dramatic tale would have been chronicled in a newspaper or memoir. Or a letter maybe.

Emily and I sat there immersed in our separate musings. Like a bolt from on high, the idea struck. "Perhaps I should check the Tolosa Historical Museum." Why hadn't I thought of that before?

The light in the hall blinked on.

"I'll take that as a yes, Em."

13

Tuesday, April 20th, noon

I dodged downtown traffic, what locals called 'heavy,' thinking they hadn't a clue. Now LA at midday, that's traffic.

I replayed the scene from last evening in my mind. Pretty flimsy evidence that Emily was trying to communicate with me via the light. Then again, stranger things had happened. But not to me, and not in my study.

Which begged the question: When the light blinked on and off on its own, was Emily trying to tell me something? I'd certainly have to pay more attention to its vagaries, especially when she and I were communing.

The Tolosa County Historical Museum is downtown off Mission Plaza. I parked my car in the nearby garage and hoofed it, noting as I approached the elegant Romanesque look of the place. It was built in 1905, one of over 1600 libraries built nationally by businessman and philanthropist Andrew Carnegie.

The brisk weather of last evening continued, and I hurried up the two sets of steep steps, pausing in the foyer to catch my breath. A small white table displayed literature and offered a warm welcome. I took in a deep breath, my senses noting with pleasure the slightly musty smell of old things, so typical of these places.

The museum had changed since I was last there. Where there had been long counters of old artifacts displayed on both sides of a single room, now the room was divided into three separate areas, gift shop to the right and display rooms on the left. *Nice.*

"Hello," I said, peering into the gift store, and then "Hello?" when silence greeted me. The volunteer on duty must be having a potty break.

I turned left, where the first room displayed vintage wedding gowns. Not today, thanks. The second room had an exhibit of old fishing photos from the late eighteen-hundreds, a good place to spend time until the volunteer returned.

The display was typical of early photos, rows of unsmiling men staring with deep distrust at this confounded thing called a camera. There were some great shots of old fishing vessels however, including one that immediately caught my eye.

The caption read: "Fishing Vessel Hesperia, sunk off Escarpa el Dorado during the great storm of December, 1893." I turned to the next picture which showed the crew posing in front the bow before the ship's fateful voyage. With mounting curiosity, I pulled the small, fold-up magnifying glass I'm never without from my purse and held it up to the photo.

I studied the grim, mostly middle–aged faces staring into the camera, wondering if any had a premonition of impending death. Impossible to tell. The man on the end drew my eye and I focused the lens over his face. Taller and younger than the rest, perhaps thirty, his face lay in shadow. Something perched on his shoulder. I held the glass closer and realized it was a bird, probably a parrot, though it was difficult to tell from the photo's sepia tone.

"May I help you?" I whirled around at the sound of the man's soft accented voice. Neal Grale, our temporary head librarian, stood at my shoulder.

I jumped back, feeling a slight shiver. "You do get around."

A disarming shrug. "I'm a volunteer for the historical society." He smiled, displaying even, white teeth against tawny skin. "Being a history buff as well as a book lover, Mrs. Kowalski."

So, he remembered my name. "It's Bella, Mr. Grale."

"And I asked you to call me 'Neal.' Remember?" He stuck out his hand and I took it, the palm cool to my touch. We laughed self-consciously, pulling away. "How may I help you...," he hesitated, "Bella?"

"I'm researching an old family."

"Are you now? Relatives?" he asked.

"No." I started to tell him more about our windmill house, then changed my mind, the memory of him regarding me suspiciously from the door of the library office fresh in my mind.

He nodded, seeming to understand my reluctance. He looked around. "I just signed on here," he said. "Thought I might get a line on my great-great grandfather. He traveled here over a hundred years ago."

"Fascinating," I said. "Are you into genealogy?"

A small smile. "Not so much. But my Mum is. We're part Maori, as you may have deduced."

I hadn't. Knowing little about New Zealand's indigenous people, I covered my ignorance by asking, "What do you know about his time here?"

"Nothing," he admitted. "He never arrived home and the family doesn't know what happened to him. People slipped away rather easily in those days, I'm afraid." He offered a rueful smile.

"I hope you find his trail," I said.

Another disarming smile. "I will. I never stop until I get an answer." He smiled again, but something in his eyes told me he spoke the truth. "About your own research, you'll want to talk to Leon. He keeps our old family records downstairs. He'll be here on Friday."

"I'll be back Friday," I said, hoping nothing else would go wrong before then.

14

Wednesday, April 21st, teatime

I worked through lunch struggling to clear a backlog of work. Now I felt tired and drained, something only a good cup of afternoon tea could fix. I rewarded myself by hoofing it down to the Cafe Noir on Fig Street for a cup of their fine Irish Breakfast.

Afternoon drizzle had usurped our morning sunshine. Not that I minded; it would be a long summer, most likely with no rain at all. The tiny drops felt dewy on my face and a new lightness found its way into my step.

It would be wonderful to settle inside by the fireplace, chilled hands wrapped around a comforting "cuppa." I stood outside and peered through the front window, eyes drawn to the flame of the hearth against the north wall. Feeling like a voyeur but unable to help myself, I perched slightly to one side, continuing to witness the conviviality that results from the ingestion of caffeine. Like a moth to the flame, my gaze lit on a familiar face. *Mike's.*

My spirit soared as it always does when we see each other unexpectedly, a common-enough occurrence in this small community. I hurried to the entrance, angling to keep him in sight through the wraparound front window. A tall, dark-haired woman approached his table. She carried a large cup.

It couldn't be, but it was—Alena Lupino, the newscaster.

She glanced around and I jumped back, afraid she'd seen me. I pushed ahead anyway. Somehow my feet got to the entrance without my mind telling them to do so. I stood there, peering at Alena and Mike through the door until I felt the hot breath of impatience on the back of my neck. "Lady, you goin' in, or what?" A thirtyish man wearing a suit, a *Wall Street Journal* tucked under one arm, stood behind me.

"Sorry." I stepped aside, unwilling to obstruct a lawyer on a coffee break, then resumed my surveillance.

The newscaster sat opposite Mike at a small table. They entered into an intense discussion, with her doing most of the talking, a lot of it with her hands, while he stared into his cup. What was this all about? First his shocked reaction at the murder scene when Alena wandered in, and now this tête-à-tête. Was she offering him a similar deal for a scoop that she'd made to me? No way. The man I knew would have been out of there like a shot.

Another possibility. Alena was also from Detroit. Maybe they knew each other there. As I considered this, Mike reached into his jacket and extracted a red spiral-bound notebook with a plastic cover, the kind reporters use, only smaller. He handed it across the table to her. She paged through it, stopping to look up at him, obviously questioning certain parts. I started to march in there and find out what the hell was going on. In the end I resisted. Later, I'd tell Mike what I witnessed between them, and insist on an explanation.

* * * * *

Wednesday, April 21st, late afternoon

Without tea, I made my way back to the paper and left early. I drove home slowly, trying to interpret what I'd seen. Was this a repeat of Mike's actions with Connie Mercado several years ago, actions that resulted in tragedy and almost destroyed our marriage?

I thought for sure he'd be home, but the spot where he normally parked the Ford 150 sat empty. And where was Sam? The old dog always came out to greet me. Disappointment and something else, a premonition of change, numbed my face.

Making my way to the front door, I caught a glimpse of the truck in the barn. Mike almost never parked it there. Maybe it had an oil leak and he didn't want to soil the driveway. He was picky about keeping the gravel pristine. Picky about a lot of things. Not always the right ones.

I knew something had changed the moment I opened the door. Despite the truck's presence in the barn, the house felt barren, and it carried the stale smell of emptiness.

"Mike. Mike?" I called, hoping against hope. And then, "Mom?" and, "Rosa?" before remembering the caregiver had taken her for an early-bird dinner at Denny's in Tolosa, her favorite.

"Sam?"

The old dog crept out to meet me, not his usual joyous greeting. "What's wrong? Where's Mike?"

He kept his tail between his legs, very un-Sam-like behavior, and half-turned toward our bedroom.

"What is it, boy? Is Mike in there?" *Oh dear God. Another heart attack?*

I tore down the hall and swore softly when I saw the empty room, our king-sized bed still neatly made. My heart became a small bird fluttering in my chest as I covered the steps to the closet.

Empty, or almost so. Mike (or someone) had removed most of his clothes, leaving behind only tangled hangers, many on the floor. I moved to his dresser. No cell phone on top. Drawers gutted. I dropped onto the bed, staring at the dog. "Mike's gone, Sam. He's gone. How could that be?"

He struggled onto the bed and climbed into my lap.

I sat there, numb, stroking his fur, trying to make sense of it all. Why not take his truck? Because it would be easily traced, that's why. But what if someone removed him by force? Would they take his clothes? They might if they wanted it to look like he'd left voluntarily.

"Have to call Ryan Scully." Sam didn't disagree. I raced for the kitchen phone and halted in front of the message center.

Mike usually parked his laptop on the desk, but now the surface stood bare save for the large write-in calendar. The photo of Ethan, his dead son, was gone from its customary place on the shelf above the desk.

That was the clincher. He'd left on his own; a kidnapper wouldn't know the photo was precious to him. I felt a great stabbing anger in my gut. Mike took his cell phone, his laptop and the photo of his son, but left me behind.

My gaze dropped to the desk calendar. The corner of an envelope stuck out from under it. I yanked it out. The writing on the front said simply: *Bella.* My hands shook so I could hardly open the flap. I tore the note inside in my haste to get at it.

It began by him saying that he had to leave town for a while, that he couldn't take me along because of Mom's illness and her inability to travel, plus the demands of my job.

Hey, how about consulting me?

"I'll contact you when I can," he continued. "Do not tell anyone, including Ryan."

Oh dear Lord. Any hope I held that there was an innocent explanation for Mike's behavior died when I read that one sentence.

He wrote further: "Contacting law enforcement could put your life in danger, and mine as well. Say I've gone back east on business. I've made arrangements with Little Mike to run the shop while I'm gone. He'll stay in touch. Destroy this for your own safety."

For my own safety. What did that mean?

The note ended with him saying how much he loved me. *Yeah, right.*

The sheet of paper fluttered to the floor and I left it there, fighting the urge to kick it across the room. I considered the burden Mike had stuck me with: to maintain a cover story that was implausible at best, and dangerous to me—and perhaps Mom—at worst.

This was too much for me to handle alone. My fingers itched to call Ryan despite what Mike said, to hear his soft brogue telling me that everything would be fine. But Ryan was a cop. His first instinct would be to launch an investigation that might endanger my husband.

A new worry: What would I tell Mom when she and Rosa got home? How could she live under my roof and not be suspicious of some cock-and-bull story that Mike had gone back east on sudden business? Just this morning the three of us had discussed a weekend trip to see wildflowers.

But even if she didn't buy this new scenario, what could she say? Silly question. Knowing my mother, sick or not, she'd say plenty.

Slumped over the kitchen table, Sam's head in my lap, the house silent except for the hum of the refrigerator, I considered my options—call Ryan, despite Mike's warning, and hope for the best, or struggle through on my own and pray Mike would either contact me or just come home.

I needed advice, but who to call? Not Amy, our former managing editor, still an e-mail buddy. She'd have his disappearance all over Facebook in five minutes.

I'd stopped cultivating close friends after Bea, my twin, died. The pain of separation, or even the possibility of separation, was too great. The exception had been Mike, the closest thing I had to a best friend. Now he'd done a bunk, as my English grandmother used to say. I hadn't felt so alone since Bea was murdered.

I remained motionless for a couple of minutes. Then I had an idea that seemed so logical I wondered why I hadn't thought of it before: Call Alena. She saw him last. The bedside clock said five-forty. She'd be at the station. I looked up the number and dialed it, my heart beating in double-time.

"KFAX News," said a chirpy voice.

"Yes, may I speak to Alena Lupino?"

"She's prepping for her six o'clock broadcast. Would you like her voice mail?"

"Yes, please."

I waited as the machine connected and was almost all the way through Alena's honeyed assurance that my call was important to her and that she would get back to me. "Get back to you, Bella?" chided my inner voice. "If they're having an affair, she's not likely to tell you. If it's something even more sinister, she's *most certainly* not going to tell you. This is stupid. You don't know anything about this woman. And you could be putting Mike in more danger."

Good point. I replaced the phone in its cradle. What now? I needed to talk to someone who had my interests at heart. I pondered some more.

Maybe Chris. My nephew had a knack for really getting to the heart of things. "Netting it out," he called it. I picked up the phone.

"Yo."

"Chris?"

"Hey, Auntie Bella, what's wrong?"

"How do you know something's wrong?"

"*Duh.* I can, like, tell by your voice."

"Oh Chris, Mike's disappeared. I came home and found his clothes gone."

"You guys have a fight?"

"No, but something serious has happened."

"Wanna talk?"

"Yes, I mean no, I can't."

"Then, like, no offense, why call?"

"Because I don't know what to do."

"I can come home."

I pulled the cell away from my ear and stared at it; he'd said, "come home." Did he really consider this home? What Chris lacked in impulse control, he more than made up for in heart. Too bad his parents didn't appreciate him. My heart filled with love for him.

"You still there?"

"What about your job with the caterer?"

"What about it?"

Oh-oh. "Tell me you won't leave your employer in the lurch." And risk his job. Not after the thousands of dollars spent for him to take that accelerated course at the Culinary Institute in Napa. Not in this lousy economy.

"Course not. Why would you think that?"

Why indeed?

"We're not busy right now. June's wedding season, then we'll be up to our asses in —"

"Chris! Language." Some things never change.

"Uh, sorry. We'll be swamped all summer, but now I can get time off, no sweat."

"That would be wonderful." More than I dared hope, really.

"Let's see, I have to work a company picnic this afternoon and I've got a dentist appointment Thursday."

At least he's taking care of his teeth.

"I'll grab the morning train on Friday. Be there around four. Can you hang that long?"

Could I? "I…I think so."

"Call if you need me. I'd skip the dentist but my tooth hurts like a son of a—"

"What did I just say, Chris?"

"Sorry. See you Friday. It'll be good to see Grandma."

"She's been wondering when you'd show up."

Silence on his end, then, "Auntie Bella?"

"What?"

"Check your bank balance."

* * * * *

Much as it pained me to admit it, Chris had indeed "netted it out." I hurried across the breezeway and raced up the stairs to my study. Breathing heavily, I sat down at my computer, avoiding Emily's eyes. I wasn't yet ready to discuss Mike's betrayal with her.

Fingers shaking so I could hardly hold them to the keyboard, I accessed the bank's website and typed in the username for our account. What if he'd cleaned us out? Surely the man I'd been married to for so many years wouldn't do anything so dastardly. But then, who was that man?

I typed in our password; got an error message. Tried again; same thing. Had he changed it? My palms sweated as I tried the third time. I hesitated halfway through. If I failed this time would the old testament god of the Internet bounce me out?

Or worse, what if Mike changed the password? That would show malice aforethought. I made myself type in the last three digits.

The Internet god smiled. Both our checking and meager savings accounts displayed balances that seemed about right. Of course he wouldn't leave me without funds. How could I even consider such a thing?

Because he's not the person you thought he was, Bella.

A new possibility struck like a lighting bolt. If he didn't take our money, that could mean abduction. Or had he kept a secret fund? Which possibility was worse? The first, definitely.

Still, he'd taken Ethan's picture, something a kidnapper, unless he (or she) knew Mike very well, might not consider. I disregarded the abduction scenario for now.

I stared at the picture of a smiling Mike on my desk, all too aware of Emily's eyes on my back. He had taken Ethan's photo with him, but what about one of me? If he'd grabbed one, that would at least prove he cared enough to have a memento. Not a rational thought, perhaps, but who could be rational in such a situation?

I rushed back downstairs and through the breezeway into the house and to our bedroom, tripping on a scatter rug by his side of the bed. Sure enough, the picture of me at Catalina Island in that awful orange sunhat, the photo he loved and insisted on keeping on his nightstand, was gone as well, leaving behind only a smeared handprint. At least he loved me enough to take a memento.

I leaned over and clasped my knees, fighting for breath. Some unknown force was squeezing the life out of me.

15

Wednesday, April 21st, late afternoon

"Where are you, dear?" Mom's voice called from the living room. I'd hoped for another hour to get myself together before she and Rosa returned. Alas, that was not to be.

"In here, Ma." It would take a minute or two to make her way down the hall with her walker. I used the time to swipe a tissue over my swollen, tear-stained eyes and run a brush through my hair.

"Are you all right?" Mom said, standing in the hall as though unwilling to violate the sanctity of our bedroom. Her mother's instinct on high alert, she looked worried.

"Just a little tired," I said, forcing a smile. "Is Rosa still here?"

She shook her head. "She had to leave. They're going to a late movie to celebrate a grandchild's birthday. She has twelve. Honestly, people should worry more about overpopulation."

She took my silence as agreement. "On the other hand, I wish I had more than one grandchild."

"Mom, I don't think you or the Holy Family order would have been thrilled about me producing grandkids while I was there. As I recall, you wanted one of us to go into the service of God and I was that person."

She nodded. "That's true. I sometimes wonder what your life would have been like if you had kept your vows instead of renouncing them."

God help me, I wanted to throttle her. "I wouldn't have met Mike and gotten married and had this wonderful life. The religious life didn't work for me after Bea died, Ma. You know that. We've had this conversation." *Several times, in fact.*

"You gave up a lot when you left Holy Family. I just hope your husband appreciates that."

A perfect opening. "He's gone for a while." She opened her mouth to say something; I put up my hand. "He had to go back east on some urgent business. He'll be gone several weeks."

She looked puzzled. "Who'll run his business here?"

"His employee is perfectly able to handle things. I don't want you to worry. Everything's under control." *Right.*

She brightened. "Can we still go and see the wildflowers Sunday after Mass? I do miss the flowers and all the greenery of Michigan. It's so drab and brown here."

"Of course we'll go. Do us both good," I said, thinking I should be canonized.

* * * * *

Thursday, April 22nd, past midnight

I sat there in the chilled and dark living room, feeling as though the walls would implode if I didn't get out of the house. Uncomfortable with calling Rosa at that hour, I left Mom alone, aware that was risky given her health problems. I drove the deserted streets of this small community, looking—looking everywhere—for Mike. Mist muted all sound and my eyes played tricks on me as I peered through the windshield at a man walking by the side of Los Lobos Road. He glanced over his shoulder. And why not—an old car slowing behind him on a dark road?

How about that man emptying trash behind Lockhart's Bakery? It was the baker. Totally obsessed, I widened my search to include the train station, car rental companies, even our airport, so tiny it seemed like a toy model, all closed and shuttered for the night.

* * * * *

Thursday, April 22nd, sometime later

Hardly remembering how I'd gotten there, I found myself at the murder scene. I pulled off the road and parked under the grove of eucalypti, the Subaru hidden from the road by their shadows.

I waited for some time, shivering in the dead cold of the car, listening to night sounds—the rustle of eucalyptus, the sigh of a sleeping ocean, my own labored breathing. Then I spied something, a sword of light moving slowly along the path.

I watched from the car, prickles of fear coursing through my body. The sword moved up, down and around the path. No, it was not a sword, but a flashlight beam. Human movement, progressing from cove to Inn parking lot. Hand shaking, I grabbed small binoculars from beneath the seat and trained them on the tall, dark figure holding the flashlight. He, for surely with all that height and girth it must be a he, seemed to be searching for something. He reached the end of the path, shining the light in a circle on the ground again and again. Then he reversed course and moved toward the cove, once more shining the light along the path.

The figure disappeared over the crest of the hill. A few moments later I heard the growl of an engine. A few seconds after that, a black Escalade passed, heading toward Mariposa Bay. Too fast for him to see me—or for me to see his license plate.

I needed help and I knew it.

* * * * *

The Wandering Nun stood in the shadow of the eucalyptus trees, hand to mouth, appalled at what she had done so impetuously the day of the murder. Because she'd thrown the knife into the bay, a killer would go free for lack of a weapon. Now she had just witnessed the same person returning to the scene of the crime, searching for the missing knife. What could she do to make things right? Even if she could swim, it would be almost impossible to locate the knife in the muddy bottom. She doubled over in pain and began to weep, for herself, for her birds—and most of all—for justice denied.

16

Thursday, April 22nd, early morning

I waited until I knew Ryan would be at the sheriff's office, then called and asked the receptionist to connect me. "I'm sorry," she said, "Detective Scully is out on personal leave."

I stared at the phone. I finally decided to confide in him and he wasn't there? "Um, Mike Kowalski's my husband. He sometimes works as a contract investigator with Detective Scully, and they play racquetball together. Is Detective Scully at home?"

"He's not," came the perky voice. "This is Marge. I've heard Mike speak of you. One of his brothers is sick and he's gone back to Ireland to spend time with him."

Ryan gone? So soon after Mike? And what about him wanting Mike to investigate the Ironwoods? "Are you sure he's in Ireland, Marge?"

"Of course, I took the original call from his sister."

* * * * *

I called myself in sick, something I'd rarely done in my years at the paper. I told Mom and Rosa I had a twenty-four-hour bug and spent the entire day in bed, greasy-haired, dry-mouthed, dozing some, but mainly tossing and turning, unable to cope with this latest thing that, like the angry bird, had come winging in out of the universe.

Ryan in Ireland, no one else in the sheriff's office I knew or trusted enough to call. As for the Ironwood brothers, forget it, especially after what Ryan said about them.

I was very aware of the forty-eight-hour guideline: If a missing person is not found within that time, the chances diminish that he or she ever will be. A new thought struck terror into my heart. What if Mike had a breakdown? Considering how he'd acted lately, that was possible, even likely.

I drifted into a restless slumber, awakening to pounding on the door. My heart hammered in my chest. More door pounding. Light leaked through the blinds; must be late afternoon.

"I'll get it!" I yelled, grabbing my robe. I ran barefooted for the door, thoughts running amok. Mike back, missing his key? Chris arriving early? The police come to deliver bad news? I adjusted the blind and peered out the side window. The *Chronicle's* managing editor stood on the porch, holding something in one hand. *Swell.* I cracked the door and stood behind it, displaying only my head and shoulders.

Margaret gave me an open-mouthed stare. "You look like hell. What's wrong?"

I pulled my robe around me and opened the door. "Just a flu bug. I should be fine tomorrow morning. Monday for sure."

She took a step back, thrusting a carton at me with both hands. "If it's flu, I won't come in. Here, I brought you some soup. From the market. I don't cook." She peered over my shoulder down the hall. "Is Mike taking care of you?"

Why would she care? "A relative died and he had to go back east for a while."

She gave me a look like she expected me to say more.

Time to deflect. "Sure you won't come in? Maybe have some tea."

She made a face. "Never touch the stuff. I'm on my way to see Alena."

"Alena?"

"Lupino. My um, friend," she said as though not sure she believed it.

"I know, but won't she be at the TV station?"

"She takes a dinner break after the first broadcast, then goes back for the second round."

"That's a lot of driving. I assumed she lived in Tolosa."

"No way, Alena has to have the best. She's got a spread up in the Heights."

Hmm. "You know, Mom likes to look at fancy houses on our drives. Maybe I'll take her by to see that neighborhood on our next outing."

She gave me a "whatever" shrug. "Lives there with her daddy. Typical Alena overkill—a flamingo-colored spread with a drop-dead view. Too gaudy for my taste."

"Sugar daddy?" I asked.

"No. Real. Bootsie."

Bootsie Lupino. Sounds like a gangster.

"I'll be going." She turned and took half a step, then turned again and looked at me, something I couldn't read in her eyes. "Sure everything's all right here?"

"We're fine," I said, which didn't exactly answer the question. I heard shuffling noises behind me. Mom stood at the end of the hall, just outside the kitchen. I gestured toward her. "I've got Mom here to help." Standing there, leaning on her walker, my mother didn't look like she could help anyone, including herself.

"See you tomorrow bright and early," Margaret said, giving me a little wave. As she made her way down the walk, she looked toward the barn where Mike's truck was parked in plain sight. Then she looked back at the house and shook her head like she was confused.

"Who was that woman?" Mom said as I bolted the front door.

"My boss, Margaret."

"Really? She certainly doesn't look very professional, with that stringy gray hair and all. Now if she cut it into a nice bob—"

"Ma, don't start. She's an okay person."

She pointed to the carton in my hand. "She brought you food."

I held out the carton. "Soup. Pea."

A thump of tail on floor behind me announced Sam's presence, undoubtedly drawn by the aroma of something that might prove to be dinner.

"Pea?" she said, wrinkling her nose. "She can't be much of a buddy if she doesn't know you hate pea soup."

"She's not a buddy, she's my boss and she dropped off some soup on the way to see her friend. End of story." I waved the carton under Sam's nose and moved toward the kitchen. "Come on, this is your lucky day."

As I poured half the soup (which looked hearty and rich) into Sam's bowl, wondering if it would give him gas, Mom asked, "Have you heard from Mike?"

"Yes," I lied, "he called this morning."

"Funny, I didn't hear the phone ring. Did he give you any idea of when he'd be back? He's got a business to run and a house to take care of." She sighed. "I swear. Young people these days have so little sense of responsibility."

I slammed the carton down on the kitchen counter. "I said, give it a rest, Ma."

"Well." A pregnant pause. "I never." She turned the walker with surprising agility and moved at a pretty good clip toward her bedroom.

"Ma, I'm sorry," I called after her. She didn't hear me—or chose not to.

I put the rest of the soup in the fridge, deciding to clear some kitchen clutter. When I'd worked my way across the counter to the desk, I realized I'd never picked Mike's note up off the floor. Or had I? Had I stashed it somewhere and didn't remember? It wouldn't be the first time I'd had short-term memory loss under stress. In any case, the note had taken feet and walked.

I thumbed through the accumulated papers on the desk, ransacked the drawer and even pawed through the trash. *Nothing, nada, zip.*

"What are you looking for, Bella?" Mom said behind me. She never stayed mad for long. Besides, she wasn't about to let me off the hook about Mike.

"Ma," I said, "did you find a…?" I started to say "note," and decided that was too much information. I wanted to avoid any conjecture on what the note said or who wrote it. Did you find a piece of paper on the floor?"

She looked genuinely puzzled. "What kind of paper?"

"Just a bill I forgot to pay. It's not important."

She shook her head. "No, dear, I didn't. Far be it from me to criticize, but you need to be more mindful of your things. Perhaps Rosa found it."

Good call, Mom. "Rosa?" I called. "Rosa?" Louder.

"Yes?" Rosa said, appearing too quickly for her not to have been listening.

"Did you find a piece of paper on the floor?"

"No, Mrs. Kowalski," she said, but not before something changed in her eyes. In a flash it was gone and she had regained her Latina composure.

"You're sure?" I pressed.

"Absolutely," she said, keeping careful control of her eyes.

"That's okay." I gave them both a wave of dismissal. "I'll find it," I said, wondering if I would.

One thing I was sure of, Rosa saw the note. Her eyes betrayed her. She knew we were in big trouble.

17

Thursday, April 22nd, evening

After Mom went to bed, I collapsed on the living room sofa, eyes fixed on the cold and dark fireplace grate, mind fixed on Alena. Who was this woman, and what was her connection to Mike? Was she a rival? Or perhaps responsible for his disappearance. Maybe both.

A forty-something woman with a glam job who lived with her *father?*

The idea planted itself slowly, but once it did, I couldn't shake it loose. Mike might be there. With her. *Hmm.* I'd drive by Alena's flamingo-colored house. There couldn't be more than one that color. It stood on the corner of Heights Drive and Dana Circle. *Hmm.*

I called Rosa and asked her to stay with Mom for a couple of hours while I met a friend for a drink. She was happy to do so.

* * * * *

I turned right on Los Lobos Road heading toward Escarpa el Dorado, a gorgeous bluff north of town that overlooked the bay. At the moment the view was lost to darkness and my own concerns. With mounting nervousness, I followed the road as it veered left past my favorite nursery, then hung another left at the development sign "Escarpa Estates."

The homes grew more lush as I wended my way up the steep hill. Another quick left at Heights Drive and another even steeper hill, culminating in a wide sweep before a hard right onto Dana Circle. Just before the turn, I spotted the house, which sat alone on the corner. I slowed down, gawking, heart doing a little thumpity, thump. Two BMWs sat in the driveway, Margaret's silver roadster, a familiar sight in the *Chronicle* parking lot. The other, a red convertible, must belong to Alena.

The house was a spread, a faux Spanish style surrounded by a high adobe wall, with the obligatory tile roof. I wondered what the neighbors thought of the color. And I also wondered about the people on the other side of that wall. Was there even the tiniest chance that Mike was among them? I'd come this far, I couldn't leave without taking a quick peek, if only to satisfy the jealous demon within me clamoring for answers. I completed my right turn, drove half a block and parked by a vacant lot.

I hoofed it down the hill wondering how I'd get beyond the wall, then spied a tall black gate. With no obvious latch or handle, how I would open the gate was another matter. A taller person could reach over and open it from inside, but at just over five feet, I was not that person.

Casting around for inspiration, my eye landed on a cooler-sized rock set in front of the wall. I probably couldn't lift it, but with no other option than to go home for a stepstool, I would give it a try. I gave the boulder a good tug and almost landed on my tush. It was fake.

I easily carried it to the gate, wondering if the molded plastic would support me—and if any of Alena's neighbors were watching. It did, and they weren't. I unlatched the gate, propped it open with a smaller rock, and returned the fake one to its rightful place.

I stood on the inside walkway, counting five outdoor spotlights. The yard was lit up like a tennis court at night. The neighbors must be so thrilled. I quickly ducked into shadows at the edge of the property.

What now? I couldn't just bang on the door and say, "Hi, I'm Bella, and I'm looking for my husband." What if I found him inside? A bit of a stretch perhaps, but it seemed too much of a coincidence that he'd disappeared right after meeting with Alena. They might even be lovers. Nothing was impossible.

I had to find out more; peeking in a window was as good a place as any to start. The ones on the west side spewed light, most likely the dining room and kitchen area, given that it was dinner time.

Keeping low and staying in the shadows, I crept to a bay window, ducked behind a convenient hedge and peered through the glass into a large dining room. Alena stood in front of an enormous breakfront near an arched doorway, talking on a cell phone. She clutched a spiral-bound notebook in one hand. It was red. The one Mike handed to her at the Cafe Noir?

My heart sped up. Until a few days ago I didn't have much faith in coincidences, but here was a big one staring me in the face. If his notebook was here, did that mean he was too?

She glanced out the window, perhaps sensing my presence. That woman had a sixth sense; she'd seen me watching her through the coffee house window, I know she did. She turned away to face the breakfront and continued her call.

A few moments later, Margaret and an extremely small—almost dwarf sized—man appeared in the arched doorway. His hair, more white than gray, was combed over a bald spot of epic proportions. Must be Bootsie Lupino.

Margaret juggled takeout cartons; he leaned on his tiny cane while hugging three plates close to his Humpty-Dumpty body. Alena started visibly when she saw the couple. Quickly she stuffed the notebook into the right-hand breakfront drawer, tapped the phone and slipped it in her pocket.

What followed played out like theater without words. The couple set plates and food on the table and beckoned Alena to join them. Bootsie extracted a packet of what appeared to be wet-wipes from his pocket and set it by his plate, despite the basket of paper napkins beside the salt and pepper shakers.

They again indicated for her to join them. She shook her head, ducked toward the doorway from which they'd emerged, and disappeared.

Bootsie and Margaret took seats beside each other, her hulk towering over him. Ignoring the food, they bent their heads together and began an earnest conversation, both occasionally looking up at the doorway into which Alena had vanished.

The news anchor reappeared a few minutes later, tension showing in every jerky movement. What was in that notebook? Did she finish her call in the other room? When they saw her, the couple stopped talking and broke apart.

The managing editor touched the back of her hair self-consciously as Alena took a seat opposite them. Bootsie removed three wet-wipes from the pack and scrubbed his hands and forearms. He took a fresh wipe to clean his plate, and another to clean his utensils. A germ freak.

Cartons were passed and silverware clinked against plates as they consumed their takeout meal in silence.

* * * * *

I stood in the shadows, pondering Bootsie and Margaret's conversation. From their body language, it seemed to be about Alena. After the TV anchor joined them at the table, the three never exchanged a word. Despite Alena's barbs about Margaret's weight, I remembered the friendly chatter the two women had exchanged over lunch at the Tolosa Inn. Whatever I'd just witnessed had somehow disturbed the dynamic of their friendship.

Was Mike in that house somewhere? Probably not. Margaret would have never told me where Alena lived if she had any inkling he was there, and Alena and Bootsie would not invite her to dinner if they had something to hide.

On the other hand, I had a strong a strong hunch that the notebook might offer a clue to Mike's whereabouts. If only I could get my mitts on it.

What was that? Something wet and cold nudged my cotton-clad tush. I stumbled sideways into the bushes, recovered my balance and whirled around to encounter a large black nose. Unfortunately, the schnozz was attached to a pit bull who, from the look of his black and white spotted body and rakish eye patch, had at least one Springer spaniel ancestor.

"Nice doggy. Nice doggy. Nice. Doggy," I said, backing away.

The white tail wagged. So far so good. I stopped. The big guy (I determined after a quick check) didn't seem perturbed. Not unusual. Dogs like me.

Or maybe "Patch" was a lousy watch dog. In any case, no good could come from hanging around to find out. "Nice *doggy*," I repeated as I backed toward the gate. He followed closely, wagging his tail, but giving me that inscrutable pit bull look I never know how to read. Like he was deciding whether to lick my hand or have it for dinner.

18

Friday, April 23rd, dawn

I dragged myself from bed, determined to get to the office early. Nothing to be gained by staying home and feeling sorry for myself.

Once showered and ready for work I felt a bit better and decided to wear the pearls that Mike had given me for our anniversary. Perhaps having them close to my heart would set up the telepathic connection I'd failed to establish last night at Alena's house. I lifted the box from the dresser drawer and caressed the blue velvet. *Mike, where are you?* Slowly, I lifted the lid.

The box sat empty. *Oh no, not this, not now.*

I spent the next half hour ransacking dresser drawers, other drawers, closets, jacket pockets, anywhere the pearls might be. And weren't. I always, *always*, put them back in the box after wearing them. It was part of the ritual. Which begged the question: Did Mike take them? If so, this action seemed unnecessarily cruel.

Forcing myself to shake off the anxiety and despair of the missing pearls, I phoned my husband's helper, Little Mike, at the shop before leaving for work. He confirmed that he'd be okay with the workload on his own, even knew a guy who'd come in and help if they got really busy. Thank goodness Little Mike was able to take over with little fuss, and no questions. What a good guy. We were lucky to have him. That knowledge didn't make up for the missing pearls, but it helped a lot.

I kissed Sam goodbye on the top of his golden head and was rewarded with a tail smack against my leg. After I came home from my encounter with Patch, he'd backed away, apparently not crazy about *eau de pit bull.*

Now, as the hood of my old car nosed through ground fog hugging Los Lobos Road, I recalled last night's experience: no Mike in sight. Instead, Alena, notebook in hand, making a phone call, Margaret and Bootsie engaged in private conversation, followed by the silent meal the three shared.

The idea hit with the force of a blow. Get inside, have a look at that notebook. Could I really do that? Wasn't going to be easy, and just the thought scared the crap out of me. The newscaster and her father would have to be away, and I'd have to deal with Patch as well. If he found me jimmying the front lock, the pit bull might not be as mellow as he was last night.

I'd find a way, I always did.

Perhaps I should wheel the car around and spend the rest of the day, at least until Chris's train time, staking out the house. Would Margaret believe another sick call? What if she phoned the house and I didn't pick up, or worse, she drove out to check on me and I wasn't home? Mom would be frantic if the managing editor contacted her.

Just keep going, Bella. You can't jeopardize your job and worry your mother. She's got enough to worry about already.

Better to ask Chris's advice later that evening, after he settled in. He'd been my lookout on a similar mission three years ago that yielded good results.

* * * * *

Enough with the aging Nancy Drew bit I thought, arriving at the paper. "You look *so* much better," Margaret said, stepping to the door of her office as I tried to slink by unnoticed.

"Oh, I am," I assured her, putting on what I hoped was an appropriately wan smile. "Just a twenty-four-hour thing."

She nodded as though she understood. "I want you to train Annie as backup for the obit desk."

My hackles rose at the implied need for a substitute. "But I don't need one. I'm always here." A lousy day off and she was hinting that my job was in jeopardy?

The managing editor raised her palms in a "no big deal" gesture. "You never know what might happen."

She left the thought unfinished and I wondered if she knew, or suspected, something about Mike. "Annie worked your desk yesterday. She did okay, but it was light for a Monday."

"Good for her," I said through gritted teeth.

The walk to my desk became The Last Mile. The paper didn't print obits on Monday, but the day could be frantic trying to meet the deadline for Tuesday's edition.

Not immediately seeing Annie, I tried to pick up the thread of what she'd done. She'd left several yellow sticky notes with questions, good ones. A few minutes later, I heard settling-in noises from her cubicle. I gathered up her notes and stepped across the aisle.

"Feeling better?" she asked, looking up from a colorful brochure she'd been studying.

"I am, thanks," I said, repeating what I'd told Margaret about having a bug. Oh, the masks we wear, the lies we tell, so as not to reveal our true selves to the outside world. One lie can lead to so many more.

Annie looked genuinely concerned and that made me ashamed. I felt in my heart that Mike would eventually be found, but her husband was gone for good. I set the notes on her desk. "Let's go over your questions. Is now a good time?"

"Sure," she said, opening her center drawer to stuff the brochure inside.

Jeez, I thought, new on the job, a recently deceased husband, and she's looking at travel literature. Perhaps some insurance money on the horizon?

"May I see that?" I asked, holding out a hand.

"It's still my break. I'm not on company time," she said, giving me a wide-eyed look.

I worked on a smile. "Didn't think you were, I'm just interested."

She held up the brochure, which displayed a photo of Casa de Maria, a spiritual retreat center near Santa Barbara. "Have you ever heard of this place, you having been a sister and all?"

I couldn't help smiling. "Aha, my reputation precedes me."

Her neck reddened. "I mean…well, Margaret told me…"

I shook my head. "Not a problem, but trust me, I am not an expert on all things spiritual." Still, I was intrigued. The brochure offered workshops and retreats in a gorgeous oak-filled setting. "I've heard of this place, and I know they're reputable." I checked the inside page. "In fact, the prices seem quite reasonable."

She sighed. "I'm looking for a place for..."

Why the hesitation?

"I could use a little peace in my life right now," she said.

Fair enough. "Do you have someone to watch your children?" The words popped out before I had a chance to consider them.

Her face clouded. "We never had kids. My husband didn't want them."

Seeing her so young and vulnerable, I wanted to assure her that she'd marry again and have a family, but bit my tongue. Hardly the thing to say to the recently bereaved.

Embarrassed, I picked up the notes. "Shall we go over these now? You did a swell job yesterday. Thanks."

* * * * *

Friday, April 23rd, midafternoon

I used my lunch hour to visit the airport check-in counters and car rental places. No one had seen a man of Mike's description, and if they had, they weren't about to tell me. One clerk suggested I hire a private detective. If I had the money I'd do just that.

After returning to work for a couple hours, I headed for the train station and waited for my nephew on the platform. It didn't seem possible that Chris had completed an accelerated course at the Culinary Institute and gone to work for a Bay Area caterer. A few months ago we'd gone to Napa for his graduation. Our hearts nearly burst on seeing him looking like the old Chris, still with long blonde hair and a boyish manner, but shoulders back, eyes forward, proud of his achievement. I remember gripping Mike's arm, both of us teary-eyed.

Mike, you son of a gun. Where are you? Why aren't you here to help me?

The train pulled up, doors whooshed open, and I felt a tap on my shoulder simultaneously. Ignoring the train, I whirled around, astonished to see the young man from the Los Lobos Farmers Market. Once again he wore the blue backpack he'd thrown at the bird. "Mrs. Kowalski?" he said, hesitantly.

"Yes?" I didn't remember giving him my name.

"May I speak to you? It's important."

"What?" I half-turned and spied Chris standing in the train's open doorway. I turned back with, I'm sure, a desperate look on my face. "Of course, of course. Wait just a moment while I get my nephew." I began walking backward, raising my hands, palms outward. "Stay there. Please."

A KFAX news van screeched into the parking lot as though late for an assignment. Celebrity onboard? A crew member jumped from the van, fiddled with camera and mic. A young stringer alighted, peered around as though looking for a victim, then headed for the young man. "Sir, do you have a moment for a quick interview? We're doing a train feature today." The young man froze.

* * * * *

When I finally returned, nephew in tow, to where I'd left the young man, he'd disappeared. Not surprisingly. The stringer, now working the crowd, had probably come on too strong. "Damn, damn, and triple damn."

Chris looked at me, worry darkening his blue eyes. "What's wrong?"

"Sorry. Someone spoke to me just as your train arrived. Said it was important."

Chris whistled. *"Really?* You think it's about Uncle Mike? "

"Could be." I turned in a circle, still searching for the young man. Several people fit his general description, but he wasn't among them. "I asked him to wait, but then that KFAX news reporter tried to interview him. She probably scared him off."

"Maybe I did," Chris said, looking like he wouldn't scare anyone. The long hair was now clipped short and he'd dressed casually in a button-up shirt, pressed down jeans and clean athletic shoes. His newfound air of authority made him look so mature.

"So, like, what do we do?" he asked, sounding like the old Chris.

"Let's separate and see if we can find him. He's about your age and he's got a blue backpack. Got your cell?"

He produced it from his pocket. "Check."

I did the same. "Check."

"Call me if you see him," I said. "Let's meet here in ten minutes."

Chris disappeared and I walked toward the station's short term parking lot. As I did so, a green van pulled out of a space on the end and took off. The young man had loaded his bicycle into a similar van at the Farmers Market after the bird incident. He appeared to be following me. And today he wanted to talk to me about something important.

19

Friday, April 23rd, early evening

"So, what now, Auntie Bella?" Chris asked, setting his backpack on a twin bed in the second spare room. Mom had been waiting on the porch when we'd arrived, with Chris jumping from the Subaru, scooping her up and, despite her protestations, whirling her around and planting a big kiss on her cheek. I hadn't seen her so animated since she'd been here.

"Ahem." Chris cleared his throat, snapping me back to the present.

"First off," I said, "you're a grown man now, so I think it's time you stopped calling me "Auntie."

He frowned. "So, like, what should I call you? You're my aunt after all."

"You could just call me 'Bella.'"

He shook his head, the frown remaining. "I don't feel right about that. How about "Aunt Bella?'"

I smiled. "Suits me. Let's see, where were we?" I set some hangers on the bed, hoping the mattress would be big enough for him. He'd grown physically as well as emotionally. No more sleeping in the makeshift quarters Mike had built for him in the barn when he lived with us previously.

I studied him, wondering if I dared tell him my idea about breaking into Alena's home. The old Chris would delight in the adventure and sense of danger in the caper. Things could be quite different with the mature young man standing in front of me. He might point out that, technically, we were breaking and entering. And I would in turn point out I'd read that, technically, breaking and entering is illegal only if one intends to commit a crime. In this case, I just wanted to have a look inside the notebook, not take it with me.

Not knowing how to broach the subject and overcome with emotion, I wrapped my arms around him, taking in aromas of the outdoors, and something deeper and muskier, a young man smell. "I feel so much better now that you're here."

He returned my hug with gusto. "We're going to find Uncle Mike."

"I'm sure of it now." I grabbed his hand, took a step back and regarded him. "So why are you doing this? You said Uncle Mike was a dick."

He grinned. "He is. I'm doing this for you."

* * * * *

Chris offered to make supper and I didn't refuse. It's not every day one has access to a personal chef. He did wonders with a package of frozen butternut squash ravioli, ladling over it a sauce of sage leaves from my garden, browned in butter and topped with toasted walnuts and grated pecorino cheese.

As I devoured the last morsel, I realized I hadn't eaten that much since Mike's disappearance. Very un-Bella-like. While Mom skipped the cheese ("Made with *sheep milk,* no thank you.")

on her ravioli, she enjoyed her meal, declaring it much better than Ensure.

Afterwards, she went to her bedroom to keep her nightly date with Vanna White on "Wheel of Fortune." The two of us relaxed in the living room, with Chris in the wing chair by the fire which he lit before settling down. I sat on the sofa, nursing a cup of savory Earl Grey tea. "So tell me what happened," he said, when we heard the theme music announcing the show's opening. His skin had taken on a rosy glow in the firelight. Sam slept with his head on Chris's shoes, a favored napping spot, comfortable as if my nephew had never left.

I took a sip of tea, fragrant with bergamot, and began to tell my story once more: finding the murdered man on the beach just beyond the Wandering Nun grove twelve days ago, Mike's reaction and his insistence that we leave without notifying law enforcement, and my insistence that we do.

I didn't spare him—or myself—leaving nothing out. Chris kept his eyes on the fire, nodding occasionally. A couple of times he made a comment like, "Why'd you hook up with this guy?" which I mostly ignored, or asked an intelligent question, which I tried to answer. Finally I got to the last development before Mike left, his meeting with Alena at the coffee house where he gave her the notebook.

"And supposedly he didn't know her before this meeting?" he asked, reaching down to pat Sam's head. If Sam were a marshmallow, he'd melt on the floor, I thought.

"Oh, I think he did. He looked panicky when she walked into the dining room of the Mariposa Inn as the detectives took our statement. Then when I got home from work a couple hours after they met for coffee, he and his clothes were gone."

"But he left the truck here."

I nodded. "To me that means he was either abducted or someone picked him up and took him to the airport, or to rent a car."

"Could he have taken the train?"

"The train?" I smiled. "No way."

Chris grinned. "Doesn't know what he's missing. You meet awesome people. But I digress." He paused to reach down and scratch Sam's ears as I marveled at my formerly teen-speak nephew using words like "digress."

"Did you check the airport check-in counters and the car rental places?"

"A total waste of time. They all said the same thing. They didn't recall seeing a man of his description at their counter. I got the sense they thought I was a wronged woman bent on revenge."

"Not surprising. Did you check his laptop to see if he made any reservations online? They send an e-mail confirmation."

"He took the laptop with him."

"Crap. Do you know his password? We could log on as him and see what he's been up to."

"On my computer?"

"Sure."

Why hadn't I thought of that? "I don't know his password. He was funny about things like that."

"With good reason, for most people," Chris said, shaking his head as though he couldn't believe it, "but you're his *wife*."

"He changed in the days after we found the body."

"How?" I had his full attention, much to Sam's displeasure.

"He slept a lot, was reluctant to leave the house and didn't talk much about what happened."

"Sounds like you were a wuss about pressing him."

I thought about that. "For the most part, yes, but one night I'd had it and forced the issue. He dug out a clipping from the *Chicago Sun-Times* that showed a younger Joe Milosch as Steve Pizniak—"

"The murdered guy."

"The article said he'd been arrested."

"Convicted?"

"I'm not sure…Wait. Mike mentioned him still doing time, so he must have been convicted."

"So, was he, like, Uncle Mike's partner?"

"I asked him that. He said no, but he'd worked in the same precinct."

Chris steepled his hands together and blew into them. "You know, maybe you shouldn't try to handle this on your own. The newspaper clipping he showed you—"

"But I told you…"

He held up his hands. "That article is something solid. It links the murdered guy to Uncle Mike. Maybe you should take it to your sheriff's detective friend and see if he'll nose around on his own."

"Can't."

"Why not?"

"One, he must have taken the article with him. I can't find it. Two, Ryan Scully is in Ireland on personal leave."

"Crap. Maybe he took the article so as not to leave anything around that could be dangerous to you."

"Could be." So like Mike, I thought. Give with one hand and take away with the other.

Chris grabbed the poker and stirred the embers. Sam gave him a dirty look, then resumed his slumbers when his idol settled back into the chair.

"So tell me about the note."

I summarized its contents, how Mike said he loved me, which caused Chris to roll his eyes, how he had to leave to protect me from something in his past that threatened me as well, how he couldn't take me with him because of Mom.

"Can I have a look at it?"

I knew he was going to ask that. "Nope."

He eyed me suspiciously. "Why not?"

"Because I can't find it."

Chris bolted from his chair, causing Sam to sigh anew. He crossed the room and bent over me, studying my face. "Aunt Bella, are you okay? Maybe you should see a doctor." He felt my brow with a hand that still retained the comforting aroma of sage.

Was I? "Look, I'm fine, or at least as fine as I can be under the circumstances. Mike took the article, and I misplaced his note temporarily. I do things like that when I've got a lot on my mind. It's a short term memory thing."

"If you say so," Chris said, looking skeptical.

"The note fell to the floor after I read it. I got distracted and forgot to pick it up. Rosa, Mom's caregiver, read it, I know she did. Something flashed in her eyes when I asked her if she'd found it."

I put my hand to my throat, thinking of the missing pearls. Had she taken them?

"Any idea what she did with the note?"

Chris's words brought me back to the present. "Maybe she threw it away." I paused. "You know, it seems strange that she appeared here the same day we found the body."

"Like someone planted her here to spy on you?"

"She left Cuba years ago."

"So what does that have to do with the price of cigars?"

"Nothing, I just mentioned it."

His eyes lit up. "You're thinking Cold War stuff? Like Uncle Mike's a secret agent?"

"Be serious, that's too stupid to even consider. You know, there's one other thing. My pearls are missing and—"

"And you think maybe she took them?" At that point Mom called from her bedroom. "She okay?" Chris asked.

"Sure. She wants a goodnight kiss." I rose from the sofa. "Come on, you too."

"Wow," Chris said, prying himself loose from the chair and Sam, "reverse grandparenting."

After attending to Mom's "lights out," we resumed our places and Sam again took up residence on Chris's feet.

"Aren't you afraid he'll cut off the circulation in your toes?" I asked.

My nephew gazed down at the dog. "Nah, he's fine. So, where were we?"

"Rosa, Cold War stuff, my missing pearls," I reminded him.

"If she bugs you, fire her ass."

I shook my head, ignoring the language. "No can do. Mom's really taken with her and Father Rodriguez gave her a good reference. If I fire her, I'll never find out what she knows about the note." *And I'll never find my pearls.*

"Got it. New subject. What makes you doubt Uncle Mike was abducted?"

"Two things, he took his clothes and he grabbed that picture of his son from the kitchen, also my photo. If he'd been abducted, he'd have left both behind."

"Unless the abductors wanted you to think that," Chris said, staring at the flames.

I grew silent, listening to the fire crackling in the grate. "I just thought of something. He took only his favorite clothes, he left what he termed 'the dogs,' usually stuff I bought him."

A slight smile from Chris. "Makes sense."

"Yes, but don't you see? Someone taking him by force wouldn't know that. They'd just throw stuff in the suitcase willy-nilly."

"I'll buy that," Chris said. "So, how about we look at the *Sun-Times* online and see if can find the article in their archive, then try to figure out his password so we can log into his e-mail?"

"Both of those are great ideas, but for later. There's something I want to do first. Here's the thing: I drove up to Alena's house last night and peeked through the window..."

Chris's blue eyes widened. "You did *what*?"

"I was curious to see where she lived." I paused. "Well, you know, full disclosure, I wanted to see if Mike was there. And once there, I decided to look around. Well, one thing led to another…"

"Aunt Bella." He dropped his voice and shook his head as if he couldn't believe what I'd done.

"Remember I told you Mike gave her a small notebook?"

"And you think it will tell you where he is?"

"Maybe. When I peeked through the window, she had the notebook in one hand and her cell phone in the other, obviously calling a number written on a page. At that point, Bootsie, that's her father, and Margaret, her friend, walked in. She threw the notebook in the breakfront drawer, like she didn't want them to see it. And when she left the room, presumably to finish her call, Bootsie and Margaret sat down and had a very serious conversation. They broke apart when Alena reappeared."

"Like, they didn't want her to know what they'd been talking about?"

"Exactly."

"Maybe they were planning a surprise birthday party or something," he said.

Why hadn't I thought of that? "Could be, but they were all so silent afterwards, I think it's something more. Actually, I'm more interested in the notebook than anything that might be going on with them. It could hold the key to Mike's disappearance. I need to get inside that house to take a look at it."

He lowered his head, slacking his jaw. "Tell me you're joking, Aunt Bella."

I toyed with a loose thread on an afghan. "Don't you see, I have to do this? I thought maybe you could help me. Perhaps divert Patch, the pit bull that patrols the yard."

"Pit bull?"

"Well, more like a pit bull, Springer spaniel mix."

He shot up, waving his hands before him like a referee. "Oh no, Aunt Bella, forget it. No friggin' way. Not if hell freezes over. I've seen this movie before. In fact, I was the star." He said the words, but his eyes held a familiar spark of adventure. He'd buy into the idea after he'd had time to think about it.

20

Friday, April 23rd, tenish

Chris didn't have to think long. In fact, an hour later, with Rosa once again holding down the fort at home, he drove my Subaru up to the Heights while I filled him in on Alena's schedule: how she left midafternoon, took a dinner break after the six o'clock news, and returned to the station later to prepare for the eleven o'clock broadcast.

"I figure you could drop me at work and then spend the day up here, checking their comings and goings. It's only for a couple of days, until we figure out the pattern, and if the old man ever leaves."

Chris turned to me, taking his eye off the sharp curve ahead of him. "Like he might go to the Senior Center or something?"

"He doesn't look like the Senior Center type. Watch the road!"

"Don't sweat it, Aunt Bella. I've got it handled."

I gritted my teeth. *Some things never change.* We drove along with Chris rubbernecking the increasingly expensive homes. Suddenly he slapped the steering wheel. "This is, like, so lame. Like this crate isn't going to stand out in this neighborhood like a sore di…"

"I mean a sore thumb," he said, as I wondered what the D-word was. I could only imagine. He was right about the Subaru though.

We drove slowly past Alena's house on the left. Nothing visible except light leaking from behind closed plantation shutters.

"What's going on here?" Chris slowed to a crawl in front of the house next door.

"What do you mean?" This house stood dark and disarrayed, a shell actually, with building materials piled in the front yard. I'd be afraid of thieves if it were my property.

"Obviously a remodel," I said. "I wonder if they work on it during the day." Why didn't I notice it before? "If construction is in a lull, or has been abandoned, you could hang out there during the day and I could relieve you at night." *Did I just say that?*

"What would I do with your car during the day? I'm telling you, this beater would really stand out."

Good question. "We'll rent you a generic one. Do you have a good driving record?"

"Of course," he said a bit too quickly. I chose not to pursue the subject.

"A major credit card?"

"Sure," he said, reaching with one hand for his wallet pocket, the other loosely guiding the steering wheel.

"That's okay," I said, hearing the edge in my voice.

"Relax, will you, Aunt Bella. I'm a good driver."

I took a deep breath. "Get a plain white sedan. Park it around the corner and up the street in front of a vacant lot. Charge the rental to your credit card and I'll pay you back."

"Can we do it tonight?" he asked, now the hopeful adventurer.

"No, we need to wait until Monday. That's longer than I'd like, but Alena only does the news Monday through Friday. I'll drop you at the car rental company and take the Subaru to work."

"Deal," said Chris turning and offering me a hand for a high-five.

"Watch where you're going!"

"Okay, okay."

21

Monday, April 26th, morning rush hour

I dropped Chris at the Tolosa Airport near baggage retrieval and car rental. Only after he disappeared did I realize we hadn't discussed Plan B, what to do if construction workers were at the site. I pulled out my phone. No, he was a smart kid, he'd figure it out.

As I turned out of the airport parking lot heading toward the newspaper office, a green van tucked in behind me. My stomach clenched. The young man again? Hard to tell. He followed me to the corner of Wide Street, turned left when I did, stayed in the left lane as I did, then dropped back to let another car get between us.

Time for a better look. I pulled into the right lane without a signal and glanced his way as the van was forced to pass me. All I could make out was a single driver, probably male, probably the same one who'd been at the Farmers Market and the train station. At the station, he'd said he had some important information for me. He didn't look threatening and I briefly considering flagging him over and asking what was so all-fired important that he had to tell me. But I lost my nerve. Maybe I just wasn't ready to know.

A block later I made another left onto Tank Ranch Road. After I'd gone a short distance, I glanced in my rearview mirror, again spotting the green van, one car between us. He followed me to the newspaper office, where I made another right into the parking lot. The van sailed right on by. A small pulse hammered in my throat. The man inside now knew where I worked.

*****

I began my work day by checking e-mail. There was an angry one from Margaret; Annie had called in sick. Perhaps because of her experience with Chastity No-Show, the managing editor was ballistic, surely more than the Annie situation warranted. Just last Friday she wanted me to train Annie as my backup. Why the change of heart? Poor kid, down on her luck. She didn't need this. There must be a reason she called in sick. Perhaps I should call or even stop by her house after work and warn her.

But Human Resources would never divulge another employee's contact information. I'd have to think of a different way to get it.

A frustrating morning all in all. At Chris's suggestion, I spent my break deep in the online archive of the *Chicago Sun-Times,* searching for the article about Steve Pizniak. Except for obituaries, the digitized archives went back only to 1997.

I checked their obits for Steve Pizniak; no hits from the *Sun-Times* site, or from a wider search. What else could I do? Just then, the phone rang. Duty called. Sleuthing would have to wait.

* * * * *

Lunchtime found me at the Tolosa Inn bakery counter, minus any tails by a green van, thank goodness. I was there to pick up a piece of Black Forest chocolate cake as a special treat for Chris. It was the least I could do after he'd spent an entire day and evening on stakeout duty. And I had another agenda, one that involved Fifi Falcone.

The plan I hatched with Chris called for me to take the late shift. But I wasn't sure I was up to spending even one night cat-napping at an abandoned construction site, hoping I'd wake up at any signs of activity next door. What's more important, I asked myself: getting a line on Mike's whereabouts, or spending a night in your own bed? *Don't answer that,* pleaded my weary inner voice.

Chris had called midmorning with welcome news—no workers at the site. Perhaps it too was a casualty of the economy. He was still parked up the street but planned to walk down and hide inside the hollowed-out shell close to Alena's driveway. He had young bones, he could sit on the floor as he waited. He was dressed in dark shorts, a blue shirt and, under heavy protest, dark knee socks retrieved from the thrift store bag. He also carried one of those long flashlights so residents would assume he was the gas man. Maybe.

According to him, no one left the Lupino house, even for a walk. Perhaps Chris was right, this was a lame idea. But it was the only one I had.

What if they both left? I'd have no idea of how long they'd be gone and unless Chris got very lucky, neither would he. Would I dash up there and enter in broad daylight? I would jump over that one if and when I had to. Chris had rented the car, a white four-door sedan, and we had a plan, which included sneaking in a lawn chair for my old bones to rest on during the midnight shift.

"There you go." The perky clerk handed me a small, pink bakery box. "Hope your nephew enjoys the cake."

"I'm sure he will." I held the box to my nose and sniffed the delectably mingled aromas of rich chocolate and tart cherries, resisting the urge to rip open the box and gobble the cake on the spot.

Time for Act Two. I grabbed my purse from the counter, looking around for Fifi. No sign of her in the café, even though the lunch crowd filled every table and people waited by the door.

"Is Mrs. Falcone here today?"

"Sure," said the clerk. "Would you like to see her?" She waved one hand vaguely toward the door that led from the coffee shop into the lobby. "She's in her office, last door down the hall." I must have looked surprised at being granted such ready access to the owner, because she added, "I've seen you talking to her before."

Fifi Falcone stood behind her desk, placing a stack of folders in a cardboard box. Other boxes were strewn about the office. She looked up in response to my knock on the doorframe and for a moment, didn't recognize me. Then her face lit up. "Ah, Bella, come in."

I looked around the untidy office. "Uh, I don't want to disturb you. Getting ready for painters?"

The smile widened. "Actually, no," she said, "but at this point I'm not at liberty to say." She gave a subject-closed shake of the head tempered by the smile. "What can I do for you? And by the way, how is Annie working out as a copy editor?"

"Fine," I said, deciding not to elaborate. "Though I do have a question about her."

"What is it?" she asked, a line furrowing the bridge of her nose.

"I know personnel information is confidential, but I'm worried. She didn't show up for work today. I know she has personal problems." *Hint, hint.*

She pressed her lips together, moved to her desk and fiddled with her Rolodex. "Right on both counts. She does have issues and I can't reveal personal information." She raised a finger to her lips. "Um, would you excuse me a minute?"

Okay, Fifi, I get it. "Sure."

Once she'd disappeared, I moved behind her desk and checked the top Rolodex card. Sure enough it held Annie's address and phone number. Working quickly lest someone wander in, I grabbed a sticky note and copied the information. I'd just resumed my stance in front of Fifi's desk when she returned.

"Sorry I can't help you, Bella," she said with a hint of a grin.

We traded smiles. "Actually, there is one other thing. Did you ever meet Annie's husband?"

She reached over and snapped the Rolodex shut. "Actually, I did. He picked her up from work once and she introduced him in the parking lot." She shook her head slightly.

"And?" I prompted.

"Well, he was a lot older, I'd say at least fifty. I thought at first he was her father." She paused as though deciding what to reveal. "Unfriendly. So unlike Annie."

"Opposites attract."

"True, but it was more than that. He wouldn't look me in the eye, and it seemed to me that he couldn't hustle her into the car fast enough. Never trust a man who won't look you in the eye."

I considered Fifi's words about trust all the way to the car. And, as I turned the key in the lock, I finally remembered what Annie said when we first talked about her husband dying. She'd asked if I was a cop. Certainly not a normal response. Unless his was an unnatural death—or she had something to hide.

22

Monday, April 26th, after dark

The rest of the afternoon had been hectic, even in a place infamous for that kind of activity. Exhausted, my personal resources drained, I chose not to bother Annie at home. Maybe tomorrow she'd show up for work and I could forget the whole thing.

One thing for sure: I didn't feel like spending the night in an abandoned house. After a hot bath and a glass of wine maybe I'd be up for it. Wine first, I determined, and had just poured a full-to-the-brim glass when Chris called.

"What?" I barked, hating myself for being short with a kid who'd put his life on hold to help me.

"The lady newscaster just left," Chris related breathlessly. "Old fart went with her."

Wow. If Alena went to the TV station and Bootsie accompanied her, they'd both be gone until at least midnight, presuming the old man came home with her.

"Be right there," I said, downing the wine in three gulps.

With a distinct wine-induced buzz, I gathered some dark clothes from the laundry pile, black tights and a dark turtleneck, then decided that was not only silly, it would make me more obvious to a rubbernecking neighbor. Better to stick to the jeans and sweater I had on, skip the watch cap, and add my gray windbreaker.

I was almost out the door, checking that my phone was charged, semi-defrosted hamburger in my pocket, along with small carrots for snacking, when I spied a small flashlight on the front hall bench. I stuffed it in my windbreaker pocket.

* * * * *

"Chris, I parked by the vacant lot and I'm heading toward the house," I said into my cell.

"Awesome. You up for this, Aunt Bella?"

Was I? "Of course. Where's the rental car?"

"Moved it after dark."

"Good. Any other change?"

"*Nada.* I'll get the gate right now." I'd asked him to reach over the top of it, pull the latch and leave it ajar.

"Sure you don't want me to come in with you?"

"Absolutely. I need you outside. Watch for Alena and Bootsie or any unusual activity."

"Like cops?"

"Right."

* * * * *

"Here, Patch." I heard rustling in the bushes and he crept toward me, tail between legs, a sorry excuse for a watch dog. He nuzzled my pocket and I offered him a hunk of hamburger. He took it, dropped it on the ground and sniffed it suspiciously.

"What's the matter, not fresh enough for you?"

He resumed nuzzling my pocket. "What?" More nuzzling. "Is it the carrots you're after?" I dug one out and he snatched it from my hand, showing no manners at all.

I spoke into the phone. "Okay, dog's taken care of. I need to get inside."

"Good luck," Chris said. We'd discussed my options for that. They weren't ideal. I would try the obvious first, see if the front door was unlocked. It wasn't, but most people hide a key outside.

Next to the door sat another fake rock bordered by a bed of azaleas badly in need of tending. Under the rock would be a logical, if not exactly imaginative, hiding place. No luck and a check of other likely spots failed to yield keys to the kingdom. "I'm going to try the back door," I said into the cell phone.

"Okay, be careful."

Predictably, the rear door was locked as well, but standing on the walkway gave me an opportunity to scrutinize the back yard as a potential hiding place or escape route. Neither option looked promising: no tall bushes for cover, and the lot was bordered by a five foot wall, a no-way-Jose for my short legs.

A garage large enough to hold three cars and several riding mowers sat at the back of the lot. "Chris, I'm going to check the garage first."

"For what?" He was practically yelling.

"*Shh.* The whole neighborhood will hear you."

"Get in the house," he whispered. "Focus."

"I'm trying." The wine had addled my brain.

"What are you *doing*?"

"Thinking."

"Don't think, *do* something."

"I am." Bootsie's car wasn't in the driveway on my first visit last Thursday, and he left in Alena's car earlier. Call it the wine, call it an impulse, but I would take a moment to check the garage to see what (if anything) the old man drove. On swift and silent feet I crossed the yard to the garage window.

A dark Cadillac Escalade stood against the far wall. I turned and braced myself against the wall, heart hammering like a sledgehammer. Bootsie was short; so was the driver who tried to run us off the park road.

Oh my god! The mission took on new meaning. One like, "Forget the whole thing. You're playing with the big boys now."

"Earth to Aunt Bella. Come in!"

His bleat hardly registered; my focus had moved to the dog, who stood in front of me. He had a small, slim box, like a key holder, affixed to his collar. What better place to hide a key than on the collar of your pit bull?

In the wake of this unexpected development, I decided to follow through despite my fear, and offered my next-to-last carrot. "Come to Mama, Patch." He took it, but got edgy when I tried to work the box loose from his collar. "Nice doggy."

All I got in return were rip-your-heart-out pit bull eyes. I ignored them, or tried to, and finally managed to slide the box open without removing it from the collar. Wonder of wonders, a key dropped into my hand.

"Got the key," I said, scurrying to the front door. "But you may have to make a carrot run."

"A what?" he croaked.

"Never mind. Inside joke between Patch and me."

I turned the key in the lock and—Voila!— heard a satisfying snick when the bolt drew back.

I stood there, feet frozen to the monogrammed door mat.

"Stay under the beam so you won't trip the alarm," Chris said.

Now he tells me! "By doing what?"

"Simple. Crawl on your belly."

Easy for him to say. "Okay, I'll try." I dropped to my knees and then, on my elbows, slithered over the door jamb into the foyer, the flashlight in my windbreaker pocket jamming into my hip. Patch stayed outside, setting up a hullabaloo guaranteed to summon neighbors.

"Stop that." Still on my belly, I turned and reached into my other pocket, with difficulty extracting the last carrot. I tossed it to him. "Go take a nap. Or something." With one last whine of annoyance, he took the carrot and held it in his mouth, standing rock still. Obviously wondering what this crazy lady was up to. Expecting the worst, I pushed the door shut in his face.

Miracle of miracles, no sound emerged from the other side. Had my luck held? Luck? What luck? At best I would find some clue to my missing husband's whereabouts. At worst I'd be arrested for breaking and entering.

"Aunt Bella, what's happening?"

"Nothing. I just shut the door on Patch."

"Still on your belly?"

"Of course."

"Good, check the walls for an alarm panel."

"I'll have to stand up to turn the alarm off."

"Just *look*, okay?"

I pulled the flashlight from my pocket, turned it on and crawled around, crimping my neck as I scanned the walls.

"Nothing in the entrance."

"Check the kitchen. Maybe they set the alarm there and leave by the back door."

"You didn't notice how they left?"

"All I saw was the car backing down the drive with the chick and old guy inside. Go!"

I returned the light to my pocket and did a slithery snake crawl left toward the dining room and kitchen beyond. My elbows were killing me, but that wasn't what did me in.

23

"Crap, crap!"

"What's wrong?"

I scrambled up and grabbed the nearest wall, putting pressure on my foot to ease the pain in my calf. "Charley horse!" I gasped.

"Work through it."

Yeah, right. Suddenly I realized I was listening to the sound of silence. No shrieking alarms, no security service pounding on the door. No barking. "I think we just got lucky,"

"Some systems just call the cops. Figure out an escape plan before you search the breakfront."

Escape plan. I looked around. "Any ideas?"

"If I see anyone coming, I'll let you know. You head out the back door and over the wall."

I canvassed the kitchen using ambient light from outside. "Bad plan. No door in sight, and that back wall is at least five feet high."

"There's gotta be a back door. Find it."

"Okay, I'm walking, I'm walking. There's a central hall off the living room. Maybe it's down there." Reluctantly, I bypassed the breakfront and moved through the wide foyer into a living room where every light blazed. My skin crawled; I felt like a target. "I'm going to turn off these lights."

"Don't," Chris said. "Adjust the blinds."

"Okay." A few quick flips of the cords. "Can you see me now?"

"Nope you're good."

Just as I was preparing to head down the hall in search of a back door, Patch began another brouhaha. "What's wrong now?"

"Another dog out front. Want me to grab Patch?"

"No, that'll make it worse."

I ran to the front door and flung it open. "Come on Patch, come to Mama."

Miracle of miracles, he did. And immediately began nosing my pocket for carrots.

"Sorry, I'm fresh out." He gave me an "entitled" look and splayed his front legs into a barking stance.

"Please, please don't bark. Let's see what your people have in the fridge." I retraced my steps through the foyer and dining room into the kitchen where stood a stainless steel refrigerator big enough to store a moose. I opened the door. A plethora of healthy choices greeted me, organic everything—tofu, cheese, veggies. Even wine. I'd had enough of that for one night.

I reached into the crisper drawer and, sure enough, found two bags of baby carrots, real ones, not the shaved down variety. I pulled out an opened bag. "There you go," I said, tossing a couple to Patch and pocketing a handful.

Patch went away happy, or at least went away. I paused a moment, staring at the freezer side of this monstrosity. People hid things in freezers.

As if on its own, my hand found its way to the handle and I pulled the door open. Condensation steamed my glasses as my eyes beheld enough food to last through the next Ice Age.

"What's going on?" Chris asked.

"I'm staring at all the food in this freezer."

"*Freezer*? Aunt Bella, your priorities—back door, breakfront, notebook, in that order. We don't have all night."

His warning snapped me back to reality. I'd begun to shut the door when I spied the Crisco can. Maybe Bootsie liked to bake cookies.

"Earth to Bella," Chris said.

Absorbed in lifting the can out, I ignored him. It felt strangely light for three pounds. I lifted the lid, and felt my eyes pop as they beheld wads of bills bound with rubber bands.

"There's a can of money in their freezer." I riffled through one bundle. "Big bills."

"Fuck!" Chris said. "Grab some." He'd obviously forgotten about the back door.

"Language, Chris, and no way," I said, replacing the lid and returning the can to its designated spot. Alena and Bootsie might not miss a few carrots, but they'd miss a few thou.

Okay, no matter what Chris thought, finding the back door would have to wait. Next stop, breakfront. Let's see, she'd shoved the notebook in the right-hand drawer. I turned the flashlight on and, with a tingle of anticipation, pulled the ornate ring handle: placemats on top, more placemats underneath. I pulled them out and checked each one. Nothing. Tried the left drawer. Same thing. The notebook had been moved.

"Find the back door?"

"Still looking," I lied.

"What did you say?" Chris asked.

I looked at the phone in annoyance. How could I concentrate with Chris carping in my ear? "Still looking for the back door. Let's maintain radio silence unless there's an emergency."

"You got it."

* * * * *

I stood in the darkened rear hallway, away from windows that faced the street, feet planted in shag carpeting, flashlight shining over four closed doors. Which one was Alena's? I wondered, my heart shifting a little. Maybe this was a waste of time. She might have hidden the notebook in her desk at the TV station. Or maybe not—if her desk was like mine at the newspaper. Everybody rifled through it looking for paper clips, rubber bands, whatever. No, my sense was that the notebook was here.

I looked left, startled by my own reflection. A door with a half-window. Relief washed over me.

I cracked it open; the hinges creaked alarmingly and I flinched. "Found the back door," I croaked.

"Awesome. Thought we were maintaining silence."

"We are, starting now." I studied the other three doors, thinking of the old TV show "Let's Make a Deal" where contestants tried their skill at selecting prizes hidden behind several closed doors. I chose door Number One in front of me and eased it open. An odor—powdery and sweet, an old man's smell—assaulted my senses. Bootsie's room, without a doubt. There was only one high window, and it faced the back of the house, so I chanced flicking on a bedside lamp.

The room could barely contain the ponderous old bedroom set shoe-horned into it. A lavender satin bedspread straight from the 1950's Sears catalog covered a double bed with ornately carved head- and footboards.

Faded family photos rested on the bureau atop a lavender dresser scarf obviously crocheted by someone, probably Mrs. Bootsie. A large woman, she towered over him in their wedding portrait. A small cushion lay on a nearby chair, its hand-embroidered letters commemorating the long-ago marriage of Bartolomeo Lupino to Maria Cavallo. I picked up the cushion and traced the writing, wondering what her life was like. Was Bootsie good to her? Did they have children other than Alena? *Time to move on, Bella.*

The three rooms at the back of the long hall were arranged in an inverted L. The one around the corner to the right proved to be a bathroom. Nothing of interest. I tried to think like a woman with something to hide. The door clockwise to the bathroom led to a cluttered office. The two might share that space; she wouldn't chance using it as a hiding place.

If I were Alena, I'd choose my bedroom. A father will normally respect his daughter's personal space. Her boudoir was behind the first door to the left off the living room. I shut the door, turned on my flashlight and played light over the walls. What a boudoir it was, with a large window overlooking the back veranda and an attached bathroom complete with transom above the door. It had been years since I'd seen one of those.

As for furniture and accoutrements, she had chosen wisely: white wicker (read expensive) bed, chest and nightstands, and a white plisse shabby-chic comforter adorning her place of repose. The largest ceiling fan I've ever seen—white wicker and brass—seemed well-suited to cooling milady's body after a night of steamy lovemaking.

I pulled open sliding doors that ran along most of one wall to reveal a walk-in closet big enough hold the contents of a Macy's warehouse. Racks on both sides displayed designer suits in every color, especially red. The far wall contained a rack of shoes, expensive ones.

Where next? Nightstand drawer of course, the perfect place for hiding something in plain sight. It too proved a disappointment, containing a hotel Bible, rubber bands and several well-chewed pencils.

A check of my watch revealed the time, 9:45, two hours plus until they returned. Unless, of course, Bootsie came home early. But he couldn't without a car. Or could he? I decided to abandon ship at 10:45 even if I hadn't found the notebook.

What was this? My eye wandered to a wicker chest next to the bathroom door. Aha, the underwear drawer, the go-to place for feminine secrets.

Patch whined behind me. I turned and he offered me a stuffed skunk. Obviously a favorite toy. "Okay, here you go." I threw it down the hall toward the living room. He ran after it. I fully expected him to return but he didn't, thank goodness. On the other hand…

No, I would not allow my mind to consider the possibility of him pooping on the rug or eating the sofa.

I pulled open the top drawer of the wicker chest, expecting to find a collection of lacy things to wear under those designer suits. So much for suppositions. My flashlight's beam revealed that she preferred standard-issue cotton low-cuts in lollipop colors, most of them with droopy elastic waistbands.

As Mom would say, "Oh, the shame of it all." Perhaps her mother had never given her the standard lecture about always wearing respectable undies to save embarrassment in the ER in case of accident.

They weren't folded either, another cardinal sin in my mother's playbook. I stirred them around; the disturbance would never be noted. The other drawers yielded a disappointing collection of T-shirts, half slips, flannel and cotton PJs and a collection of Beanie Babies.

Beanie Babies? Give me a break. I slammed the bottom drawer shut with my foot. As I did this, a strip of red plastic appeared between drawer and dresser frame. Red plastic, hmm. I looked, looked again and ran my finger over the plastic edge. The notebook? Shoving the drawer closed had partially dislodged it from its likely hiding spot in the gap to one side of the drawer slider. (Hiding things in that handy-dandy space was an old trick I'd learned in junior high.)

I tried to force the drawer. No way. Gripped the plastic edge and gave one royal yank. No dice. "Chris, think I just found—"

"Mayday, Mayday! Over."

"What's wrong?"

"Old man's here. Someone in an Escalade dropping him off."

"Crap." The notebook would have to wait. I ran to the rear door where the dog stood. "Here Patch," I called softly. *Get dog outside.*

"Mayday, Mayday, old man's heading toward the back."

Oh, Jeez. I turned and made a beeline for the front, noticing as I did unrolled toilet paper on the bathroom rug, Patch in the middle of it—where else? I reversed course to snatch up the paper, then reversed course again when I heard shuffling noises coming from the back veranda.

"Come *on*, Patch!" I begged over my shoulder. An anxious second while he debated his options, back door and his person, or front door and me, the purveyor of carrots. He opted for me.

Heart beating wildly, I waited for the sound of creaking hinges. Now! I eased my way out the front, dragging Patch by the collar. I broke into a gallop as I neared the front gate, Patch hard at my heels. Chris pulled me through the gate, slamming it in Patch's face. He set up a howl.

We scampered next door to the safety of the construction site. Would the old man investigate the racket? He either didn't hear it or was inured to the dog's barking. Ditto the neighbors. We were in the clear. Except for the toilet paper. And the stuck notebook.

24

Monday, April 26th, late

"Wow, that was wild!" Chris said, eyes alight. We sat across from each other at the kitchen table with mugs of hot chocolate. *Safe.*

He's too fond of these adrenaline rushes, I thought, and the chocolate and sugar are making things worse. "What did we learn?" I said, taking a slurp of foam and topping off the cup with another mountain of whipped cream from the can at my elbow.

Chris cast his eyes down as though he hadn't done his homework, but two grin lines betrayed him. "Uh, that Patch likes carrots."

"Be serious. At least I know where the notebook is."

"Do you think they'll notice it hanging out of the dresser drawer?"

"How could they not? I just hope Alena sees it first."

Chris took a robust swig. "You still don't know what's inside."

"True. How do I solve that?"

He dangled before me the key I'd accidentally taken in my rush to escape. "We go back and have another look. Maybe tomorrow night."

"Impossible. That gig's over." I stood up, working a sudden cramp out of my calf. "Between the dog inside and the notebook hanging out of the drawer, they know someone's been in the house."

"You think?"

"I know."

"Tell me about the driver of the Escalade," I said, once again taking my seat.

"Didn't see much, just a tall dude."

"Did you get the license plate?"

He gave me a "be serious" look.

"While I was in the backyard I took a quick look in the garage."

"You did *what*? What a waste," Chris muttered.

"It wasn't a waste. There was another Escalade in there. Probably belongs to Bootsie."

"So there's *two*?"

"At least," I said. "The problem is, I'm not sure which one, if either of them, the murderer jumped into at the Mariposa Inn. I didn't tell you, but I went back to the scene the night Mike left."

Chris whistled. "Why?"

"I'm not really sure. Guess I thought it might give me a clue to Mike's whereabouts. I saw a tall man searching the path. He left in a black Escalade."

Chris's eyes widened. "Cool. The murderer returning to the scene of the crime?" I nodded, and he said, "Could be, like, the same dude who brought Bootsie home tonight. What was he looking for?"

"Again, I'm not sure. Maybe the knife. As far as I know it hasn't been found."

He held up the key. "So what do we do with this baby?"

"Get it back tonight before they miss it."

He turned the key over in his hand. "We should make a copy first."

"What for? Besides, the hardware store's closed. Key goes back tonight."

"Like, how?"

"Like, simple. You drive up and toss it over the wall. Wipe it free of fingerprints first," I said, thinking of mine all over the house. They would be a problem only if they called the cops. *Not likely.* "If you do, I'll make you potato pancakes for breakfast."

* * * * *

Rather than watching late news, I logged on to the Internet and searched for the Lupino name. The results, though not surprising, sent my pulse into a tailspin. There, big as life, was a picture of Bootsie sitting on a bench at Belle Isle, a Detroit landmark, with Johnny Staccato, another mobster. The two were undoubtedly hatching some nefarious scheme.

The Lupinos, along with the Staccatos, were well-known Detroit crime families. Bartolomeo Lupino Junior (aka Bootsie) was the second son of Bartolomeo Senior, now deceased. The old don had arrived in the fledgling Motor City in the mid-thirties to begin a life of New World crime. Accompanying him were his wife, young son (Bootsie), and a suitcase full of cash.

Unlike other families involved in money laundering, drugs and prostitution, the Lupinos, since the 1960s, had specialized in construction, especially public works projects. Their nefarious activities within the industry included extortion, payoffs and infiltration of labor unions. The FBI had been trying to nail them for years. Bootsie, known for secrecy about his private life, was reputed to have one son and several daughters by two wives. I remembered that picture of him on the dresser with the first Mrs. Bootsie. What happened to the second wife, I wondered?

Okay, I thought, pushing back from the computer, Bootsie's definitely a mobster. What drew him here? Why the money in their freezer? And why didn't the Lupino house have more security? Pretty stupid. Or arrogant.

25

Tuesday, April 27th, early morning

I lay there, trying to awaken and start my day, but a powerful dream kept reclaiming me. Each time it did, the images changed and became stronger.

A woman in religious habit, fiery hair barely contained by her veil, wanders the path. A heron watches her from a nearby branch. She moves from side to side, searching for intruders bent on frightening her birds. She turns a face alight with fervor to me and, as I watch, it morphs into Annie Milosch's sweet countenance. The heron moves restlessly as though to take flight. Annie turns from me, and hurries on her way, searching for the tortured soul of her murdered husband.

Sometime later, I reawaken. Sunlight peeks through the blinds. Again the dream pulls me away from the earthly world. The scene changes. Emily Divina stands on the widow's walk of our old mill. She looks intently out to sea, waiting for her lover to return. A heron perches on her shoulder, making a fearful racket.

The radio plays in the kitchen, Mom listening to NPR—some new crisis in the Middle East involving chanting and protests. I try to rise; the dream shackles me to the bed. I have become the Wandering Nun. The heron flies from my shoulder, burrows under my veil and attacks the nape of my neck.

Gasping for breath, slapping at my hair, I force myself awake. I gaze around struggling to make sense of the quickly fading images. Four women wandering the same path, each with a mission: The Wandering Nun protecting her birds, Annie searching for her murdered husband, Emily seeking her lost fisherman. And me—seeking Mike.

* * * * *

A short time later, I stood at the kitchen sink pouring steaming water over tea leaves in the pot. The herby aroma filled my air passages, helping to clear my dream-fogged brain. I took a deep breath, inhaling the mist into my lungs. I breathed out, I breathed in, I breathed out—and then I knew. Emily, our resident ghost, had used the dream as a medium to warn me that Annie and I were both in real danger. Why Annie? I now strongly suspected that Joe Milosch was her husband. Everything fit: the date of the death, Fifi's description of him as a mature man, Annie's obvious fear for her own safety.

The dream had another message as well. What was it? I continued to stand there, inhaling the steam and massaging my temples to stimulate circulation, hoping to invoke the other images of the dream, understanding only that it concerned Emily. But

I'd been awake too long and that part of the dream had vanished into the mist.

26

Tuesday, April 27th, after work

"Hello?"

"Hi Annie, it's Bella." Silence at the other end of the phone. "We've missed you at work for the past two days. I think you should know. Margaret's very upset. Are you okay?"

More silence. "You there? I asked if you were okay."

"Yes…no…well not really."

"I'm sorry. Anything I can do? If you need someone to talk to, I can come over."

"No! It's not safe."

"What's going on, Annie? Does this have something to do with your husband's death?" I hoped she would confirm what I now suspected. That her dead husband was Joe Milosch.

"I can't tell you."

"Maybe things aren't as bad as they seem."

A laugh, bitter. "Trust me, they are."

More silence, and I continued, "How about meeting somewhere in Mariposa Bay? There's a cafe not far from the jetty." Better to ask her about her husband's identity face-to-face, where I could judge her reaction by her body language.

A long silence while she pondered what I'd said. "No, not inside. Meet me at the jetty around seven."

"I'll be there."

"Good. Park and stay in your car. I'll find you. And…leave your cell phone at home." The line went dead.

* * * * *

I pulled into a parking space opposite the giant Mariposa Rock, which loomed large behind me. I remained in the Subaru as Annie instructed, checking other vehicles for a sign of her. I glanced back over my shoulder at the piled granite that forms the jetty. Good. The sea was calm. When it's not, waves break over the rocks in spectacular fashion, throwing spray in all directions. Gorgeous, but a bit sinister. Rogue waves are a problem along this coast. Nearly every year some unwary soul is swept away.

At seven-fifteen, not knowing whether to be anxious or annoyed, I yanked my cell phone from my purse and called her. "Leave it at home," she'd warned.

No way. Also no answer, and no answering machine. I decided to wait a while longer and then—do what? Go home, I guess.

By seven-twenty Mariposa Rock behind me was throwing long shadows. Before I could talk myself out of it, I slipped from the car and traversed the sandy path that led to the rocks. The sight of the parking lot, empty now save for my car, sent a tingle of apprehension up my spine.

Approaching the jetty, I halted, spying a dark shape on the rocks. A seal? Closer now, I saw a human form and ran toward it. Closer still, I deduced from the slim form and long, trailing hair that the prone form was a woman. *Oh, no, could it be?*

I stood on tiptoe in front of the immense pile of rocks. "Annie!" I called. "Annie?"

I tried to climb the pile, but I'd worn clogs that slid dangerously. I kicked them off to the foot of the rock pile and tried bare feet. Worse. The stones were both slimy and sharp, making the task impossible. I stumbled down, turned and studied the form from afar. Whoever it was looked very dead. The bile rose in my throat.

Cell phone. I reached in my pocket. Damn. On the seat. Barefoot, sharp little stones cutting into my toes, I ran to the car and called 911.

27

A Mariposa Bay police car arrived in less than five minutes, followed by two ambulances and a fire truck. That brought people running from all directions. *Where were they when I needed them?*

The cops immediately set up a barrier to keep them out. All the lights, noise and confusion, so similar to Joe Milosch's murder scene, just about did me in. How could this be happening again? I forced myself from the safety of my car, retrieved my shoes and hurried over to meet the officers.

The unformed officer in charge, Steve Howe, according to his badge, asked, "Where's the body ma'am?"

I pointed toward the jetty. "Over there. Hurry!"

A posse of officialdom poured from the vehicles and did exactly that. I stood behind the squad car, leaning against it for support, arms folded in a vain attempt to stay warm, almost paralyzed with shock.

The second officer had just pulled out pen and pad when his radio squawked. "Dixon here. What you got?" he asked into his shoulder. His eyes widened at the answer.

"Ma'am," he said, "there's no body out there."

What? "There has to be. I saw it."

"Maybe a rogue wave washed her away when you left the scene."

Something in his tone and narrowed eyes suggested that I'd been negligent. Or worse, delusional. I flung my arms out. "See?" I screeched. "The ocean is calm."

Dixon shrugged. "Rogue waves happen even in calm seas."

"Wait. Wait just a minute. I tried to climb those rocks, but they were so slippery I couldn't get to her."

"Her?" asked Howe. "So you know for sure it's a woman?"

"Yes, of course, I saw her hair and…"

Dixon picked up on my hesitation. "You know this woman?"

"I work for the *Central Coast Chronicle*—"

"Reporter?" The two exchanged glances.

"Obituary editor."Another shared look, this time accompanied by discreet eye rolling.

"Continue," said Howe. Not a request.

"I'm pretty sure she works for the paper. As a copy editor."

"*Pretty* sure?"

"Look, as sure as I can be."

"Her name?" Dixon asked in a heard-this-before voice.

"Annie Carter. And—" Was now the time to reveal my suspicion that Joe Milosch was her husband, and that Annie feared for her life?

"And?" prompted Dixon.

I gulped a deep breath, knowing full well I was not just opening a can of worms, but crawling inside. "I think she was the wife of Joe Milosch, the man murdered at the Mariposa Inn recently."

"You *think*?" Dixon asked.

Not every question requires an answer.

"Better kick this up a notch," Howe said. "Call the Ironwoods. I'll get County Search and Rescue."

* * * * *

Even from a mile away, the Wandering Nun heard the helicopter overhead, saw its light reflected on the water. Another tragedy in the bay. One more thing to frighten her birds. Soon they would leave, never to return. She put hands together and prayed to God that somehow the knife would be found. Only then would peace return to the bay. Only then would her birds be safe.

* * * * *

Mariposa Bay Detective Frank Ironwood arrived without his partner, Rick. Just as well; Detective Frank was relentless enough for two. As I sat next to him in the squad car, he made me repeat my story over and over, and then one more time for good measure. Meanwhile, frenzied activity on the jetty increased, with boats taking to the water. A Search and Rescue helicopter continued to circle, its spotlight transforming the area into an eerie lunar landscape.

After I told the detective for the umpteenth time that Annie and I had agreed to meet here, he asked, "At her request or yours?"

"Mine," I said, wondering where he was leading me.

"Purpose of the meeting?"

It was hard to keep the irritation out of my voice. "It seemed as though she needed a friend after her husband died."

"And her husband was?"

"Joe Milosch, I told you."

"Interesting," he said, making note of the name, circling it, and writing "Attention Rick" to left of it. He turned to me. "And you initiated the call?"

"That's true."

"Did she give you her contact information?"

Aha, a different question. I hesitated and he picked up on it. No way was I going to involve Fifi Falcone. "Of course." I assumed my best why-do-you-ask? act.

Underneath it *was* an act. If this could happen to Annie, Mike might face the same fate. The mere thought brought on waves of dizziness. I leaned my head against the vehicle's side window.

"Ma'am?" the detective asked. "Are you okay?"

"Of course I'm not okay," I wanted to say. "I've just found a drowned woman and now her body has disappeared, and my husband is missing and might be dead, and there's some connection and I don't know what it is."

I drew a deep, enabling breath. "This has been a bit much, and your haranguing isn't helping."

His uptight demeanor softened slightly. "Would you like me to call your husband, Ma'am?"

Husband. I thought fast. *Can't tell him Mike's out of town.* We weren't supposed to leave the area. "He's laid up with a virus." I fumbled in my pocket and handed him my cell with Chris's number displayed. "Would you be good enough to call my nephew please?"

* * * * *

Chris arrived quickly, having gotten a ride with a former high school buddy, and the detective dismissed me.

"You want to go straight home, right?" Chris asked, slipping behind the wheel of the Subaru.

"Not yet. I have an idea." The sight of my nephew after this latest ordeal had revived me to a remarkable degree.

He sighed. "I was afraid of that."

* * * * *

Annie lived a few minutes drive from the jetty in a small bungalow near Spence's Fresh Market.

"Why are we doing this?" Chris muttered.

"I just want to see if she's here."

"Aunt Bella, like, you saw her body on the rocks. Trust me, she's not here."

"I need to be sure."

He was right. She wasn't there, or if she was, she was well-hidden inside. After we parked in the market lot and hoofed it back to her house, I pounded on the front and back doors calling, "Annie, Annie?" while my favorite sidekick peered into darkened and locked windows.

As I stood at the foot of the back steps contemplating our next move, I heard behind me, "Aunt Bella!"

"What?"

He pointed toward the street. "Law's here."

Crap. I peered around the corner. Sure enough, two squad cars sat in front of Annie's house. We looked at each other and, with no time to waste, made for the back fence. I'd like to say I climbed it, but full disclosure: Chris hoisted me to the top, where I balanced myself on shaking arms while he scaled it like a gymnast. He hauled me over from the other side and I dropped to the ground like a sack of potatoes. We made for the car, thankful it was parked close by.

* * * * *

After checking on Mom and finding her fast asleep, all I wanted was a warm bath to soothe arm and thigh muscles still aching from fence climbing. But this latest Evening from Hell was not over.

Chris's belongings sat by the back door: duffel bag and clothes piled in a wash basket, a set of clean sheets on top. No doubt where he'd dumped them when the Morro Bay PD called. "What's this?" I asked.

He suddenly developed eye contact problems. "Um…like, my girlfriend's coming for, like, a few days, and well…" he nudged the tile with one sandal, "we'd like some privacy."

"Girlfriend?" "Privacy?" I exploded. "You're a kid."

"I'm twenty-one," he reminded me with a lopsided grinned. He reached up to sweep a blonde lock off his face, obviously forgetting his now-short hair. He brought his hand down and stared at it. Again, he dug his toe into the tile.

"Where did you two meet?" I asked, wondering if I really wanted to know.

"She works with me," he said. "She's a great cook."

A promising start.

"What's her name?" I asked, stalling for think time, remembering Miranda, his girlfriend when he'd lived with us before. That relationship had turned sour, resulting in a brush with the law. He'd learned a lot from that experience. At least I hoped so.

"Milly."

Expecting something like Brittany or Skye, I was taken aback by the old-fashioned name.

He pulled his smart phone from his pocket, worked his thumb and index finger this way and that as though taking measurements, then thrust the device at me. "Here's her picture. Isn't she gorgeous?"

"My," I said. "My." The girl who stared back at me had what my English grandmother would call a "handsome" countenance. Long of face, strong of jaw, dark hair pulled back into a pony tail, she wore large, heavy-framed glasses that gave her an owlish look.

Seeing Chris's expectant face, I said, "She has an inner beauty."

He beamed, apparently hearing only the "b" word, dropped the phone into his pocket and grabbed a box. "I'll take this stuff to the barn. I pulled my old futon out of the storage room. Opened up, it's big enough for two."

"Wait," I said, "you sleep out there. Milly can take your room." I gave him my best "Not in my house" look.

His eyes widened. "You're kidding. That is, like, so last century."

"No, Chris, I'm serious. What will Grandma think? And what if Uncle Mike came home unexpectedly and found you two..." Not wanting to say "shacked up" I let my voice drift.

"He's not coming home, Aunt Bella."

A bolt of shock zigzagged through me. Had he changed his mind after being here such a short time? He backtracked. "I mean, not right now."

"Okay." I sighed. "Here's an idea. How about you take the sofa in the living room and Milly takes your room as I suggested?"

"Works for me," he said, grinning. Of course it worked for him. The sofa was just down the hall from the third bedroom. And the door locked from the inside.

"Thank goodness that's settled," I said.

28

Wednesday, April 28th, early morning

After tossing all night, I overslept and had no time to read the *Chronicle*. Upon arriving at the office I stared at the headline that screamed back at me from the stand outside the building: "Woman reputed to be murdered man's wife disappears from jetty, feared drowned!" Thank goodness Mariposa Bay law enforcement had identified me only as "an anonymous caller."

I'd barely stowed my purse in my desk drawer when Margaret sailed into my cubicle. "Who do you suppose the anonymous caller is?"

I jumped. Why ask me? *Steady, girl.*

I turned her question into an observation. "Seems like not having a copy editor is a bigger problem."

She nodded, heaving out a breath so deep the papers on my desk rustled. The odor of raw onions permeated the air. "We'll hire a temp until this gets resolved."

"Margaret," I said, backing away slightly, trying not to fan the space between us, "whether she's dead or not, I don't think this is going to get resolved. At least not in the sense that Annie's returning to work."

"Well, duh. Nothing worse than having an employee you can't count on. One way or another, Annie's finished here." So much for compassion.

* * * * *

Wednesday, April 28th, dinner time

A wonderful aroma, earthy and yet sweet, tingled my senses as I stepped through the back door. Chris had been working magic in the kitchen. I was surprised that he had time; Milly's train arrived at four. I lifted the lid from a pot resting on the stove. Yum, curried rice, liberally buttered and sprinkled with fresh cilantro. Another pot held fragrant golden chicken broth and root vegetables.

Hearing voices from the living room, I hurried in to meet Chris's new girlfriend. What's the old adage: Expect the best, prepare for the worst?

I needn't have worried. The scene that greeted me was pure Norman Rockwell updated for the twenty-first century.

Mom sat wedged between the two young people on the sofa, clasping Chris's right hand and Milly's left. All were immersed in "Diners, Drive-ins and Dives" on TV. Sam lay at their feet, looking as though his world was complete.

"Oh, hi, Bella. Have you met Milly?" Mom lifted both of their clasped hands like a boxing referee. Milly struggled to her feet.

"That's okay, stay where you are Milly, " I said, reaching over to grasp her free hand. We exchanged pleasantries while Chris and Mom beamed. Milly looked much like her picture, tall and lean with an arresting, if not beautiful, face. Behind big glasses her green eyes held an intelligent spark.

I like this girl.

"What's for supper besides that lovely curried rice?" I asked.

"I've already eaten," Mom said, slightly off-topic. "Milly made me some chicken broth. It was so good I ate the whole cupful."

I eyed my smallest teacup, the spoon still in it, sitting empty on the coffee table. At least she'd eaten something and better yet, kept it down.

"That's great, Mom," I said and meant it. She still looked pale, and pitifully thin, her wig slightly askew. But for the first time in days, her cheeks held a hint of color and there was life in her eyes.

"Me and Milly are grilling ahi tuna wrapped in bacon with rum and apricot sauce," Chris said.

"Great. I'll make a salad."

Milly patted Mom's knee with her free hand, a gesture that might have been condescending, but wasn't somehow. "Mrs. Rogers, maybe you can eat a little more soup with us."

"I might just do that," she said.

After we finished dinner, including a superb white wine Milly brought from Napa, and a crème brulee that descended magically from the heavens, Mom yawned and excused herself for Vanna and an early night. As soon as we heard the bedroom door close, Chris leaned forward, scratching Sam's back at the same time. "Aunt Bella, anything new with Uncle Mike?"

I glanced at Milly to see her reaction. From the look the two exchanged, I knew he'd filled her in on the Mike situation. I shook my head. "Still no word. I check my e-mail constantly."

"Have you ever tried hacking into his account?" Milly asked, gathering up forks and knives.

"Hacking?" I asked, wondering if I should be worried about her absconding with the silver.

She nodded. "That might tell us something about his whereabouts."

"I see what you mean. I tried, but I couldn't figure out his password."

The pair exchanged a "not-good" look, then Chris said, "Let's try again. I'll bet me and Milly can figure it out. She's a good hacker."

"Good idea," she said. "While Chris and I do the dishes, make us a list of Mr. Kowalski's birthday, driver's license number, any old addresses you know of, any nicknames he liked, his parents' names, pet names, anything you can think of. We can try various combinations."

"Won't my provider just shut me out if I keep entering passwords?" I asked, gently discouraging Sam's repeated hand licks. He was only trying to be helpful.

She smacked her forehead. "They might."

"Some hacker you are," Chris said, and flicked her on the forearm with a dish towel. Sam barked at him, a first.

29

Thursday, April 29th, midmorning

At work my mind kept returning to our unsuccessful effort to hack into Mike's e-mail. Last night we'd discussed it further. Chris and Milly both felt strongly that for security purposes he would have used a nonsense combination of letters and numbers, something like S5G7, for his password.

I didn't agree. He might be an ex-cop, but an eight-year-old's concept of Internet security was better than his. And his memory wasn't the greatest. No, he'd definitely use some word or combination of words he could remember.

A mental picture of Sam sitting next to us in front of Chris's laptop last night flashed through my mind. He'd whined at every mention of Mike's name, as though expecting him to emerge from the screen.

Mike's favorite nickname for Sam was "SamLab." That had possibilities. I declared myself on break and logged on, trying out the made-up word, and then SamLab1 and 2. *No hit, no surprise.*

I grabbed a pencil and paper and began to doodle, hoping it would help my thought process. It didn't, so I started writing down words, whatever came to mind, as fast as I could. After a few minutes, I checked the list. One word stood out: AggieMay.

I circled it. That's what Mike calls me when he wants to be especially irritating. Besides Mom, he's the only person in the world who knows my middle name is Agnes May, after my two grandmothers. Isabella Rogers Kowalski is at least tolerable. Isabella *Agnes May* Rogers Kowalski is not.

With shaking hands I logged on and entered his user name and AggieMay.

The magic word produced a list of e-mails in his inbox—thirty-seven of them! Some dated back to before he disappeared. There were the usual junk ads and forwarded jokes. He certainly hadn't been reading his mail regularly. One address caught my eye: ngrale@mynet.net.

Neal Grale? Why was the library manager sending Mike e-mails? It was dated the morning after the Milosch murder and the subject line was blank. As my finger hovered over the mouse button to open the file, I sensed a presence behind me. The hair rose on the back of my neck. By the time I gathered my courage to turn around, the lurker had disappeared.

* * * * *

Thursday, April 29th, early evening

"Where you goin'?" Chris called from the kitchen as I set my purse down on the hall bench and made for the breezeway and my study in the old mill.

"Have to see a man about a dog," I said, imagining the puzzled expression the old saying would bring to Chris's face. I wanted to be alone when I rechecked Mike's e-mail on my own computer.

I climbed the steps, saluted Emily's portrait as I entered the office and logged on, using AggieMay as the key to the kingdom.

I looked, and looked again, a sick feeling rising in my throat. The inbox had only one new message—an ad from a Canadian pharmacy. Mike (or someone) had cleaned out his inbox. Who, and why? To keep me from seeing something I shouldn't?

Quickly I checked old mail, recently deleted mail, saved mail and all his special folders. The message from Neal Grale was indeed gone, as though I'd imagined the whole thing.

Needing some explanation about the missing message and, with other unanswered questions about the man himself, I e-mailed Neal at the library. Would he like to meet for coffee at Lockhart's Bakery Saturday morning?

I didn't say why.

30

Saturday, May 1st, midmorning

Mrs. Lu, the new owner of Lockhart's, bustled from table to table in the crowded eating area, asking if everything was okay. The smiling nods of the patrons affirmed that the bakery hadn't changed. She and her husband had recently bought it from Gary Lockhart, who was now enjoying a well-deserved retirement.

Neal Grale was there ahead of me. Laptop computer open in front of him, he signaled to me from a small corner table while I waited for coffee at the counter. He'd accepted my e-mail invitation immediately without asking the purpose of the meeting.

"Not having a treat?" he asked, as I settled in opposite him. "Those maple bars with bacon look delicious."

"They're a new addition by the Lu's." I set my coffee to one side so as not to spill it and grabbed a napkin from the dispenser in case I did. "Want to share one? My treat."

He patted his slim midsection. "Afraid not, have to watch *eev*-erything I eat."

I doubted that. He appeared to be one of those naturally slim people. I pointed to the laptop. "Catching up on library business?"

A big smile. "Actually no, I'm pursuing a lead on my great-great grandfather."

"Really? A lead? That's exciting."

He closed the computer. "I'll tell you about it later. Let's discuss your concerns first. I assume you have some, though you didn't mention them in the e-mail."

"I bet you wonder why I asked you."

"Hey, if a lovely lady invites me for coffee, I rarely say no." He raised his hands, palms out, then lowered them and sipped his brew, observing me over the top of the cup. What was there about me that he found so interesting? As for me, I was struck by his good looks, especially his pale green eyes which told me...

Actually, I don't know what they told me, but that didn't bear any relevance to the subject at hand. "As you may know, Neal," I said, "my husband has taken extended leave..."

I was tempted to say "of his senses," but held my tongue.

He set his coffee down, and cocked his head. "I didn't know that. I do hope it isn't a health problem."

"No, no, nothing like that. He had to go back east on business, and you know how things like that can drag on."

A thoughtful nod. "I see, but I don't understand how that relates to me."

"Uh, Mike's not the greatest technically, and while he's away I'm monitoring his e-mails. I logged on the other day and noticed one from you. Would you mind telling me what it was about?"

A frown line appeared on his brow. "I don't quite understand. You didn't read it?"

"Not at the time. I was interrupted and then when I checked back, it was gone."

"Perhaps your husband deleted it," he said carefully. I knew what he was thinking: Mike didn't want me to read it.

"I wouldn't ask if it wasn't important ..." I didn't know how to finish the sentence.

He shook his head. "I'm sorry, Bella, I really am, but I'm don't see how—"

"I understand," I said, cutting him off. We sipped in silence.

"Look," I said, a few moments later, pursing my lips to fight back tears, "I can't tell you any more, but I *need* to know. It's a matter of life and death," I added without meaning to.

He reached across the table and took my hand, shaking it slightly. "Of course, then. It's no big deal. Let me back up. That day we first talked, almost three weeks ago?"

I nodded. The day of the Milosch murder, though I didn't say it.

"Anyway, that day, not long before you arrived, a man came in, removed a bunch of travel books from the stacks, took a seat at one of the tables and began thumbing through them."

"Why did you notice him, of all the people in the library?"

"Why? He looked like a troubled man, and people reading travel books usually look happy because they're planning vacations. We got to talking and he m*ee*ntioned my accent, and of course, I said I was from New Zealand."

"And..."

"Well, now that I think about it, he said something like 'bet that's a good place to lose yourself,' or words to that effect. I told him New Zealand is indeed a great place to get away from it all."

"I've heard that," I said, a plethora of alarms going off in my head. Mike in New Zealand? On another *continent,* at the bottom of the world?

He fingered his paper napkin. "Especially the South Island, with all the open spaces, ranches and temperate rainforests. He introduced himself as Mike Kowalski."

"Which is why you figured he was my husband when I came in later?"

"Eexactly. He gave me his e-addy and asked me to send him more information, things that wouldn't be in the guide book. I sent him information on places I particularly like, Stewart Island off the south coast, where I used to live, and Te Anau on the west side."

He stopped. "Maybe I shouldn't be telling you this. He might be planning a surprise trip for you."

I forced a smile. "That's okay, we share everything. However, your e-mail seems to have dropped into a bit bucket somewhere. I need to tell him about it when he calls me tonight. He calls me every night," I added in a classic example of overkill.

"I'm sure he does. Give him my best regards."

"I will." We sipped in a more congenial silence. "Neal?"

"Yes?"

"Why were you watching me from your office door as I left the library that day?"

"Was I? I was probably deep in thought about something else."

"That wasn't how it seemed."

Again he cocked his head, the gesture giving him a cocker spaniel look. "I remember now. You looked troubled. I remember thinking two troubled people with the same last name had visited the library that day."

"Troubled?" I heaved a deep sigh. "Neal, you don't know the half of it."

"I sensed as much." He looked deep into my eyes. "You know, I don't *need* to know, don't *want* to know, but if I can help in any way, please call on me. I mean that."

"I know you do," I said, thinking, *What a sweet man.*

He opened his computer. "Now, want to see what I found out about my great-great grandfather?"

"Absolutely. Maybe you should start by telling me his name."

"Kawana, and he was the son of a chief."

"Kawana?" I rolled the unfamiliar name around in my mouth. "That's impressive."

"Thanks, I think so." He turned the computer sideways and edged it toward me. The screen displayed a black and white photo of a man's face, the image greatly enlarged. The man had a dark complexion.

"Kawana, at about age thirty. My great-great grandmother died in childbirth and Kawana left the baby—"

"Your great grandfather?"

"True. Kawana left him with other members of his family in New Zealand to find work on the west coast of California. Unfortunately, his family never heard from him again."

"What a tragedy, especially for your great grandfather, to never know his own father." I pointed to the screen. "Where did you find that picture?"

"Right under my very nose. It's one of the photos in the present fishing exhibit. Here I'll show you." He clicked to the next photo, which displayed the crew of the Hesperia before their fatal wreck off Escarpa el Dorado, the image I saw when visiting the museum. He pointed to the younger, darker-skinned man on the end. The man had a bird on his shoulder. I looked closer. "Kawana had a parrot?" I asked.

"Apparently," Neal said. "For companionship, most likely." Again he pointed to the photo. "What do you think of that bit of good fortune?"

"I think it's terrific, but how do you know it's him, besides his appearance, of course?" There may have been many fishermen of other races on the Central Coast at that time.

"I did a bit of nosing around in the archives myself, then asked Leon, the curator, for help, and he found a crew list from the Hesperia, dated December 21st, 1893, the day they set off on their final voyage. Kawana's name was on that list."

"Imagine that," I said, "another bit of serendipity."

He grinned. "It was, indeed. Of course my evidence is only circumstantial, but how many Kawanas would there be here in 1893? He was a fisherman in New Zealand, and so it would be reasonable to assume he fished here as well." He clicked back to the enlarged photo. "Besides, he looks a bit like me, don't you think?"

"The spitting image," I said, though I thought the resemblance slight at best. If Neal was satisfied, I was happy for him.

He lifted his cup and drained it, smacking his lips. "Have to get to the library." He reached over and closed the computer, dropped it into a leather bag and slung that over his shoulder. "Stuff needs doing in regard to the Kids Craft Fair. Hope I was able to shed some light on the contents of your husband's e-mail. Kathy will be back in a week or two, but..." Here he hesitated. "But I may stay around for a bit. I like it here. Nice people. Let's stay in touch. "

"Yes, lets," I said, surprised that it felt to good—so right—to say that. There was something else I needed to tell him, something about another image, but I couldn't bring it into focus.

Still trying to summon the thought, which remained gauzy and illusive, I turned and watched him go, waving over his head. He stopped at the counter, pointing to the maple bars as a clerk hurried over. Clutching two small sacks, he doubled back. "One for each of us," he said, handing me one. Then he was gone for real.

I nibbled on one end of the donut. The salty bacon made a lovely contrast to the sugary maple frosting and fluffy dough inside. Could be habit forming. So could Neal Grale.

I returned the bar to the bag for later, reflecting on his bombshell—that Mike might be in New Zealand. Somehow I assumed he was close by. So much for assumptions. A lump formed in my throat, replacing the happy feeling of a few moments ago.

I sat there a few more minutes, swallowing down the lump and pondering my next move.

His passport! I had no idea if it still lay in his top dresser drawer.

* * * * *

I barreled into the house, barely acknowledging Mom and the kids immersed in a cooking show. In our bedroom I yanked open the drawer and rummaged beneath the handkerchiefs he'd left behind. The passport was gone.

I sank down on the bed and sat there awhile, resting on my elbows. Tried to push myself up, but someone had poured cement over my arms. I sank back and curled up on my side, hugging his pillow. Where would I find the strength to get up again? Did it matter?

Of course it mattered, I thought a few minutes later, jumping up and adjusting both attire and attitude. I had a husband to find, a sick mother to care for, and a nephew and his girlfriend whose day I didn't need to ruin with my personal pity party.

31

Monday, May 3rd, early morning

I'd no sooner walked in the door than Margaret asked me to clean out Annie's desk to make room for the temp who would replace her. I didn't mind taking on the additional task. Obituaries were light and keeping busy would take my mind off my own problems.

Milly had gone back to Napa yesterday and Chris was moping big time. I was glad he could stay a few more days. Mom and I needed him, moping or not.

The story of Annie's disappearance continued to be big news, with much speculation in the media about where and when the body would be found.

I sat back in her chair, desk wiped clean, paperclips, rubber bands, pens and pencils in the center drawer's allotted spaces. Beside me sat an untidy pile of papers I'd pulled from the side drawers. These I turned my attention to, consigning most to the round file.

I was about to toss a brochure when its cover caught my eye. Casa de Maria, the retreat center south of Santa Barbara, the place we'd discussed her first day on the job. I turned it over.

What was this? Annie, or someone, had jotted light pencil notes on the back. I squinted at the neat printing. A date, April 28th. I checked her desk calendar, thinking: That was the day *after* I saw her body on the rocks. Had she planned to escape there only to be killed the day before? What a cruel twist of fate.

Or…I sat and thought things through. Maybe, just maybe, there was another explanation. Perhaps she had faked her own death, and set me up as the person to report it. She might be hiding out at Casa de Maria right now, the last place in the world anyone would look for her.

If it weren't for this brochure in my hand...

I studied the penciled-in date. Another maybe: She planned the setup on the spur of the moment as we talked on the phone and had no chance to return to the office for the incriminating brochure. I decided to do her a favor and buried it in the bottom of my handbag.

32

Saturday, May 8th, early morning

The man in the beat-up sedan hit a button on his cell phone. "Broad's leaving town. Turning on to the 101 going south."

"I'm five minutes away," said the tall man in the Escalade.

* * * * *

The Subaru and I buzzed along the 101 freeway. I told Mom and Chris that I needed a solo drive down the coast to clear my head. Neither of them questioned that, and I headed south to see if Annie might be hiding out at Casa de Maria.

Maybe ten miles later, I pulled out to pass a pokey driver. As I checked my rearview mirror, I did a double take. There was a black Escalade a few vehicles behind in the right lane. My heart did a little flippity-gibbet.

By the time I got to Santa Rosita, thirty miles south, I'd spied the car several times, always a few vehicles behind, always in the right lane. Again I told myself it was another Escalade, but the raised hairs on the back of my neck said otherwise.

I stayed to the left for several miles, passing slower traffic. Somehow the Escalade remained behind me in the right lane.

The last thing I wanted to do was lead the driver straight to Annie. What to do? A deep inhale and exhale to clear my mind. Turn around and go back? No, I had to be smarter than that.

I drove for a while wondering how I could lose this guy. And then I had it. I stayed in the left lane until close to the 246 exit. At the last second I whipped in front of a car in the right lane, bracing for a sickening crunch of metal. Didn't happen. Took a quick look. The Escalade with a tall man behind the wheel had no choice but to go on.

I barreled up the onramp, did a quick stop, hung a quicker left, crossed over the freeway and made another left northbound. After I'd gone about a quarter mile, I glanced in my rearview mirror. So far so good.

I drove north for several exits, executed the same maneuver in reverse, and then headed south, congratulating myself on my cleverness.

But as I neared the Casa de Maria exit, I noted a green van, again several vehicles behind in the right lane. My pulse raced. The same young man who'd followed me intermittently since that day at the Farmers Market? Maybe, maybe not, but still not knowing his motives, I decided to be careful not to lead him to Annie. Hugging the left lane, I passed the Casa de Maria exit, moved at the last second to the right lane at the next one, then barreled off the freeway.

The tactic worked and I took surface streets toward Casa de Maria, deciding on a whim to park on an innocuous dead-end street and walk in. If I sensed someone following me, either on foot or by car, I'd just walk right on by.

* * * * *

Saturday, May 8th, late morning

I hoofed it along the narrow road, working up a sweat. Once I had to jump to the side when a Lamborghini shot past me, the drivers seemingly heedless of the fact that the road had no shoulder. I trotted along, torn by conflict. On one hand, my actions could lead anyone looking for Annie straight to her. On the other, it was my one chance to find out more about Joe Milosch and his exact connection to Mike. Maybe we could help each other by trading information.

Annie, if she really was alive and hiding out, could use a helping hand. While not expensive compared to most retreat center standards, Casa de Maria still charged daily rates comparable to a good hotel. Where would she get the money? No sense wasting energy thinking about that. She might not even be here, and this sojourn would turn out as advertised to my family, a day of solitude and peace.

So far it had been anything but.

The retreat center stood at the end of a winding road, the buildings canopied by dense foliage. I slipped through the open gate and headed toward Administration. Both my pulse and my gait slowed and a welcome sense of peace and tranquility came over me.

An unfamiliar aroma, wild and earthy, filled my senses. So far, I'd seen only two people strolling the grounds and neither resembled Annie. With her limited mobility, I didn't expect to find her out walking.

Still, I checked for her presence at some small sanctuaries adjacent to the road: a graceful fountain on one side, a Bench of Dreams on the other, a peace garden dedicated to the victims of Hiroshima and Nagasaki.

Where the road ended, past dormitory buildings on the right, I turned left, walked a short way and climbed wide steps to the administration building.

A plain woman somewhere between thirty-five and fifty sat dwarfed behind a huge computer screen. She stood up when I entered, her pale eyes behind round glasses friendly tho' wary. The same could be said of her smile. "May I help you?" she asked, removing the glasses.

"I'm looking for one of your residents. Anne Carter?" A flicker of recognition in the eyes? Perhaps. She slammed her glasses back on, locking them against her forehead with the flat of her hand. "I'm sorry, but we don't reveal the names of our guests."

Why did I expect this to be easy? Suddenly the problems getting here, being followed not once, but twice, and the long hot walk, took their toll. I found myself taking out my frustrations on the woman. "But I *have* to find her. It's important, for *both* of us. Annie is disabled and she may be in danger. Her abusive husband is looking for her," I fibbed. "We're coworkers and I have to warn her. I found your brochure when I cleaned out her desk, and we'd talked about Casa de Maria, and it's the only place I can think of that she might be." I leaned my elbows on the counter, exhausted, not just from the tirade, but with all the difficulties and uncertainties getting here.

The glasses came off again and a frown line creased her smooth forehead. "If you're only coworkers, why are you so involved in her affairs?"

"Well, you see I used to be a nun and now I'm not, but I just can't help getting involved—"

"I understand," she said, offering the small conspiratorial smile of a fellow nun.

"Besides," I said, "my husband is missing and somehow if I can help Annie, maybe I'll find him."

"I don't follow your logic, and I still can't tell you if your friend is here, but I do have a suggestion. Walk with me to the door." She came around the counter and headed for the entrance, motioning over her shoulder for me to follow. She slid open the glass door and pointed outside. "See that path there, just beyond where those two cars are parked?"

"Yes?"

"Take it."

Yup, definitely a nun.

33

Saturday, May 8th, midday

I found her perched on a large boulder, reading, cane resting beside her. "Annie?" I said softly, so as not to startle her. Thank God she was alive.

She jumped, dropping her book and knocking over the cane. She stared at me, blue eyes enormous in her thin face. "How did you find me?"

"Long story." I indicated the rock big enough for two. "May I sit?"

"I'd rather you didn't," she said. "I'd rather you just go away and leave me alone." When I did nothing of the sort, she repeated, "How did you find me?" adding, "I'm supposed to be dead."

"Well, it's obvious you're not. I was cleaning out your desk and found the Casa de Maria brochure with the scribbled arrival date—one day *after* your disappearance. She looked away, shoulders stiffening beneath her white T-shirt. I added, "I'm not the enemy."

"I know that." It took a moment, but her face softened. "You look like you're going to have a stroke." She scooted over and grabbed a bottle from a small pack. "Sit down and drink some water. I don't want to be calling 911." She almost managed a smile.

"Why are you here?" we said at almost the same moment.

We both smiled and I gestured, "You first."

"Pretty simple. I want some peace in my life." She hesitated. "You understand?"

"I do. But staging your own death is not exactly the best way to begin."

"Shh!" She peered around. "You can never tell who might be here. Sorry, but—" She studied the trees as though criminals were lurking. "This isn't the best place to talk." She pointed through the foliage to a tiny building perhaps a hundred yards away. "Let's go there."

A sign on the door said "Meditation Chapel." Expecting to enter the chapel proper, I was surprised to find myself in a small, dark anteroom with only a guestbook on a small table and several folding chairs stacked against the wall.

"In here," Annie whispered, and I trailed her into the chapel, also small and dark, but with cushions scattered on the floor. On the far wall was a sight that snatched my breath away: an illuminated circle at least eight feet in diameter with a cross at its center. Both circle and cross were formed from daylight streaming through countless small holes.

"A mandala," Annie whispered. "This one symbolizes the universe."

"You've been reading their brochure." I touched her arm, still warm from the sun. "Let's talk."

She shrugged. "Okay."

"Who's making your life hell, Annie? What made you stage your own death and run away?" I asked, lowering myself onto one of the cushions, wondering how I'd get up again.

Annie remained standing, hands clasped, one atop the other, on her cane. "The same people who killed my Joe."

"Joe Milosch?"

"How do you know his name?"

"I put two and two together: the timing of his death and your grief, your reluctance to place a death notice in the paper, your fear of law enforcement involvement."

She nodded. "We lived a secret life."

"I thought as much."

Two women lumbered through the door. Chatting away in loud voices, they waited in the anteroom for us to finish inside. But they'd broken the mood. Annie rushed out, brushing by the women, leaning heavily on her cane, earning stares from them.

I followed and without thinking, grabbed her arm. "Is there somewhere else we can talk?"

She pulled away. "I've changed my mind. I don't want to talk. Why don't you get in your car and just go home." Her eyes blazed.

Struggling to maintain the personal space that seemed so important to her, I said simply: "I'd like to help you, and I think I can. And maybe you can help me find my husband."

Her eyes flickered with hesitation, then moved to the dormitory building on her left. Options were being weighed. I held my breath. "Maybe my room?"

* * * * *

We settled ourselves in Annie's spartan quarters. At her invitation, I perched on the side of the high, narrow bed, legs dangling. Annie choose a straight chair close to the door. I turned to face her. "Have you any idea who's trying to kill you, Annie?"

Her face crumpled. "The…the…same people who killed Joe. They think I know about his past life and…and…they're right."

His past life as a crooked cop, I thought, remembering the newspaper article Mike had shown me. "Any idea who 'they' are?"

She moved her chair still closer to the door, once again distancing herself from me. "Why should I trust you?"

She had a point. The only way I was going to get trust was to give some back. "My husband Mike knew Joe in Chicago. Now he's missing—"

"He's missing?" A hand went to her mouth. "That's awful. Was he kidnapped?"

The now-familiar lump formed in my gut. "I don't know for sure, but I think he left on his own after we found Joe's body at the Inn."

"You found Joe's body!" she shrieked. "Why didn't you tell me?"

"I didn't figure out it was him for a while."

"What we you doing at the Inn?" she asked in an accusing tone, as though we had no right to be there.

"Well, every year we celebrate our anniversary there, except this year, we were going to that remote motel up the coast at Punto Solitario, but my mom is sick and we didn't want to be so far away—" I stopped, aghast that I revealed these intimate details.

She looked at me like I'd lost my mind. "Why wait all this time to tell me you found his body?"

I felt myself blush. "I guess I didn't want to add to your grief."

"Wait a minute," Annie said, as though a light bulb just went on. "Before, you said your husband knew Joe in *Chicago*?"

I nodded, unaware that my life was about to unravel. "Joe served in his precinct."

She blinked in astonishment. "Joe was *never* a cop in Chicago, and he *never* worked there."

My throat began to close. I put my hands flat on the bed to stop the room from spinning. "He must have. Mike's from Chicago."

She shook her head. "Joe told me everything. He and his partner in the Detroit PD, whose name I don't know— it may very well have been your husband—had information on organized crime within the department. Joe went into witness protection after it all came down."

"Witness protection?"

She nodded. "That's why he wasn't supposed to tell me about his past, but he did anyway."

"Did he tell you his real name?"

Again she nodded."I always called him Joe. Steve Pizniak's past was buried by the Marshal's Office, and that was just fine with me."

Easy for her to say. "Mike showed me an article from the *Chicago Sun-Times* showing Steve Pizniak after his arrest for racketeering. Said he went to jail."

Annie folded her arms, hugging them against her waist. "Joe was a cop in the Detroit PD, he worked undercover, and the Mob found out about it. He went into witness protection. If your husband said he went to jail, he's lying."

"My husband is not a liar!" I shot back, and covered my mouth with my hand.

Annie looked at me as though my unconscious gesture said otherwise. Mike had indeed bent the truth on several occasions during our marriage. The details were none of Annie's business. I'd already revealed too much about us.

"Well," she said, "something doesn't add up. Joe lived in Detroit. He graduated from San Giuseppe High School in 1972. I have a yearbook at the house that says so."

"Why didn't you bring it with you?"

"I forgot it in my hurry to get away."

Understandable. I thought a moment. Nineteen-seventy-two? That was the year Mike graduated from high school. What was I to make of that? Also, why would someone in witness protection keep a yearbook from his former life? Steve/Joe was either too cocky or not too bright.

"What about the *Chicago Sun-Times* article?" I asked.

"Fake. Has to be."

A fake? Silence between us as I attempted to think this through. Her late husband lived and worked with Mike in Detroit. He worked undercover and went into witness protection when the Mob found out about it. Where did that leave Mike?

"Did you and Joe marry in Detroit?"

She shook her head. "Vegas. Joe had been there a long time. Moving here was supposed to be another new beginning."

"So, you only know what he told you about being from Detroit."

"I have the yearbook," she countered.

"That could be fake too. Mike and I were married in Detroit after he moved there from Chicago." Only after I made that smug statement did I realize how idiotic it sounded.

Annie looked at me like she'd like me to leave; I wasn't ready yet. "You say you don't know the person who killed Joe. Any ideas?"

She stared at the wall for a bit, then turned back to me. "The whole Detroit Mafia has lots of lieutenants. It could be anybody."

"But this isn't like a big city. Why would they be here on the Central Coast?"

"Joe figured they wanted to muscle in on some construction contracts."

"That makes no sense. There's no construction here big enough for the Mafia."

Her thin shoulders hunched in a shrug. "I only know what Joe told me. He thought the first thing they'd do is put someone they trust in a prominent position. Someone with a public face."

"Like a politician?"

"That too. But he was thinking more about the media. You know—to butter people up."

I stared at her, speechless. Alena came to mind. And why not? Her father, Bootsie, was a known mobster.

Little men with big hammers pounded on my temples. Dear God, why had I come here? I should have left well enough alone.

Now I had a whole new set of questions to torment my days and ruin my nights.

"Joe told me to disappear if something happened to him," Annie volunteered.

"Why didn't you?" I said, sounding sharper than I'd intended. I leaned forward, touching my chest. "I mean, if *I* could find you, anyone could."

Annie looked around the room as though it were a suite at the Hilton instead of a cell worthy of a cloistered nun. "I'm tired of running. I thought maybe if I escaped for a little while, things would settle down and I could come back to Mariposa Bay." She smiled. "People are so nice there."

"Tolosa County's the friendliest place in the U.S.," I said, repeating the claim of a recent magazine article.

"Was there something specific that made you decide to run?" I asked.

Fear returned to her eyes. "Someone in a big black car drove by my house. Several times."

"An Escalade?"

"Maybe. I'm not sure. And when I came home from work one night, my lock had been jimmied. Someone broke in. I was afraid to go back to work after that."

"I can see why. Did they find the yearbook?"

"I don't think so, it was still in the same place."

"Why didn't you call the police?"

A tear formed in the corner of one eye. "Whoever broke in killed my dog, the only thing I had left after Joe. I found Skipper's body in the back yard. It was a warning about what would happen to me if I said anything about the Mafia being on the Central Coast."

I got up and put my arms around her, feeling her tremble. "Annie, you're in grave danger. Better get out of here while you can. Do you have money?"

She nodded, reaching for her purse. "A little."

"Enough for a flight?"

She held up a wad of bills bound with a worn rubber band. "All my savings."

"Good. After I leave, call a taxi and take it to the Santa Barbara Airport. Get on the first flight going anywhere. Pay cash for your ticket. Can you do that?"

She gulped. "As long as it's not too far away. Can you drive me to the airport? I took the train to Santa Barbara, and a taxi here."

"Better not. Someone in a black Escalade followed me part way here. I lost him around Solvang, but he could resurface." No sense telling her about the green van. I would deal with that on my own.

"Oh God." She jumped up and started throwing things into a small bag. I watched, wondering if I'd given her the right advice. She stopped folding a pair of skinny Levis. "What?" she asked.

"You told me not to bring my cell phone. Why?"

"Because, when you saw my 'body,' you'd have to go somewhere else to make a call. That would give me time to get away, and the cops would naturally assume that I was washed off the jetty by the surf."

That actually seemed plausible. "So you set me up and took a huge chance besides. Someone else might have showed up before me. Someone able to pull you off that rock."

She shrugged. "They didn't."

"Annie, do you have a house key with you?"

"Sure. Maybe when this is all over I can go back home."

Maybe not, Annie.

"I need to look at that yearbook. Where would I find it?"

She reached into her pocket and extracted a key from a small ring. "On the top shelf in the front hall closet. Good luck."

34

Saturday, May 8th, early afternoon

I was no less hot and sticky on the walk back to my car and now I carried the burden of Mike's past life, plus worry that he might be involved, even unwittingly, with the Mafia.

I felt for Annie's key in my pocket. A look at that yearbook would confirm what she'd told me. The book might be fake; I had a hunch it wasn't.

After discussing Annie's options, we agreed she should spend the night at Casa de Maria behind locked doors and take a taxi to the airport at dawn. That way, if anyone asked in the office, the nun wouldn't be so likely to tie my arrival with Annie's departure. I doubted she'd cough up the info even if she suspected, but we couldn't be too careful.

A block and a half from my car, my gut clenched. The green van sat at the curb of a stately home near the next corner. Somehow the driver found his way here.

Head down, eyes averted, striving for casual, I crossed the street and, once close to the vehicle, kept as close to the far edge of the sidewalk as I could get without stepping on someone's lawn. Do rich folks alarm their grass? I wondered. I was perhaps ten feet past the van when common sense finally prevailed. I wheeled around and retraced my steps.

The driver was sleeping, head resting on the side window, mouth agape. Sensing my presence, he bolted up and stared at me with unfocused eyes. I motioned for him to roll down the window. Instead he opened the door and hopped from the van, facing me on the sidewalk, palms out at shoulder height. *I've got nothing to hide, lady.*

The smell of fast food clung to him, a mélange of grease and salt and something savory, maybe ketchup. I motioned for him to lower his hands. They dropped to his sides. In his early twenties, the kid was of medium height, with a squarish build, and today, dressed casually in shorts, surf shirt and river sandals.

"Why are you following me?" I asked. "It's been going on since that day at the Farmers Market, and then at the Tolosa train station when you said you had something important to speak to me about. Well, speak!" *Right, Bella. Show him how tough you are.*

He shrugged, the gesture belying the unease in his grayish eyes. "Just doing my job, Ma'am."

"What do you mean by that?"

"Your husband offered me cash and wired it to me. I wasn't about to turn it down."

"My husband Mike? Is that who wired the cash?"

"Um, yes Ma'am."

Mike was alive! I could hardly speak; I forced the words out. "Where…did he wire it from?"

"Can't really say. But I need money for school."

School. Presumably he wasn't a hardened criminal. I stared at him and he returned my stare, also not about to back down. Something about that stubbornness seemed familiar. "What are you supposed to find out about me?"

"Nothin.' I'm supposed to keep an eye on you. He thought you might be in trouble. Or danger."

Try both, buddy. Needing to touch something real, I placed my hand on the van's fender.

"Ma'am?"

"Yes?"

"If it's okay, can I still follow you? I need the money."

"Why not," I said, motioning over my shoulder. "Everyone else is."

* * * * *

Pulling onto the northbound 101, I glanced in my rearview mirror. Sure enough, the kid followed, this time right on my tail. I stared at the van in my rearview mirror. He never said what he wanted to speak to me about at the train station. And there were questions I should have asked him: *How did Mike choose you? Where were you supposed to do if I was in danger?* And most important, *Do you have a way to contact him?*

These and other noisy thoughts tumbled in my mind like loose coins in a clothes dryer. Hoping for a calm perspective, I popped a Mozart tape into my player and let the music swell around me.

Annie swore that her late husband worked in the Detroit PD. That Steve/Joe never lived in Chicago.

So what did that mean? Either Mike's newspaper clipping was a fake, or she was lying (unlikely). Or Joe lied to her and the yearbook was a fake. I had her house key in my pocket and I couldn't wait to get my hands on that yearbook.

We'd gone over her story again before I left and she added more details. According to her, Steve was never arrested, he'd gone into witness protection in the mid-nineties after turning state's evidence against a prominent mobster, name unknown. He then moved to Las Vegas. As Joe, he worked low level jobs, bouncer, bartender, finally deciding a few months ago, upon the advice of a friend to move with Annie to the Central Coast.

Like the name of the mobster, this friend was also unknown to Annie. According to her, keeping in touch with friends from your former life was a witness protection no-no. So was telling your back-story to someone in your new life, as Joe had done. He ignored the rules and that probably lead to his murder.

I glanced in my rearview mirror. Kid right behind me. Why hadn't I gotten that young man's name, to say nothing of having my questions answered?

The 246 exit had fast food. I signaled a turn and pulled off the freeway. Sure enough, he followed.

I'd treat him to a coffee or ice cream, find out his name, and ask him, *beg* him, if I needed to, to tell me what he knew about Mike.

35

Saturday, May 8th, midafternoon

We settled across from each other at a small table in the fast food restaurant, the large plastic clown keeping a close watch on us. "Okay, I've had a chance to think about this and I need to know more. Who are you and why are you following me?" I took a sip of my café mocha. Sensing whipped cream on my upper lip, reached for a napkin.

The kid was way ahead of me. A smile crinkling the corner of his eyes, he handed me one. "I thought you'd never ask." A long pause. "I'm *Ethan*."

The silence between us lengthened. Sometimes I'm slow to catch on. He reached into a pocket. The Nevada driver's license he handed me identified him as Ethan Earnhardt, age twenty.

I handed it back. "Doesn't mean anything to me."

The smile widened even as his eyes flicked with uncertainty. A nervous sip of sweet tea. "I'm Mike's son."

The news lay like an oil slick on the surface of my brain. "That's impossible. You're dead."

He patted his shirt, arms and face as though checking. "Don't think so."

I leapt to my feet, gripping the table until my knuckles turned white. "Why didn't you tell me before?" I shouted. People turned and stared.

He put up his hands. "I dunno. He asked me not to. But that makes no sense with all that's happened. I was going to tell you at the train station, then things got nuts and I lost my nerve."

More silence, except for the clatter of ice dropping from the soda machine into someone's cup. I studied him. "Mike" was written all over him, from the square build, to the gray eyes, to the strong jaw. "But…but, what about the accident?"

He looked down at his hands, the same as Mike's, also square, with long fingers and flat nails. "My mom," he hesitated, his voice breaking, "was…was killed. I got out of the lake alive, made it to shore somehow. I don't remember any of this. People told me about it later, after I came home from the hospital. I was seven."

I thought of the picture of Ethan Mike kept on our kitchen message center, and how he'd destroyed all photos of Grace, his wife, before we were married.

"You know for sure your mother was killed?"

A sad nod. "I went to her funeral."

"So…so, what happened to you after that?"

"Because of things going on in Mike's life at the time, he had to disappear for a while."

Aha, so this wasn't the first time he'd done a disappearing act. Somehow I wasn't surprised and continued to press. "Where'd he go?"

He shrugged. "I dunno. I got shipped to Las Vegas."

"Las Vegas? Did you know a guy named Steve Pizniak?"

He looked puzzled. "Should I?"

"How about Joe Milosch?"

He considered. "Maybe I heard the name, but I can't put a face with it. Why?"

"Never mind. If you were only seven, who took you to Vegas?"

"My step-grandma. She raised me. Has a business there."

"Step-grandma?"

""Grandpa Boo...er...Grandpa's second wife, now ex-wife."

Did he start to start to say "Bootsie?" *Oh my god!* "Is Bootsie Lupino your grandfather?"

He didn't have to answer, his look said it all.

Needing time to think I asked, "And you've been in Las Vegas ever since you were seven?"

"More or less. As I said, Mike…" His voice dropped away.

"Mike. You call him Mike."

"Seems weird to call him Dad."

"Understandable."

I stared at a poster on the wall showing a pre-anorexic model sipping a huge chocolate shake. I looked again, seeing the scenario as though it were emblazoned on her forehead. Joe Milosch's body, Mike's fear, his disappearance. "Mike's in…in," I could hardly get the words out, "witness protection, isn't he?"

He fingered the design on his drink cup. Hedged. "I heard that."

Okay, I'll accept that, I thought. He's protecting someone, either Mike or his step-grandma. Or both.

"Okay, let's assume Mike is now, or was, in witness protection. I've always heard that people in that program get new names and whole new identities. Do you know if he ever used a name other than Kowalski?"

He shook his head. "I don't think so, at least not that I heard."

"So today, as we speak, he has a different identity, that of a former Chicago cop, but uses his real name. Does that seem weird to you?"

He shrugged. "Maybe."

"Why do you go by the name Earnhardt?"

"I used to go by Kowalski, but after Mom died, my step-grandma, Jayne Earnhardt, changed my birth certificate to her name. Mike went to Chicago for a while, but then he came back to Detroit."

"You know that for a fact?"

That's what Grandma Jayne said, and she had no reason to lie."

"Have you seen your grandpa him lately?"

He shook his head. "Not since I was seven. I wouldn't know him if I ran into him on the street."

"But he'd know you?"

"Prob'ly."

Annie didn't know the name of the Mafia guy that Joe (as Steve) had testified against.

Could it have been Bootsie?

Did Mike testify against him too? His own father-in-law?

"One other question," I said, reeling from information overload, but needing to press on. "If you were supposed to be keeping an eye on me, how come I only saw you a few times?"

He gave me a lopsided smile so like Mike's that it both broke and captured my heart. "Just because you didn't see me, doesn't mean I wasn't there."

* * * * *

Saturday, May 8th, late afternoon

When we parted in Solvang, Ethan dropped a bombshell. He'd remained here as long as he could. He had to go back to Las Vegas to get ready for the summer quarter at his college. Was I okay with that? No, but I had to accept it. On the drive back to Tolosa, I'd been aware of him behind me. No Escalades, thank goodness.

He peeled off at Tolosa and I continued on to Mariposa Bay. Only later did I realize I'd once again failed to get his contact information. Too much on my mind, I guess.

I was desperate to get home, but checking Annie's house for the yearbook had to be my first priority. I marched up her front walk like I owned the place, then unlocked and pushed the door open. The house had taken on the lonely, musty smell of abandonment. I peered around; everything in place. If someone had been in the house, at least they hadn't tossed it.

Shutting the door revealed the closet behind it. I reached on tip-toe up to the top shelf and put my hand right on the yearbook, dated 1972. Almost too easy.

I scanned the yellowed pages, seeing nothing of interest at first, just faded photos of high school activities: games, dances, projects. Grads were pictured in alphabetical order at the end of the book. I found Steve Pizniak immediately, a typical pimply faced teenager. The caption under his photo said: "Most likely to marry first."

I leafed to the K's. Not many, but there was Michael Kowalski, smiling at the camera and looking very much like Ethan. So he *had* gone to high school in Detroit, had known Steve Pizniak. The caption under Mike's photo: "Most likely to marry second."

I leaned against the wall, knowing the yearbook was genuine, not faked like the newspaper article. *Mike, Mike, why did you lie to me?*

Hand trembling, I leafed back through the activities' pages, and sure enough, Steve and Mike were pictured with their dates at the senior prom. The caption read: "These two are rumored to be serious about these pretty sisters from Saint Sabina Girls Academy."

The girls looked young, painfully so. One must be Grace. I'd never seen a picture of her before. Mike refused to have any in the house, claiming it brought back too many painful memories.

But there was more to it, Mike, wasn't there? You knew Steve Pizniak in Detroit, not Chicago, and, in fact, went to school with him there. You even married Grace, his girlfriend's sister. *You and Steve Pizniak testified against Grace's family, that's why you both had to go into witness protection. Only then did you go to Chicago. Why didn't you tell me all this? I'd have kept your secret.*

I stood for a long time, eyes riveted on Grace. I'd always wondered what she looked like, this ghost woman who'd inhabited my marriage. Here she was, if not in the flesh, at least as close as I'd ever get. Petite like me, coming only to Mike's shoulder, she had a strange little face, attractive but almost birdlike, olive skin, and penetrating, close-together dark eyes. Something about those eyes bothered me.

I studied her sister, Steve's girlfriend. As tall as Steve, she and Grace didn't even look related, much less like sisters. Why do we look at eyes first? Something about this girl's reminded me of someone familiar, but the rest, lean body, bobbed dark hair, unusual in that Age of Aquarius era when lanky hair, and lots of it, was the norm, I couldn't match to anyone I knew.

Wait a minute. Wait *just* a minute.

Ethan mentioned Bootsie married a second time, and had a second family, Alena and Bret. She was—*oh my god*—Mike's former sister-in-law. That was the connection between the two, why Mike had ducked under the table when she walked into The Wandering Nun restaurant. But that still didn't explain why they met at the Cafe Noir and why he gave her the red notebook.

The day's events tumbled down on me like an avalanche. I couldn't wait to get home, to a place of safety. Before returning the book to its place in the closet, I stole one last glance at the prom picture.

Was it Alena?

36

Saturday, May 8th, early evening

Something wrong. Our house too quiet, air sluggish, sour smelling.

"Mom?" I called. "Chris?"

"In here." Chris called, his voice tense. I tossed my purse on the hall bench and made quick tracks to Mom's room. She lay in bed, white as the sheet tucked under her chin. Her eyes were closed, the lids translucent, like a baby's.

"She had a bad spell." Chris chewed his lower lip, his worry obvious.

"Mom," I said, leaning over the bed and taking her hand. "What's wrong? Is it the chemo?" She opened her eyes and offered a whisper of a smile. "Maybe."

"Maybe?" The word came out louder, and harsher, than I'd intended.

"Aunt Bella?" Chris said, a reminder to use my indoor voice.

I gulped a deep breath and gripped her hand tighter. "I'm sorry, Mom, it's just that maybe we need to take you to the emergency room, see what's wrong."

"No, no." She rolled her head from side to side. "I'm not going. You can't make me."

"I'm not going to make you Mom, but—"

"I have those tests next week." She heaved a deep sigh. "That's enough."

She was scheduled for tests on Monday. Studying her now, it seemed the immediate crisis had passed. She was weak and pale, but she still had her spark. And maybe she had point. She'd see her oncologist soon after the tests and this latest problem could be discussed then. Weak as she was, there was no point in hauling her out of her own bed and depositing her into the bedlam of a typical ER on Saturday night.

"Rest now," I said, lifting the bell beside her bed and tinkling it softly. "Ring if you need me. I'll be close by."

I motioned for Chris, pale as Mom, to follow, leaving the door open to hear the bell. Chris offered to make popcorn, but I thought the smell might be too much for her queasy stomach. Instead I poured us each a glass of wine. It seemed weird to share alcohol with him. I had to keep reminding myself he was of legal age.

We took our glasses into the living room, where Chris made a fire as I settled back on the sofa and tucked an afghan around me. The whole day, being followed, first by the black Escalade and then by the familiar green van, had been way beyond strange. To say nothing of my conversations with Annie, and then with Mike's son Ethan, capped by revelations in the yearbook that Joe Milosch and Mike had gone to school together.

Mike was alive, I was sure from my conversation with Ethan. Did he know by now that his son had followed me today? He knew I wasn't an idiot, that sooner or later I'd figure out who was tailing me in the green van. And why.

So Mike had married into a Mob family and then became a cop. Or was it the other way around? I would deal with that later, when I felt calmer. Right now, Mom came first.

* * * * *

Saturday, May 8th, late evening

I awoke to a cold, empty room, fire burnt to embers. The wine, barely touched, sat on the coffee table. Chris must have removed it from my hand before I spilled it.

I tiptoed through the dark starless night to bed, stopping first to check on Mom. She slept peacefully, the nightlight throwing a faint glow onto her face. Chris had hauled two chairs into her room. He was asleep sitting up on one, his feet on the other.

My heart swelled with love. What did I do to deserve such a good nephew? Should I tell him about Ethan? No, not now. He had so much on his plate already with his job, his girlfriend and his beloved grandma's illness.

37

Monday, May 17th, midmorning

Mom and I sat in the doctor's reception area. They were running behind; we'd been here way too long. Maybe that was unfair, I decided, surveying other frail looking patients. They had serious problems that often took more time than anticipated.

Chris had taken the early train home. His boss called over the weekend, needing him to work a big retirement party on Tuesday. That was okay, the guy had been more than generous.

Mom sat beside me, trying to concentrate on a *People* magazine article about the latest misadventures of a young performer with substance abuse problems. The magazine shook, making a rattling sound in the otherwise silent room. She was nervous, and with good reason. When the receptionist called to schedule the appointment, she'd stressed that "Doctor" wanted to speak to me as well. I hadn't told Mom. Now I wished I had. At least she'd be forewarned.

"James Bryan." The nurse called the man ahead of us.

I patted her arm. "You'll be next."

She let the periodical slip to the floor. "I'm so sick," she said. I reached over and gently smoothed her thinning hair while we waited. Lately she had refused to wear her wig, saying it made her too warm.

"Helen Rogers," the nurse announced, startling us both. I helped Mom to her feet and followed her into the doctor's office.

She half turned and made a backhanded gesture of dismissal. "I'll go in by myself. "

The nurse put her arm around Mom's thin shoulders. "Today Doctor wants to see your daughter as well."

"Oh." Mom made a small, strangled sound as though someone had punched her in the gut.

The nurse led us into his office. Doctor Lebovitz sat at a small round table with two other chairs, one for the patient, one for the patient's trusted advisor.

A good idea I decided. Doctor didn't face patient across the forbidding expanse of an immense desk. Seated here we would be on an equal level.

"Hello, Mrs. Rogers, Mrs. Kowalski," he said without consulting her chart on the table before him. I gave him a point for preparation, and another for not calling her "Helen." With a wide smile, he gestured for Mom to sit on his right, with me on the left.

He had a kind of nebbish Woody Allen look. No, I thought, studying him closer, more like PBS commentator David Brooks, but with better teeth. "Well now." He began to rearrange papers on the table. "How are you feeling, Mrs. Rogers?"

"Awful," she said. "I feel just awful."

"That's understandable." He pushed his glasses up with his index finger, paused and took a deep breath. "Mrs. Rogers, I'm sorry to tell you this..."

Mom leaned forward gripping the edge of the table. Time stopped.

"But… you've said you wanted to be kept informed of your condition," he continued. Profound silence followed.

"And?" Mom asked.

"The chemo's not working as it should. The tumor has metastasized to your liver."

Her knuckles whitened around the table. "I'm going to die?"

I can't be hearing this.

Now I saw why the doctor's chair had wheels. He scooted over and put his arm around my mother's shoulders. I gave him another point for empathy, even if it was a bit studied. "In time, yes. But none of us know how long we have. And we can perhaps slow the liver tumor growth with more chemo."

Mom shook her head resolutely. "No more, if it's not going to take away the cancer."

The doctor nodded. "Absolutely. That's your choice."

"What's your guess on time?" I asked, and wished I could cut out my tongue.

He frowned at my lack of tact, tightening his grip on her shoulders. "I can't really say."

"Oh dear, I've had my last Christmas."

Hmm. Funny she should focus on that.

"As I said, Mrs. Rogers, we can only guess. You may very well be around next holiday season. In the meantime, let's look at the glass as half full." Again he pushed up his glasses and I noticed that he wore no wedding ring. "There's Memorial Day coming up soon, Fourth of July, Labor Day, Columbus Day, Halloween..."

She looked at him like he'd lost his mind. He did not mention Thanksgiving and Christmas.

Christmas. What would this year's holiday be without Mom, and without Mike? He and I had made love so tenderly last Christmas day. Just thinking about it aroused me. I looked at Doctor Lebovitz. He *was* attractive in a nerdy kind of way.

My God, Bella, you're a monster. Here is your Mom receiving a death sentence and you're thinking about having *sex* with the doctor who's delivering it? Maybe it was just a doctor-patient thing, as when women fall in love with their obstetricians. Except Doctor Lebovitz was an oncologist, my mother his patient. That seemed to cross some kind of line.

"Mrs. Rogers," he continued, "here's a bright spot. You'll feel better than you have for some time because we're going to stop treatment."

"And then…?"

He gave her shoulders an extra squeeze. "And then there are pain meds whenever you need them."

Thank goodness they'd dropped all that nonsense about terminally ill people becoming addicted.

"Tell me it's not going to hurt too much." Her words brought quick, hot tears of frustration to my eyes. If only there was something I could say, or do, that would make this moment, and all the moments to come, easier for her.

Another squeeze, as I pondered the likelihood of accidental bruising by an over-enthusiastic doctor.

"Again, as much pain medication as you need." Which didn't exactly answer the question, but he couldn't really. No one knows how another will react to pain. Here was my mom, who had pretty much relied on my dad for everything. Now, facing the end of her life, she was on her own. Little I could say or do would help her in the end.

"I think it's time for Hospice," Doctor Lebovitz said.

Her reaction was immediate. "No, no Hospice. My daughter doesn't want a bed in the living room of her lovely home."

"Mom, one, my home is far from lovely, and two, I don't mind."

"And I'll be out there on display with no hair and bottles of stuff dripping into my arms for everyone who traipses through the house to see." She began to cry, her first tears since the doctor delivered his verdict.

"It won't be like that at all. I promise."

I rose to go to her, but the doctor gestured for me to remain seated. "A good cry never hurt anyone."

I loved him for that.

"We don't have to make a decision about Hospice today. Think about it for a while. In the meantime, as I said, Mrs. Rogers, you're going to start feeling better almost right away."

"Physically maybe, but not mentally," I wanted to scream. Instead I said to Mom, "We can work around the bed issue."

"I'm sure Hospice can be flexible." Doctor Lebovitz removed a card from her folder and handed it to me. His hand touched mine and I felt a spark of electricity between us. He noticed it too. Behind the nerdy glasses, his eyes widened. A shiver passed through me.

The doctor ducked beneath his professional cover. He indicated the card still in my hand. "Call them when you're ready. Next week would be fine."

His takeaway message seemed to be: "Don't wait too long."

* * * * *

Monday, May 17th, dinnertime

I threw two frozen entrees in the microwave. The turkey and dressing smelled festive, like Thanksgiving, but Mom and I mostly just pushed the food around our plates. When we'd abandoned any pretense of eating, I fed them to Sam, who acted like he'd won the canine lottery.

Afterwards, I made a fire and we sat in the living room, each with a mystery novel. Sam settled himself as close to the fire as possible, head resting on his crossed paws. Sensing our anxiety, he remained watchful.

She sat in the wing chair by the fireplace wrapped in my warmest afghan, her feet on the ottoman. I curled up on the sofa, book resting on my raised legs.

I glanced around thinking how many important discussions we had had in this room. Mike sitting, like Mom now, in the chair by the fire, me curled up in the dent I'd worn in the sofa cushion.

Just as well that Milly and Chris were gone. Mom and I needed time alone. We both understood that we had finite time to repair our troubled relationship. An evening of reading mysteries, an activity we both loved, seemed the perfect place to begin some serious mother-daughter bonding.

As often happens, she had a different take on things. "I want to talk about my will."

Oh please, not tonight. "Ma, you've had a rough day. There's plenty of time."

"No. There is not. You heard Doctor Lebovitz."

"Okay." I closed my book with a thud. "What's on your mind?"

"There's a copy of my will at the house," she said, referring to her home in Detroit, "another in my safety deposit box, I'll give you the key. Mister Lambs, the executor, has the original."

"Mister Lambs," everyone called him that. I had no idea what his first name was, I hadn't thought of him in years. He and Dad had been carpool buddies forever. Both were pressmen, a job now automated by computer typesetting.

"I have a request."

The beginnings of a headache stirred in my temples. Shouldn't have had wine with supper. "Anything, Ma. You know that."

"I want you to bury my ashes next to your father and Bea."

What? Waves of hurt and jealousy washed over me. "You don't want to be buried in California?"

"No, I don't. Why would you think that? I've only been here a few months. My roots are in Detroit. I had friends there. I had a life."

How could she be so unfair? "We've tried to get you out and about, but it's hard. I have to work, and you're sick, Ma. You can't get out and make friends the way you did there."

She jutted out her chin. "I spent almost fifty years with your father, and after Bea's horrible death, I want to be near her, near them both."

What about me? I wanted her to be buried here, where I could keep her close—and she wanted to be close to Bea. It was as though my twin had reached out from the grave and snatched her from me.

"Bella, you two made a decision to come to California with, excuse me for saying so, very little thought that you'd be leaving me alone after losing my daughter and my husband within two years."

Was this decision her way to punish me? "We asked you to come with us."

"That's true, but you kids needed to be on your own, just married and all, and after the changes in your lives." She referred to me leaving religious life, and Mike's loss of his family shortly before we met.

Correction. Loss of his wife. *Ethan was alive.* Every time I thought about that, shock waves catapulted through my body.

"We did think about you, Ma. You said you wanted to live near your friends. That they were your support system."

"They were, and still would be if most of them weren't ill themselves or dead. I don't begrudge your coming out here, but it would have been nice if you'd visited sometimes."

I stared at her, chin wattles resting on her chest. She looked shockingly old. How could I have been so thoughtless? Worse than that, heartless. "I'm sorry," I mumbled. "I just never thought..."

"That's the problem, you just never think."

"Oh, I think all right," I flared. "I think you preferred Bea. After she was killed, you were left with your second-choice kid." *What had I just said?*

"That's absolute bullshit!" my mother replied, the first time I'd ever heard her use a Class-A swear word. "You deal with the child who needs you most. And Bea needed me. If you had children of your own you'd know that." She stopped, apparently appalled at what *she'd* just said.

"Oh, Bella, I'm sorry." She looked aghast, eyes wide, pale lips forming a perfect "O." "I didn't mean..."

My hand did a listless wave. "It's okay, Ma. I'm sorry too." A good daughter would have hauled her tired butt off the sofa, dragged herself across the room and hugged her. I couldn't move. I wanted so to reach out to her, and *I couldn't.*

Like a dog with an old bone, I wasn't quite ready to bury my hurt. "You always catered to Bea."

She stared at me, a soup of pain and anger in her eyes. "You really think that?"

I chewed my lip, biting back hot tears.

"If that's true, and I'm not saying it is, it's because she needed me more."

"Needed you more? Ma, look at me, I'm a sniveling bunch of neuroses, I'm afraid of water, I'm afraid of height, I have terrible panic attacks. Why didn't you see that?"

"I did see it. I'm not as insensitive as you suppose."

"I never said you were insensitive."

Her hand shot up. "Let me finish. You have always faced your fears, Bella. You may have felt frightened, but you didn't let it stop you. Bea, God love her, had plenty of neuroses, as you call them, and she turned her fears into something that wasn't so nice." She breathed in as though there wasn't enough air in the room.

"Ma, are you okay? We can talk about this later."

"You've asked me that three times. I'm fine, and I want to talk about it now." She gripped the chair arms. "It pains me to say it of my own daughter, but she was a bully. That was her way of controlling all of us, I see that now."

"Hmm." What she said was true. Growing up, Bea was always messing with me: challenging me to jump off the garage roof with an umbrella parachute (result, one broken arm), sneaking up behind and pushing me off the boat dock into Lake Saint Claire.

She let a friend's canary out of its cage, knowing it would send me screaming from the room, her laughter hard at my heels.

Contrast this with the picture my nephew Chris had painted of Bea as a mom, terrified of the park slide and having to back down the steps while all his friends watched. Could those traits coexist in the same person? Of course they could, we're all a walking mass of contradictions. "I loved her anyway."

"What did you say, dear? Please don't mumble."

Her words provided the first clue that I'd said the last bit aloud. "I said I loved her anyway."

"Of course you did, dear. We all did. Especially your father. She always could wrap him around her little finger."

What she said was sadly true; I'd never had the same clout with Dad. Poor Pop. Like many parents who lose children, he lost the will to live after she died.

After our exchange, we retreated to the safety of the printed page. At last she put her book facedown on her lap. "Chris says you're pretty good at solving murders."

Wow, was this a one-eighty or what? "He's telling tales out of school."

"He didn't provide many details. I mean, why say something like that and then clam up?" She looked at me expectantly. "Well?"

"Well, a few years ago, I guess you could say I solved the murder of the woman who owned the land where the sewage treatment plant was to be built."

"The same plant you're still fighting over?"

I rolled my eyes. "Don't get me started. About the murder, the solution stumbled over me, rather than the other way around."

"Janet seemed to have heard about it in Cleveland. As you may well imagine, she was very worried about my safety here, with you running around solving murders all the time."

How like that woman *my brother-in-law married.* "It was no big deal. I didn't want to worry you."

"She also said that wasn't the only murder you've been involved in."

"When did she tell you all that?"

"After I got sick, when she and Ed found out I was coming to California. They wanted me to move down to Cleveland with them."

"I'm sure they did." They wouldn't tender that offer unless there was something in it for them. Like getting Mom to change her will.

"So, tell me more about these murders you've been solving," she said, a gleam of anticipation in her eye. A vicarious thrill, perhaps.

"I don't want to talk about this any more." Thank goodness we hadn't told her about the Joe Milosch murder. Of course she'd seen it on TV, but since we weren't identified as the couple who found the body, she hadn't made the connection.

"And now there's the murder of that unfortunate young man at the motel."

"It isn't a motel, Ma, it's an Inn," I said, hoping to derail this conversation. *Fat chance.*

She swiped the air. "Whatever. Are you snooping around on that one as well? Is that why Mike left town?"

"Of course not. How could you even think such a thing?" *If she only knew.*

"Honestly, Bella, you get me so mixed up, I forget what I wanted to say in the first place. What I think is not the point."

God give me strength. "What is, then?"

"I was thinking," she said, contradicting herself, "since you have to take my ashes back to Michigan, sell the house and tie-up my affairs there, you could do something for me. For us as a family."

"What's that?" I asked with a sinking feeling.

"Put those good instincts to work and find Bea's murderer. We'll all rest easier knowing the killer is behind bars."

Huh? "Ma, I won't be able to stay that long. There's work, remember? Also the Detroit PD said Bea's killing was a random act. I wouldn't know where to start."

She gave me a wise-woman smile. "I know you better than anyone, even that husband you love so much. You may not remember it, but you were always the daughter we dispatched to find anything from misplaced car keys to a runaway cat. You have, I don't know, this sixth sense, it's hard to explain. I'm not surprised you're solving murders."

How do I reply to that?

"I know you can find Bea's murderer if you put your mind to it. Since you have to be in Detroit anyway, why not do it?"

Because I might get killed, Ma.

"Promise me, Bella."

I chewed on that awhile, then said, "Okay, Ma, I promise." I could always take it back in the morning when she wasn't so tired and emotional.

"Good," she said, pushing her afghan aside and groping for her walker. "I'll sleep better knowing that."

Only then was I able to struggle to my feet, little arrows of pain shooting through my head. "Let me help."

"I don't need help, I need a goodnight kiss."

Of course she did. Quickly I crossed the room and enveloped her thin shoulders in a hug, giving her papery cheek a big kiss. I didn't realize until I felt wetness on my cheeks—and saw tears in her eyes—that we both were crying.

Sharing tears, a good place to begin.

38

Tuesday, May 18th, sometime after midnight

I retreated to the safety of my novel and awoke on the sofa, stiff and cramped from sleeping in one position, my book t-boned on the rug, the room shrouded in cold and darkness. I glanced over at the armchair. Empty. *That's right, Mom went to bed hours ago.*

I lay there awhile, feeling, if not good, at least satisfied that we'd made a good beginning on repairing our broken relationship. What was the quote, "Put aside childish things?" Perhaps I was starting to put aside my own childish things.

At last I summoned the strength to haul my tired-beyond-belief butt from the sofa and off to bed. Once in the hall, I stopped dead, the only sound the sudden hammering of my own heart. Something wrong. With Mom. I flung myself headlong toward her room.

"Mom! Mom!" Her frail body made barely a lump under the covers. I flicked on the overhead light and, afraid to go forward, but unable to move back, edged closer.

Her eyes were open, seeing nothing. All color had leaked from the irises, leaving behind the milky color of death.

I felt for a pulse and held a small mirror under her nose, hoping against hope for the tiniest bit of fog on the glass.

* * * * *

Numb with shock, not knowing what else to do, I called 911. Time passed and paramedics screeched into the driveway, siren screaming. I opened the door and waited. A light snapped on at the house across the road.

I couldn't stop shaking, the sirens and lights reminding me of the incident with Annie on the rocks. Maybe in my heart I expected that, like Annie, it would prove a false alarm, and Mom would be alive.

"In here." I led the young man and woman down the hall. They quickly verified that Mom was indeed gone but insisted on transferring her to the hospital for an official confirmation of death. I asked to ride in the ambulance with her; they suggested I follow in my car.

In cold and darkness I cranked the heater up high, hoping warm air would stop my shakes. I kept one eye on the ambulance taillights and the other on my gas gauge. The needle sat on empty.

"I will not run out of gas. I will not run out of gas." I repeated as I attempted to keep up with the ambulance. "Bella," I said, gripping the wheel so hard I half-expected it to whimper, "don't worry about the ambulance. Just head for the hospital."

A few miles down Los Lobos Road, the engine sputtered, coughed and then somehow gained a second life. I prayed to Saint Jude, the patron of hopeless causes, to infuse some heavenly fumes into the tank. Who would I call if I ran out of gas? Not Saint Jude. Not my undoubtedly-wide-awake neighbors whose number was not in my cell phone directory. My mother had just died and I was about to run out of gas following the ambulance taking her to the hospital.

Without warning, it started to rain, a few drops at first, then a mini deluge. I flicked on the wipers. *Are you happy, Mom? It's raining. That's what you wanted. How about you Saint Jude? Has she got you messin' with me from up there already?*

Peering out the windshield, I pictured myself making a long walk in the rain. Sure enough, a few miles down the road, the engine died for good. Saint Jude had obviously thrown up his hands and gone back to bed like any sensible saint.

I coasted to the shoulder and punched phone buttons for Triple A, then realized we'd dropped our coverage, not for the first time, to save a few bucks. *Okay, chronically pound-foolish Bella.* Whose number in your meager cell directory can you call at four in the morning?

* * * * *

"Stay here, Bella," Margaret said as the hospital receptionist ushered us to the waiting room. "I'll rustle us up some caffeine. I also need a ciggie."

The managing editor, used to calls at odd hours, had not hesitated, arriving within minutes of my call. At her suggestion, we tacked a note on the windshield for the Highway Patrol and she delivered me to the hospital. After I signed all the papers she'd drive me back to my car and call Triple A using her card. Despite her sometimes-odd ways she really was a nice person.

That thought was verified a few minutes later when she handed me a steaming to-go cup. "Here, I got lucky. Irish Breakfast with three sugars. Good for shock."

"Exactly what my English grandmother would recommend." I held the steaming brew to my nose and inhaled, my soul soothed by the smoky fragrance. The simple tea ritual is so much more than the sum of its parts.

Margaret lowered herself into the chair beside me. "Still no word? Why is this taking so long?"

"Someone from law enforcement has confirm her death, and they called Doctor Lebovitz as well. He lives in Dos Pasos."

She gave me a funny look, as though wondering how I knew so much about my mother's doctor. Little did she know I'd researched him on the Internet.

"The nurse told me Doctor Lebovitz doesn't have to come in when a patient dies, but he usually does, to offer condolences. Old school, I guess." Another sign of a caring doctor.

She had no reaction to this statement, taking a sip of her black brew, and saying instead, "Why isn't your husband here with you at a time like this?"

I almost choked. "Mike?"

"You have another?"

"No, no, of course not." I took a long draught, playing for time. "Um, he's still gone."

"Gone?" she asked. "*Gone?* What does that mean? Have you guys split?"

"He had to go back east on business."

"Back east, where?" she asked, her dark pupils contracting.

"Detroit," I said, without thinking.

"I thought he was from Chicago."

"He is," I said, knowing it wasn't true. I looked up to see Doctor Lebovitz approaching.

Saved.

"I'm sorry about your mom," he said, offering a firm handshake. "I liked her a lot, she was a very feisty lady."

"She was indeed," I said, and meant it. He tried to pull his hand away; I kept it.

"She died in her sleep," he said. "Probably never knew what hit her. A good death. Now she won't have to go all the way down." Another discreet tug as he attempted to rescue his hand.

"You're right," I said, "a good death." I pulled his hand toward me and wrapped my arms around him. He seemed surprised—shocked even. Though I needed him to hold me, I felt his spine stiffen and his hands dropped to his sides. After an awkward second or two, he patted my back with one hand as one would an over-enthusiastic puppy.

I stepped back, aghast. Again I'd gone too far. "I—"

He held up his newly-liberated hand. "It's okay. Go home. Lack of sleep does strange things to people."

* * * * *

On the ride back to my car, I realized something was bothering me about my earlier conversation with Margaret. I turned to her. "Please don't tell Alena about Mike being gone."

She looked puzzled. "Why would I do that? You hardly know her."

Strange response. A more likely one would have been, "Alena doesn't know Mike." Somehow she knew the two were acquainted.

39

Tuesday, May 18th, early morning

The storm passed, as storms will. In the milky gray of predawn, I sat sideways on the window seat in my study, legs drawn up beneath me. I had my back to Emily's portrait, not yet ready to face those penetrating eyes. My headache hung around like an unwelcome guest. I thought my conversation with Mom last night was a new beginning for us—in reality it had been the end. How could that be?

I rested my shoulder against the large bay window that lets in an abundance of midday light, but does little to keep out morning chills. My hands were clasped around my knees for warmth, the closest I could get to the fetal position without actually being in bed.

I had much to do, but I needed this time to get my head together, both physically and mentally. Thank goodness Margaret had promised to bring in our new temp to staff the obituary desk today.

I made a mental check list. Chris still didn't know about his grandma and I debated whether to call him immediately or wait until tomorrow. Best to wait. There was nothing he could do and he was working that big party tonight.

I also had to make arrangements with the mortuary to have her remains cremated. Where would I find the strength to do this? To consciously, and with knowledge aforethought, reduce her physical being to ashes?

There were also the inevitable, difficult calls to make, especially to Mister Lambs, her executor, with the news that I'd now be selling her house. Most disagreeable of all, to Ed and Janet in Cleveland. Just the thought of that conversation tightened the headache's grip on my temples. Maybe I could put it off until tomorrow.

Also, there were her clothes and personal effects. It seemed heartless to give them to the Goodwill so soon. But what good would it do to leave them in the closet for six months when someone could be using them?

And what to do about Mike? Should I shoot an e-mail into cyberspace, hoping it would somehow reach him? *Touch him?* If only Ethan would contact me, I'd go through him. Why, oh why, had I not *insisted* that he give me contact information?

From somewhere I gained the strength to turn and face Emily, giving me a peek view of the bay, the color of pewter in the morning light. Once again I pulled my legs up and wrapped another afghan around my shoulders, letting it trail in warming folds around me.

My eyes found focus on Em's face. "Thanks for being worried about me, old friend. I'll get through this okay, I know I will. I wish I could cry though." I hadn't been able to shed a tear since finding Mom's body. Instead there was this terrible, all-consuming numbness.

Before entering the room, I'd made sure the light switch in the hall was in the off position. "Em, let's try something different. I need guidance. I'm going to run some thoughts by you, and I don't want you to turn on that light unless you disagree. Okay?"

The light remained off.

"First, there's one item I can't get out of my mind. Doctor Lebovitz said Mom had a 'good' death. Something about that bothers me, as though people who cling to life until the very end—and why wouldn't they?—bring upon themselves a 'bad' death. The word 'good' seems judgmental somehow, but I don't think 'easy' is much better. Obviously I need to think about this some more."

Emily thought so too.

"Remember, I'm ruminating here. I mean, do you think some people control their own deaths? Here was Mom pretty much dependent on someone else all her life, but she didn't want to lose her dignity. Also, she didn't want to inconvenience me at a time when she knew my life was difficult. I think she willed her own death, either consciously or unconsciously."

Darkness from the hall.

"Oh, this is so embarrassing, I had an 'over the top' moment with Doctor Lebovitz. I couldn't seem to let go of his hand and even hugged him in the waiting room. That was natural, don't you think?"

The darkness continued.

"Not surprisingly, I've got a theory about my attraction to him. Dying reminds us of our mortality, and what defines us as mortal more than sexual attraction? It's like gorging on food at a funeral. Both acts remind us we're alive. Hope you agree with me, Em."

She did. Apparently.

I sat in silence for a few more minutes, willing myself to get up and act on my mental to-do list. My head felt better, but bone-numbing lethargy remained. None of this was easy.

"Another thing. She asked me to take her ashes to Detroit for burial next to Dad and Bea. But I can't go right now, with Mike missing. I can go later. Which begs the question: Where am I going to store her ashes in the meantime? It seems disrespectful to store them in the closet with her clothes. Don't answer that."

She didn't.

"I can't go right now. I'm afraid if I do, something will happen and it will be a long time before I come back. And what would I do with Sam? I know I promised Mom I'd investigate Bea's murder. The truth is, I'm afraid of what I might find. I've always felt that it was more than just a random, in-the-wrong-place-at-the-wrong-time killing. I don't have to keep that promise, do I? I mean, I was going to rescind it in the morning."

The light came on, and stayed on, glowing more brightly than it ever had.

"Oh Em, I was afraid you'd feel that way," I said, through a sense of grief so intense I thought it would stop my heart. With it came tears. Buckets. I welcomed them, as a way to keep from dying myself.

40

Tuesday, May 18th, still early

"Mrs. Kowalski, you okay?"

"Whaat?" I struggled to my feet, afghan drifting to the floor. "Oh, Rosa, hi," I said, goofily. "I must have fallen asleep." I had called her with the news about Mom, and I was still too groggy to make sense of her sudden appearance. "Why are you here?" I asked, with singular lack of tact.

The insult stung, I saw it in her eyes. "I came to see if you needed anything. I was worried about you. I pounded on the door, but you didn't answer so I used my key." She leaned over and dropped it in my hand. "No use for it now."

"Thanks," I indicated the easy chair beneath Emily's portrait. "Sit down a minute. Would you like tea or something?"

"No, thank you," she said, continuing to stand there, her eyes opaque with unexpressed thoughts.

Of course, she wants her money. "Have a seat then and I'll write you a check."

"Very well." She settled into the chair and folded her hands primly in front of her, toes barely touching the floor. I sat down at my desk.

"You have Mass for your mamá at Saint Patrick's?" she asked as I reached in the drawer for my checkbook.

Would I? I hadn't thought that far ahead. "We'll do that in Detroit where her friends are," I said, deciding on the spot. "She didn't know many people here."

"She knew you, she knew me, she knew Debby." She touched her heart, eyes dark with disappointment.

Oh dear. I struggled for words. "I…I just can't right now, Rosa."

She nodded understanding but hurt remained in her eyes. Again she touched her heart. "You have a good heart. Your mamá was a difficult woman, and you have many troubles now."

I did indeed, and wondered how much she knew. As if reading my thoughts, she pulled a piece of paper from her sweatshirt pocket and offered it to me shyly. "I found this in the kitchen the day your husband left."

I knew it was Mike's note before I even opened it.

Again she reached into her pocket. "Your pearls."

So, she *had* taken them. "Rosa," I said, struggling to control my anger, "those items were not yours to take. Did you read the note?"

She bit her bottom lip, the look in her eyes saying "yes."

"And what about the necklace?" I fingered the pearls I never thought I'd see again.

She blinked rapidly, obviously searching for an answer that would satisfy me.

"Okay," I said, taking a deep breath. "I'm trying to understand. Were you curious about us, about our lives?" That would explain the note, but not the necklace.

"Not curiosity, not at all," she said quietly. "You were in trouble. I knew that, and I thought if I read the note I could help, and well …" Her voice dropped. "I took it."

"I don't understand."

She held up one finger. "Your mamá is, was, a very, how do you say, 'curious' lady. I did not want her to find it."

She had a point. There would have been hell to pay if Mom had read the note.

She held up another finger. "I took the note and the pearls to my sister—"

"Your sister?"

"To weave a spell so that the note's power to hurt you would be diminished."

"A Santeria spell?" I asked, thinking of the West African and Latin American rituals.

"Not exactly. My sister has developed her own practices, the same as Santeria in many ways, but in some ways different. She helped our family to endure the bad years in Cuba."

"Don't they…" I paused. How could I say this diplomatically? "Isn't that against your Catholic faith?"

She shook her head. "Not at all."

No other explanation was forthcoming. Who was I to judge? She had tried to help and, who knows, perhaps she had. I crossed the room and hugged her tight, savoring the warmth of another human being. "Thank you so very much. And please thank your sister."

She gave a solemn nod, which could mean anything. "What will you do now?"

"I'm going back east for a while to bury her next to Dad and my sister, sell her house and settle her affairs. I may even get lucky and find Mike."

Once again she put her hand on her heart. "You will, eventually. My heart says this." She hesitated. "You have something else you must do there. My sister and I will pray for you."

I studied the woman before me, so simple and yet so elegant in her Latina stoicism. Could she really know that Mom had tasked me with finding Bea's murderer? No point in troubling this good woman with still another burden of my heart.

I sat down at my desk. "Let me write you that check." The light in her eyes when she saw the amount was all the thanks I needed.

On impulse I reached for the pearls now on my desk and handed them to Rosa. "Please ask your sister to keep these until I come back. I'm going to need all the help I can get."

41

Tuesday, May 18th, late morning

Margaret had given me the day off, but after my time with Rosa, I realized how much I needed the company of others. I could help the temp at the paper, then spend the afternoon making arrangements for Mom. The day was shaping up to be a wicked hot one, the first of the season. My back and shoulders were drenched with sweat as I stopped for the light where Los Lobos

Road dead ends at Fig Street, pulling into the far-left lane. A black Escalade pulled up on my right in the other left lane. *Oh dear. Not today, of all days.*

I glanced at the driver, surprised to see his window open. Hands on the wheel, he stared straight ahead. There was no missing the Roman nose and short stature of Bootsie Lupino. More than ever I was convinced he was the one who tried to run us down on the park road the night. Did he recognize Mike as his former son-in-law?

Immobile with shock, I failed to notice the green light until a host of horns erupted behind me. I slid around the corner into the left lane and slowed so the SUV would stay ahead in the right lane. So far so good, except for another cacophony of horns.

When I saw his blinker go on for the turn onto Tank Ranch Road I gave into what Mother Superior called "Saint Impulse," following him around the corner, again staying two cars behind.

Several minutes later he again turned right, this time on Wide Street, staying in the airport lane. Sure enough, he made a quick right up the hill into short term parking in front of Wings, the airport restaurant. Meeting someone for breakfast, no doubt.

I circled around the lot's perimeter. On the second pass, a spot opened up opposite him and I tucked the Subaru into it. Now to wait and see what happens, I thought, eyeing Bootsie's car in the rearview mirror.

My wait was short. With obvious difficulty, Bootsie struggled from the vehicle. Leaning on the side panel with one hand and gripping his cane in the other, he made his way to the back of the vehicle and peered around, shading his eyes from the sun. A few moments later, another Black Escalade pulled into the spot next to him. A convention of Escalades?

One of the Ironwoods alighted and walked toward Bootsie mopping his brow. "Christ, it's hot out here." Frank or Rick? I wasn't sure until he turned my way and I saw the scar on his chin. Rick, of course. Interesting. I wondered if Frank would show up in a third Escalade.

I grabbed an envelope from the door pocket and jotted down both license plate numbers.

Bootsie slapped the back of his own SUV. "Forty K wholesale for dis piece a crap. Wouldn't you think dey could make da air conditioning work?"

The detective muttered something noncommittal. While the men continued to talk, I made myself small in the seat, angling the rearview mirror to keep them in view. They were unaware of me; people in old cars tend to be invisible. A plane approached the runway and landed, making it impossible to hear their conversation.

A few minutes later, two men approached on foot from the direction of the terminal. One of them, perhaps in his late thirties, carried a black brief case. But it was his companion who caught my attention. I'd seen him before.

The four men shook hands all around and Bootsie hugged and kissed the young man on each cheek. "Bret my son, how was da flight?" He stepped away, extracted a wet wipe from his pocket and scrubbed his lips and hands.

Bret? What kind of good Italian boy is named Bret?

"Detroit to LA was okay. What's not to like about first class? The stewardess had big tits." He clenched his fingers as though holding two softballs. Bootsie chuckled. Bret pointed toward the small jet, still on the tarmac. "What's with that piece a shit? How come they can't fly a real airplane for Chrissake?"

"Because this is the sticks," said the man who'd accompanied him.

I studied this man, who was perhaps my age. Where had I seen him before? *Focus, Bella.* Hmm, maybe I'd only seen a picture. Hmm. A picture. That was it.

Mike had shown me a *Chronicle* photo of Sheriff's Detective Darrell Vader receiving an award that Mike felt was undeserved. My husband suspected he was crooked. Hmm. Maybe Ryan Scully had a hunch there was illegal hanky-panky going on between Vader and the Ironwoods. Maybe that's why the Sheriff's Office wanted Mike to investigate, though Scully never came right out and said so.

Two mobsters, a cop and a sheriff's detective meeting in the Tolosa Airport parking lot. No sign of Detective Frank. Yet.

Panic welled in my throat. I was sole witness to this cozy gathering. Should I hightail it out of here? No, the Subaru engine starting would announce I'd been here all along. I made myself even smaller in the seat. I'd feign sleep if necessary and hope one of them didn't pop me just for the heck of it.

"Papa, what kinda meeting is this?" Bret whined, his raised arms taking in the landscape. "I come to California, I expect, you know, beaches and broads. Instead I get a *parking lot*? Can't we at least have a beer?"

"You smell like a brewery already," the old man answered. "And lemme tell you about dis here meeting. It's secret. Like da ones back in da day. Public place. No smart phones, no computers. No microphones, no Feds, no witnesses."

Except me. I thought about the online photo of Bootsie and Johnny Staccato sitting on the Belle Isle park bench. Plotting someone's demise, no doubt. Was that what this meeting was about?

Bootsie turned to Vader and Ironwood. "So wadda you two jokers got for me? Everything cool?"

"Sure, sure Boss." Ironwood answered for both, while Vader stared off in the distance. "I hired some clown in a beater to watch the broad, lemme know if she leaves town. Got a call a few days ago. She went to Santa Barbara. Shopping. Dames. Go figure."

Oh no! I was the broad/dame. Why was I not surprised? But shopping in Santa Barbara? Rick, you don't want Bootsie to know I managed to lose you.

"Don't shit me," Bootsie said, obviously thinking the same thing. "You fuck up, I call the dealer, he repos your Escalade. You drive dem fancy wheels at my pleasure, *gumba.* Got dat?"

"Ab-so-lutely," Ironwood answered, drawing out the word.

"Good. Your brother da Boy Scout wants to save your ass, but he don't play along wid us and what's he drive? A '97 Honda. Remember dat." He slapped Rick Ironwood lightly on both cheeks.

So, Detective Frank was not directly involved. A good guy at last. But wait a minute! Now my solo interview with him took on new meaning. Was he trying to find out if I'd seen Rick's license number as the Escalade pulled out of the Inn? Also, if I'd noticed a weapon at the scene. A knife his brother carelessly left behind?

"You jokers get a line on dat missing Polack cop?" Bootsie continued.

I struggled not to turn my head. That could only be Mike.

"With Milosch dead, him and mebbe da broad are da only ones who can blow dis deal."

"Give us a break, Boss. We're working on it," Vader said. "He seems to have vanished."

"He vanished all right," said Bootsie. "He's in friggin' New Zealand!"

Oh my god! They must have looked at Neal Grale's e-mail.

"Now, which one of you goons wanna take a trip out dere and find him?" the old man asked, lifting his chin.

"New Zealand's a big place," Detective Rick said. "Any idea where he's hiding out?"

"I'll bet Kowalski's wife knows," Vader said. "Broad's a loose cannon."

"Leave her alone, you hear, *gumba*?" Bootsie said. "You get involved, things get messy. And you too, Ironwood. "

"Of course," said Detective Rick.

"Call off your goon in the beater. Don't follow her no more, hear?"

Why hadn't I seen the beater car? Because I was too busy looking for Escalades.

"Anything you say, Bootsie," Ironwood answered, not sounding happy.

"I got a plan to find out what she knows. Pretty soon she's gonna get an e-mail." Bootsie kissed his fingers. "*Perfetto.*"

Oh swell.

"So, Bret." Bootsie turned to his son. "Change subject. The sewer's goin' out for bids in a year or so. Mebbe federal money available. Dat's why I brought you here. Keep you in da loop, so to speak."

"Federal money?" said Bret. "How did that happen, with the economy and all?"

"I put the screws to my DC connections. Poor slobs in Los Lobos don't got no money. They're in da toilet." He laughed at his own joke, then again kissed his fingertips. "The most expensive sewer in history and we're gonna get da contract. How sweet is dat?"

So it was true. The Mob was planning to muscle in on the Los Lobos sewer, and I was their target. The blood rushed from my head. I gripped the seat hard, gulping deep breaths to keep from passing out.

"Very sweet, Papa," Bret agreed. "But what about the Mercados? I hear they got construction tied up around here."

"Good boy, you been doing your homework, but I got dat covered. Alena's news director at KFAX, and your step..." The rest of what he said was lost in the roar of an approaching plane.

Alena news director? News to me. Perhaps Bootsie had given her a promotion to impress his son. He also said something about "your step." What did that mean?

"We control a major part of da local media, da part that counts," he continued. "Everyone watches KFAX." He stopped. "Though we may have a problem with Alena. Not your concern," he said this as though thinking out loud.

A problem with Alena? What was that all about?

Bootsie gestured to Ironwood and Vader. "Den dere's our law enforcement friends here. Tell him your plans, boys."

"Major big time sting," Vader said. "We plant some stuff on the Mercado brothers, we..." A plane roared down the runway and took off.

Damn and double damn.

Silence returned and Bootsie spoke: "Hell, we make da Mercado brothers look so dirty dey can't get a contract to build a dog house. We glad-hand da right people, pay off da others, and bingo bango, we own Central Coast wastewater construction. Just like we did in Michigan. Why—"

Ironwood cut in. "Yeah, and don't forget all those old plants up and down the coast that need upgrading. You guys can be in shit city for years." He slapped Vader on the back. "Me and my buddy here can grease the skids for you."

"Dat's why you're on our payroll," Bootsie said. "Who says da Mob's lost their *cogliones*?" Again he got physical with Detective Rick, socking him in the arm. "We got balls of steel, Baby!"

There was more, plenty more, but I'd heard enough. All I had to do was remain invisible until they left. And try to stay one step ahead of Bootsie's plan. For that I would need help.

* * * * *

The meeting lasted maybe fifteen minutes more, then broke up quickly. Vader once again accompanied Bret to the terminal. Ironwood and Bootsie stood behind their SUVs continuing to strategize in tones too low to hear, probably about my fate. If I'd stayed home today I wouldn't have known any of it. I shivered at the thought.

My thoughts returned to the dynamic duo. Surely it was risky for Vader and Ironwood to be seen in a public place with known mobsters. All it would take to be outted was someone with a cell phone.

Cell phone. Hmm. I turned on my phone's camera and angled it over my shoulder at Bootsie and Ironwood. If they caught me, things would get ugly fast.

Click. Click. I lowered the camera and checked the image of the two men. Perfect. They shook hands and the Mariposa Bay detective left.

Bootsie peered around. He started towards the restaurant, took three labored steps leaning on his cane, and apparently changed his mind. He looked around again and stepped in front of some bushes, waited a few moments, fussed with his trousers, and took a whiz. That completed, he put himself back together, pulled a wad of wet wipes from his pocket and scrubbed his hands before climbing back into the Escalade. Before pulling out of the parking lot, he made a call on his cell.

I knew what I had to do: Go home, check my e-mail, and keep checking it. Then I too would make a call, an important one.

42

Tuesday, May 18th, midday

My hands shook as I turned on my home computer. The wait for it to boot seemed interminable.

I stared at the screen. *Unbelievable.* There was an e-mail from Mike, sent within the hour. My still-shaking hand clicked the open button, and I read the brief text. He wanted me to meet him in Punto Solitario, at our fantasy motel up the coast.

The message said to meet on Sunday, in five days time. He'd reserved room twelve and I was to come directly there without checking in. I gaped at the e-mail, half-afraid it would vanish. Mike was the only one who knew about our fantasy place. How ironic that I would get one from him now, as I waited for Bootsie's e-mail.

Or was it? I read the post again, especially the part about not checking in. That sounded fishy as a week-old flounder. I slumped in disappointment. If this was the e-mail the old man talked about, he lost no time in sending it. Maybe the call he made from the Escalade was to some flunky who did it for him.

How had they gotten Mike's e-address? *Think, Bella, think.* From Ethan, who was Bootsie's grandson? Or from reading Neal Grale's e-mail? The latter seemed the most likely.

And how would Bootsie know about Punto Solitario? *Because you blabbed to several people, Bella, that's why.* I made a mental list of people I girl-talked with about Punto Solitario: Alena, Margaret, Annie, maybe even Fifi Falcone. I couldn't remember for sure.

I reached for the phone, then realized it might be bugged. Our Internet connection was through the phone line. Maybe that's how they got his e-mail address.

I pulled my cell from my pocket and stared at it. Could be bugged as well.

Enough is enough, I decided. Convinced the e-mail was a setup and someone told Bootsie about our fantasy motel, I drove to the only pay phone in Los Lobos and placed a call to J. Edgar's finest.

* * * * *

My call to the Bureau unleashed forces I couldn't imagine. They were very interested in what I had to say about Joe Milosch's murder, Mike's subsequent disappearance and the Lupino family shenanigans. They'd been trying to get the goods on Bootsie's operation for years, and a federal prosecutor had an open file on him. My information might provide them with an opportunity to finally indict him. The photo of him and Rick Ironwood was pure gold. Too bad I didn't get one of Vader as well, but he'd get his in time.

The FBI had searched my house for bugs and found none, followed me and determined that no one had me under surveillance. Bootsie had called off the dogs, supremely confident that I would fall into his trap.

As I suspected, the FBI has tools to track electronic transmissions that are unavailable to the general public. They confirmed that the e-mail invitation to meet Mike at Punto Solitario had been "spoofed." (Think getting an e-mail for cut-rate Viagra from your maiden aunt.)

It was sent from newscaster Alena Lupino's home computer. She must be in this up to her slightly sagging neck. But, if that was true, it made no sense for her to meet with Mike, and for him to give her the notebook. What changed between the time Joe Milosch was killed and the date of their meeting? She must have discovered that he was a target. But if so, why send me the spoofed e-mail now, an action that showed involvement in Bootsie's nefarious scheme? I relayed all this to the FBI, but they remained noncommittal.

Maybe someone else sent the e-mail using her computer. I'd have to think about that.

How the culprit got Mike's e-mail address—unless it was in the notebook—was also a conundrum, but the Bureau explained that getting someone's e-mail address was no problem with today's technology.

For me to meet the old man, and any other family members who cared to show up, in a remote motel room was foolhardy in the extreme. Still, Bureau agents asked me if I would be willing to keep the date and wear a wire. I thought they were kidding. The FBI never kids.

They claimed the situation wasn't as dangerous as it sounded. They investigated room twelve of the motel and found a connecting door between it and room eleven. When the time came, they'd create a distraction, open the door and pull me into room eleven as the Lupinos dealt with the disturbance. Simple. Except for that old devil in the details.

I told them I'd have to sleep on their plan, a virtual guarantee of insomnia. But sometime in that long night I realized that if the Lupinos were in jail, Mike would be out of danger. I agreed in a moment of misplaced bravado. The agents also explained that permission to fit someone with a wire required them to obtain a court order, which could take thirty days or more. I'd have to postpone the motel date, which surely would arouse suspicions on the Lupinos' part. The federal prosecutor's open file expedited the process and the order came through in days, almost unheard of according to Agent Karen Grady, who was assigned to me.

I used the time to take care of Mom's affairs and notify people who needed to know about her death, including Chris, who wanted to come home immediately to help. I said it wasn't necessary. No way would I involve him in this latest brouhaha.

43

Sunday, May 23rd, early morning

I dragged myself out of bed and into a hot shower without my usual two cups of tea. After hours of tossing and turning, I'd overslept. The FBI would be at my door in fifteen minutes.

I was crossing the front hall from kitchen to living room, at last savoring my first bracing sip of tea, when the doorbell rang. I turned. Agent Grady peered through the side window. I had to look twice. She was dressed in a gray work shirt and trousers instead of a dark business suit.

After fumbling with the locks, I finally got the door open and Agent Grady introduced her colleague, Matthew Vance. He wore an identical uniform.

"We even have hardhats in there," Karen said, nodding toward a nondescript white van in the driveway. They would park near the motel, ostensibly to work on phone lines. Grady would record the transmissions from the "wire" attached to me, while Vance directed the backups stationed in the next room and elsewhere on the property.

Both Grady and Vance were tall and both had a fresh-from-The-Academy look about them. Were they experienced enough for this assignment, I wondered?

No worries. Grady immediately took charge. Standing in the front hall, she studied me for a few moments then nodded her approval to Vance. She'd instructed me to wear loose clothing to conceal the transmitting device. Apparently my long-sleeved blouse and sweat pants were good choices. I felt like a dork. I mean, who wears a satin blouse with sweat pants?

But today was not about fashion. I showed them down the hall to the kitchen on the right. Here they would fit me with the wire. A few pleasantries and a lot more instructions later, Agent Grady pulled the "wire," which was smaller than a computer thumb drive, from her bag and held it up. "Ready for J-Edgar?"

"Who?"

She laughed. "Inside joke."

I was tempted to say I didn't want the old megalomaniac between my breasts, but restrained myself.

"I'll wait in the living room." Agent Vance pulled a cell phone from his pocket and loped across the hall.

Agent Grady helped me out of my blouse and draped it over the back of a kitchen chair. I shivered, feeling naked and vulnerable standing there in my bra. She blew on her hands and then rubbed them on her pant legs. "Cold hands."

"Hold still now." Even though she warned me, I flinched several times as she taped the tiny wireless device between the cups of my bra. She handed me my blouse and, after I buttoned it, stepped back to view her handiwork. And frowned.

"What's wrong?"

She didn't answer, calling instead, "Hey, Matt, I need to you."

"What's up?" he said, placing a hand on each side of the doorway and leaning forward as though stretching tired muscles. Tall as he was, this kept him from having to meet my eyes.

She pointed toward me. "What do you think? Can you see anything?"

He leaned forward even farther, studying my chest like a general studying a field map. Heat rose in my face and neck. "Uh, maybe," he said, "she's got no…"

He didn't finish, but I got the message. My boobs weren't big enough to hide the device.

"Okay, Matt, thanks. Got it." He returned to the living room and presumably his cell phone. Karen Grady turned back to me. "Got falsies?"

Did I? "I think so, though it's been years since I wore them."

She made a "go" flick of her hand.

I returned shortly with ancient foam falsies, hard as hockey pucks. She stuffed them into my bra, pinching me only once, and nestled J-Edgar between them, taping him securely. When my blouse was buttoned, she again stepped back to admire her handiwork, smiling at a job well done. Vance, once again summoned from the living room, agreed: no telltale outlines.

I noticed, however, that the middle button was loose. "Uh…"

Agent Grady checked her watch. "Not now, Bella. Let's roll. We're behind schedule."

The blouse, loose button and all, would have to do.

44

Sunday, May 23rd, a little later

As I opened the door of the old Subaru, Sam appeared from nowhere and tried to muscle his way into the back seat. "No, boy," I said, pulling him back by the collar, "not now. We'll have a walk later." He gave the agents a baleful look, turned his back and made his lonely way back to the barn. These strangers had obviously spoiled his day.

Sam's world had shrunk considerably since Mike disappeared and Mom passed. His world would shrink even more if I were hurt or killed today. But I could not, no, *would not,* allow myself to think that way.

Once I was settled in the driver's seat, Agent Vance said, "Remember J-Edgar is voice-activated, so don't talk to yourself or play the radio. We'll follow at a discreet distance. Good luck."

Thanks, I'll need it. I thought about Mom saying I always took on challenges even when they scared me. *You were right, Ma.*

Agent Vance headed toward the van and Karen took over, activating the device and putting a finger to her lips.

I pointed the car north on Highway One, somewhat comforted that the agents would be close by. Agency backups would be in the adjoining room. *FBI protecting, FBI protecting.*

The ocean north of Mariposa Bay sparkled in the morning sunshine. A few miles up the road, a gaggle of surfers rode breakers near Cuyamaca pier. The scene reminded me of the New Year's Day Polar Bear Dip a few years ago. An old friend down on her luck was murdered as hundreds of people frolicked in the waves nearby. I checked my watch. Behind schedule.

I pulled around a horse trailer and shot ahead, doing almost eighty, A few minutes later I passed Hearst Castle. Lights flashed in my rearview mirror. Highway Patrol. *Swell.*

"Pull over on the right shoulder," intoned a disembodied voice. I looked around; Bureau van nowhere in sight.

The HP officer pulled up behind me, lights flashing. I *so* did not need this. Where was the FBI? I reached over and with shaking hands, tugged open the glove box to get my registration. Long moments passed as I pawed through wadded paper napkins, old receipts, a creased map of Utah. Everything but the needed document.

Ouch. Crimp in the neck. I straightened up, massaging the area and glancing in the rearview mirror. The HP guy spoke earnestly into his microphone. And then—he didn't. The lights continued to flash. And then they didn't. Instead, the vehicle pulled around me, the officer giving me a small salute. *FBI protecting, FBI protecting.*

I pulled out onto the highway, barely missing a fast approaching vehicle that appeared from nowhere. The Subaru shuddered and the driver gave me the finger as he whipped around me into the oncoming lane, empty, thank goodness. My right leg (not to mention the rest of me) trembled at the near miss. I feathered the gas pedal, determined to drive the speed limit and not worry about time.

A few miles farther, San Simeon pier stood in dark, stark relief to the blue of the ocean and the glint of midmorning sun. On the way back I would treat myself to lunch at their historic store and café.

Passing the old Piedras Blancas Lighthouse caused my stomach to plummet to my toes. Only a mile to go. Time to watch the ocean side of the road for the tiny motel. It would be easy to miss. Then I saw it. The Punto Solitario Motel, L-shaped and low-slung, with a dark blue roof, bright blue trim and a neglected air, apparent even at this distance. What a dump. How could we have even considered spending a night here?

As I passed a farmhouse about three hundred yards south of the motel, I remembered Agent Vance's words: "If anything, *anything*, goes wrong, head for the beach. Worse case, hide in the scrub between the motel and the farmhouse."

I studied the coastal dune scrub which extended from highway to oceanside cliff. There's a reason it's called 'scrub,' I thought. Wouldn't hide a decent sized rabbit.

Nothing can go wrong, I assured myself. *FBI protecting, FBI protecting.*

I forced myself to turn left into the gravel driveway. As I did, I caught sight of the Bureau van pulling into a spot a few hundred yards north of the motel. Tears of relief stung my eyes.

The restaurant on the left had a long-abandoned look, the office directly in front displayed no current signs of occupancy. No doubt closed for the day at the behest of the FBI.

Rooms eleven and twelve formed an L at the north end of the building, with number twelve closest to the highway. Noisy, no doubt. Enough to hinder voice transmissions?

Mine was the only car in the lot and my heart leapt with sudden hope. Maybe the Lupinos had failed to show up. *Maybe one of their henchman dropped them off.*

I peered around, pulse pounding. The FBI might not be the only ones with backups at the ready. I pondered my next move. The Hilton this was not. Ostensibly a working motel, the entire place wore a shroud of neglect. Dingy beige curtains on filthy windows were bunched together as though fastened with safety pins, the doors warped, with cracked and fading paint. Even the meager landscaping had turned up its toes, the victim of inattention and salt air.

Why did I agree to this insane plot? I thought of Mike and forced myself from the safety of the Subaru.

45

Sunday, May 23rd, an hour later

I was about to knock on the door of number twelve when I remembered the spoofed e-mail said to just come in. I shivered with fear as I turned the knob and poked my head inside. "Hello?"

I waited. No answer. Strange. The room seemed empty. I pushed the door all the way open and set one foot inside. "Hello?"

Still no answer so I put the other foot inside. "*Yoo-hoo?* Anybody here?" I propped my handbag against the door to hold it open—a quick escape.

Traffic noise filled my ears, and the room smelled like old plumbing. Worst than that. A plugged sewer line. I peering around, heart pounding, feeling like I wasn't alone.

A quick glance confirmed the agents' description. On the left wall sat a swaybacked bed covered with a chenille spread, lime green where it wasn't stained, and the connecting door, now closed. I hoped the FBI remembered to unlock it. Beyond the bed was the bathroom, which I avoided because of the stench.

In the room itself, north- and south-facing windows were covered with the beige curtains *de jour.* They hid the van from sight. I resisted the urge to peek to make sure it was still there.

Beneath the window, a rabbit-eared TV perched on a scratched round table. Two folding chairs and a 1950's pull-down lamp the color of an overripe pumpkin completed the décor.

Traffic noise waned. "Hello?" I called again. A response this time, like a moan, from the other side of the bed. *What the—?* Alena lay on the carpet, wrists and ankles bound with duct tape. Several overlapping bands stretched across her mouth and chin, extending into the long hair at the nape of her neck.

"Oh my god, Alena, who did this to you?" I asked, though the answer was obvious. Bootsie said at the airport there was a problem with Alena. This must be his solution.

Before I could whisper this disturbing event into the transmitter, the connecting door opened. I turned toward the sound, expecting the FBI. Instead Bootsie shuffled in, leaning on his cane. The door slammed shut behind him. Cold, naked fear surged through my veins.

Cane in his left hand, gun in the right, the diminutive don looked fragile—and dangerous. "Well, well, look what da wind blew in." He eyed my handbag propping open the front entrance.

"What's dis?" He moved around me with surprising vigor, turned his back and swept the purse aside, using his cane like a golf club.

"Gun," I whispered to J-Edgar as this door too slammed shut.

He veered toward me, eyes black and opaque as pebbles. Had he heard what I just said? Apparently not. "Get away from dere," he said, prodding me with his cane until I stood beside the bed, my back to the connecting door. He moved opposite, so close I could feel the heat of his body, smell his garlic breath.

Conflicting emotions surged through me: extreme claustrophobia, humiliation and anger at the cattle-prodding, terror of the gun. Hope that by now agents were in the next room.

"Bootsie." The word came out like a sigh.

"Mr. Lupino to you, *puttana*." He spat the insult, leaving a speck of saliva on his whiskery chin. "Whore," he said, in case I didn't get it.

My hackles rose. *Steady, girl.* The gun danced before my eyes; I forced myself to ignore it. "Where's my husband, *Mr. Lupino*?"

"Dat's for *me* to find out." He tapped his chest and raised his chin. "Why you think you was invited here today?"

I decided to play dumb. "I don't understand any of this." The old don shrugged dismissively.

Alena had managed to scoot herself around to the foot of the bed. She watched her father's back, eyes wide with terror. Or was it an act designed to frighten me into doing their bidding? I studied her demeanor for clues.

No, the emotion was real. No woman, especially Alena, whose hair was her pride, would willingly allow it to be duct-taped. Whoever did this was a sadist.

"Why do this to your own *daughter*?" I asked, wondering how a frail old man had managed to subdue a woman as fit as Alena.

Not with drugs, she seemed alert. An accomplice. Who? Certainly not…Or was it?

"Why?" he squawked. "My own flesh and blood gonna sell her father down da river. Wants outta 'da life.'" The gun wobbled dangerously.

So Alena wanted out. And if she wasn't involved, someone else was. And I knew who. Past being terrorized, I got mad instead. "Will you quit waving that thing around?"

Intent on his rant, he didn't hear, or chose not to. "Well, she gonna get outta da life. No problem." He trained the weapon on me. "And take her lover with her. Murder-suicide."

"Oh come on," I said. "No one will believe that. We barely know each other."

The old man's eyes flickered and my heart skipped a beat. I knew before I even turned around that Margaret Cavalier stood behind me. "Papa Bootsie can do anything," she said.

46

Nerves jumping, I whirled around. The managing editor had entered through the connecting door, on cat feet as always. She must have been behind me that day at the paper and, thanks to my large monitor, seen me checking Mike's e-mail. From there it would be a simple matter to get his e-address and delete the one from Neal Grale, so I wouldn't see it.

Margaret placed her hands on her hips and gave me a sickening, simpering smile. I glanced at the door behind her. Closed, and still no FBI backups. *God. Help!*

A pregnant pause and a staring contest, with all four of us at a standstill. I kept my eyes on the managing editor, recalling the cozy scene with Bootsie at the Lupino dinner table, also the conversation I'd half-heard at the airport. The mobster said to Bret, "Your step—"

"Step." I blinked, and blinked again. Bootsie had said "stepsister." I didn't hear the whole word because of the airplane noise. Margaret was Alena's and Bret's older sister, their stepsister, as was Grace, Mike's late first wife. Why hadn't I seen that before?

I recalled my finger tracing the name Maria Cavallo on the embroidered cushion in Bootsie's bedroom. *Cavallo/Cavalier.* My finger had obviously sent a message to my brain, one I ignored until now because Margaret was nice to me, bringing me soup, helping out the night Mom died. She assumed a name similar to her mother's to hide her connection to the Lupinos, and with good reason. As managing editor of the *Chronicle,* she was primed to direct and control the print media coverage of her family.

"Margaret," I said in a loud voice for J-Edgar's benefit.

"I'm not deaf," she replied, eyeing me. Did she suspect a wire? The moment passed and I recalled what Bootsie said about a murder-suicide pact, with Margaret claiming they had ways of making the scenario plausible. Of course they did. Alena and I wouldn't protest. We'd be deader than dirt.

Margaret wrinkled her hawk-like nose. "Still stinks in here." Then she pointed to Alena. "How are you doing little sister?" Alena remained silent, terror in her eyes.

Margaret must have helped Bootsie tie her up. Where was the FBI then?

"Toilet's still plugged," the old man said, stating the obvious.

"Doesn't matter, we'll be out of here soon enough." She turned her attention to me, holding aloft a notebook. Red and spiral-bound. Mike's, without a doubt. "We want only one thing from you," she said, "your husband's whereabouts, and this piece of crap doesn't tell us anything."

I fixed my eyes on the red cover. Margaret, or more likely Bootsie, must have seen it poking out of the dresser drawer. She waved it under my nose. "Recognize this?"

"Never seen it in my life," I lied.

"Bullshit, Bella," she said, slapping me smartly across both cheeks with it like a Nazi general in a bad movie.

I ducked, rubbing my face, which burned more from humiliation than pain.

"Papa Bootsie found it after you were in his house, bitch."

Hmm. Not difficult to figure out there was an intruder with the dog inside, toilet paper all over, and the notebook disturbed. How did they know it was me?

"Your finger prints were all over da place," Bootsie said, confirming my worst fear.

"Law enforcement's not the only ones who can lift prints," Margaret added. Again she waved the notebook. "This little darlin' has contact information for the U.S. Marshal's Office, among other things. A regular how-to book for entering witness protection. My younger, more beautiful, more famous, more *everything*, half-sister," she gestured toward the bound woman, "thought she'd follow *your* husband and our *other* former brother-in-law, Steve, aka the late Joe Milosch, into the program. Wrong!"

Margaret pulled her lighter from her pants pocket. With obvious delight she flicked it and positioned the flame under the pages. The edges curled and smoldered for a moment then burst into flame. "Tell us where your husband is." She thrust the mess so close to my face that my bangs singed.

I leapt back, waving my arms to ward off imminent asphyxiation. "No idea."

Still holding the pages, she advanced until I was backed up against the wall. Noxious fumes filled my throat. The smell of my own singed hair filled my nostrils. I threw my hands up to protect my face.

"We know you've heard from him."

"I haven't. He said it would be dangerous if I knew anything." Lame words, but true.

"Ouch, ouch!" Hot melting plastic reached her fingers. She dropped whole mess on the rug and danced around in pain, accidentally stepping in front of Bootsie and the gun.

"Get outta da way." He shoved her aside and, using foot and cane, stomped out the flames, leaving only wisps of smoke and the acrid smell of burnt carpet.

Margaret's tough-girl persona melted like ice cream on a hot sidewalk. She licked her burnt fingers, tears caused by more than the burn flowing beneath her glasses. I saw that Bootsie was special to her, she was the daughter of his first family, and he'd shoved her roughly to one side when she interfered with the gun. Even now he showed no concern for her pain.

But Margaret was hard as a shoe-leather cookie and she recovered quickly. "Here's the deal, Bella. You tell us where your husband is and you get to live." She gave Alena a look of fake pity. "If we like your answer, we may even spare my little *step*-sister."

Bootsie swung the gun at Alena, who begged me with her eyes, making my skin crawl with guilt. My own life had been in danger before, but never had someone else's fate depended on me. "You can't do that. Please, please. I'll do anything." I fell to my knees, retching from the odor of smoldering carpet.

"Bella, you know what you have to do," Margaret said, her voice quiet, almost kind. Why the change? From the corner of my eye, I saw her uninjured hand extend toward me. "Here, let me help you up."

Without thinking, I grabbed it.

Sucker. She twisted my hand viciously, sending me sprawling onto the carpet. I landed on my boobs, J-Edgar digging into my chest. The falsies may have protected it, but they didn't lessen the pain. I shifted position, gathering my wits, spitting out carpet fibers, mulling my options.

Okay, so she'd just shown me who was top dog. Now what was I to do? *Try focusing, Bella.*

"Alright already, I get it." I lifted my head.

"We know he's in New Zealand," Bootsie prompted. "Probably hiding in a big city, da safest place."

I struggled to my feet with as much dignity as I could muster. Maybe I could fake them out. I struggled to think of some New Zealand cities.

"Um, Auckland?" I said.

"Bull crap!" Margaret said. "I saw you hesitate." She held up a finger. "One more chance, Bella."

Only one? A shiver shot up my spine. I stalled for time. "So I was wrong about Auckland." I raised my hand as though about to impart profound thoughts. "Actually, he's in Perth."

Oops, that's in Australia.

I failed and now I'm going to die, I thought, pressing my lips together to stem the flow of tears.

A long beat of silence.

"Good girl," Bootsie said, exchanging a nod with Margaret. They'd mistaken my fear of imminent death for acquiescence. And if they didn't know Perth was in Australia, I wasn't about to tell them.

"I need to take a piss." Bootsie turned to Margaret and handed her the gun. "Try not to plug her while I'm in da can. I want dat pleasure." Turning his back, he shuffled toward the bathroom.

"Papa Bootsie," she called over her shoulder, "that one's backed up. Use the one next door."

"Dat's right." He reversed direction, shuffling toward the connecting door.

"Make it quick," she said.

So, she felt vulnerable without Bootsie. Maybe I wasn't a dead woman after all, at least not yet. Now was the time to grill her for J-Edgar's benefit. "Margaret, what's your part in all this?" I resisted the urge to sniff. Smoke from the carpet had declared war on my sinuses.

Her brow creased. "What do you mean?"

"Your family business."

"I don't know what you're talking about."

"Sure you do. Nothing's secret on the Internet. There's a whole bunch of stuff out there about the family business. Check it out. Knowledge is power, my dear."

"Not for you, *my love.*" She waved the gun at me. "You're fresh out."

Touché. "I wonder why you guys chose this place. You hiding out?"

She snorted. "Lupinos don't 'hide out.' Others hide from us. Like your husband, for instance."

"Okay, why is he hiding from you?" My nose dripped like a hose in need of a washer.

Her eyes narrowed to pinpricks. "Why all the questions?"

I fingered the loose button on my blouse. "I'm just curious and I'm probably a dead woman anyway."

She nodded and I swallowed hard.

"Think about it," she said. "What's going on in Los Lobos that's worth millions?"

I pretended to think. "The sewer?"

"Very good. More precisely, the wastewater treatment plant, the most expensive one for its size in U.S. history." Exactly what Bootsie said.

"Los Lobos is putting out construction bids soon. Do you really think you can muscle in on that?"

"I know we can," she said with a smirk. "No one has more experience in waste management than the Lupinos. Garbage pick-up, recycling, public works."

"But," I said, repeating what Bret said at the airport, "there are family-owned construction companies locally that have been in business for generations. You don't stand a chance against them."

She tapped the side of her forehead like I was the dimmest bulb in the chandelier. "Wrong, dummy. It's a matter of paying off the right people, plus, of course, a good public relations campaign. A few suggestions in the media that the major local construction company can't handle the job. A whiff of payoffs on their part, a juicy scandal involving drugs. Voila! Our family gets the contract." She stared at me with hard eyes. "Why do you care?"

I took my time with her question, trying to stay cool. "I'm just trying to understand what drove Mike away. I risked my life to come here, and I expected to see him today. Instead, I find you guys. You see, I get it." I glanced toward Alena, who gave me a piteous look. "There's no way you're going to let us go, no matter what I tell you."

Margaret didn't answer; I persisted. The FBI should have enough to nail them for racketeering, but an admission of murder would ice the cake. "I know Joe Milosch and Mike were partners in the Detroit PD, and I think they both went into witness protection because they testified against your family."

"Go on," she said in a too-quiet voice.

"I'm guessing you, or someone in your family, accidentally ran into Steve, now known as Joe, around town."

"Lucky guess. Bootsie noticed him first, followed him for days. In fact, he saw him and your husband at the state park."

That's why he decided to run us over.

"Did Milosch want in on your new project? Is that why he had to die?"

She shrugged. "Not exactly. At least not then, though he would have in time. He was my first husband. My only husband. Him showing up here at the same time we did, how's that for a rotten coincidence?"

Wow! Margaret and Milosch were married. She was Prom Girl in the yearbook photograph. At first I thought it was Alena, but she'd been in grade school in 1972.

"Bootsie murdered him because he could identify you guys?"

She shrugged one shoulder. "We don't do murder. We outsource it. In this case, *I* outsourced it," she said tapping her chest with pride.

Eureka! An admission of murder for hire. I thought of Detective Rick Ironwood and his Bootsie-provided Escalade He had been the tall man with the black Escalade searching the Wandering Nun grove for his missing knife, the murder weapon.

"Bootsie takes care of me. I'm his favorite, you know," she said, interrupting my thoughts.

"Speaking of Bootsie..." Keeping the gun trained on me, she backed up and banged on the door. "Papa, hurry up. If you're not out in one minute, I plug her."

"*A...a...achooo*!" The sneeze came from nowhere. My loose button took flight and scored a direct hit on Margaret's midsection.

47

"What the...?" She clutched her stomach as though she'd been shot. The gun hand wobbled dangerously. That wasn't the worst; J-Edgar had slipped. Without thinking, I hitched him up. *Oops.* My hand dropped to my side.

Not quick enough. Sparks shot from Margaret's eyes. "You're wearing a wire, you little bitch." In a flash she was all over me, burnt fingers forgotten, ripping open my blouse, digging inside my bra, grabbing the transmitter. She yanked J-Edgar out, adhesive and all, taking a good piece of skin with it, and hurled him against the connecting door. Alena whimpered.

"Papa, get out here! Now! She's wearing a wire! I told you we shoulda checked her." Her eyes were wild. Without warning, she grabbed me and wrenched my arm behind my back.

I screamed in agony.

"Shut up." A frog-march toward the connecting door. "Open it." Where *were* the FBI agents?

I opened the door and she shoved me into the next room.

"Papa," she hollered once we were inside. "I *need* you."

"I need *you*. I'm having a heart attack," Bootsie croaked. A thud like a body falling came from the bathroom.

"Oh, no!" She tightened her grip on my arm. "Hang on, Papa. I'll be right there." She steered me toward a straight chair, spun me around and shoved me into it. "Take off your blouse."

"What?"

"Take off your blouse. And quick. Or I swear I'll use this." The gun loomed large and I did as I was told.

"Margaret, call 911!"

"Can't do that, Papa. Take deep breaths, put your head between your legs. I'm coming." She advanced toward me, pupils dilated, blouse in one hand, gun in the other. She slipped behind me and tossed the gun out of reach on the bed. Using the blouse, she tied me to the chair, knotting the long sleeves together.

"Stay there!" she added unnecessarily. Abandoning the gun, she ran toward the bathroom. And like her father, disappeared inside.

The bathroom, it seemed, was a black hole.

Sounds like stampeding wild boar echoed through the wall. What now? *Get the hell out of here, that's what. Get help for Alena.*

I tugged against the restraint—and promptly landed on the floor. The satin fabric didn't hold the knot. I jumped to my feet, grabbed my blouse and bolted for the entrance, running headlong into Agent Vance.

"What took you so long?" I demanded.

48

Sunday, May 23rd, a few minutes later

Dazed, shaken and once again fully dressed, I found myself in the parking lot, flanked by Karen Grady and Matthew Vance. A tsunami of relief washed over me as we waited for other agents to accompany Bootsie and Margaret on the "perp walk" from room eleven to two waiting vehicles. In room twelve, another female agent had drawn the unenviable job of freeing Alena from duct-tape hell.

Thanks to communication technology, more agents, Sheriff's Department vehicles, an ambulance and the press converged upon the motel within minutes. Tires crunched on gravel, vehicle lights flashed and people spoke important sounding words into all manner of devices. A few balanced TV cameras on their shoulders including one from KFAX, Alena's station.

Conversation was nigh impossible. "Let's debrief in the motel office after the perps are gone," Karen shouted into my ear. She stood on tiptoe. "Look, here they come."

Mesmerized, I watched as the room door opened and Margaret, then Bootsie, emerged, accompanied by the agents who'd been planted in the bathroom. A hush came over the spectators, the silence broken only by waves hitting the beach. Margaret's gray hair hung in snakelike tendrils; Medusa without power. She struggled against her restraints, swearing like a sailor on steroids. When she saw me, she spat, barely missing my shoes. "You'll get yours," she vowed, eyes red with rage.

What did she mean by that? *That this might not be over?* My mind refused to accept that possibility.

Bootsie's head was bowed. If he saw me, he gave no sign. The pair were escorted into separate vehicles and whisked away, leaving behind only shadows and spewing gravel.

"What will happen to them?" I whispered to Matt.

"Nothing good. The prosecutor won't go for capital murder because Bootsie cut a deal with us, fingering Detective Rick Ironwood as the stabber of Joe Milosch." He sighed. "But a conviction can be a bitch without a murder weapon."

Funny a hired killer would choose a knife, when a gun was faster and more reliable. Ironwood must be particularly sadistic. I shivered anew.

"Still, Bootsie will spend the rest of his life in prison," Matt continued.

"Good. What about Margaret?"

Matt drew an index finger across his throat. "She hired it done."

"And Alena?"

"She'll most likely testify against them and enter witness protection." *Just like Mike.*

"So, if Rick Ironwood is the killer, do you think Detective Frank knew, or suspected? He came alone to the house and interviewed me a few days after the murder. Wanted to know whether I saw the license plate of the Escalade at the Mariposa Bay Inn, and if I'd noticed a knife at the murder scene."

"Interesting. No way to tell, but we'll follow up with him." He patted my arm. "Great job today. It was tough, I know."

"You don't know the half..." I started to say as a KFAX reporter advanced toward us, mic in hand. She witnessed the scene with Margaret and probably guessed I was part of the sting operation. Matt and Karen each grabbed an arm and propelled me toward the motel office.

* * * * *

Karen closed blinds while Matt arranged three chairs around a scratched desk behind the reception counter, then made a pot of coffee from a pot sitting on a table in the corner. I headed for the restroom, running water hot as I could stand it over my hands, and splashing it on my face. I couldn't warm up. The mirror confirmed what I already knew—I was a mess, hair spiky and wild, brown eyes haunted, deathly pale except for two crimson blots on my cheeks.

The siren song of caffeine lured me back to the office. I sat at one end of the desk, Matt at the other, Karen in the middle. Not knowing what else to do, I concentrated on the floor. A worn path on the gray linoleum spoke of many trips from desk to counter. This down-in-the-mouth motel had undoubtedly been the site of other dramatic events over the years—drug deals, infidelities, maybe even suicides.

I sat there, still shivering and gripping the warm mug while they arranged papers and made calls. Finally I took a sip, feeling it warm me all the way down.

"Some points we'd like to clarify with you," Matt said, tapping a pencil on the desk.

"Stop that!" I yelled.

He looked surprised, but dropped the pencil. Noticing me shivering, he asked, "You up for this?"

"I suppose," I said, trying to tamp down sudden anger, "and there are things I'd like to clarify with *you*. Like, why weren't backups in the next room like you promised?"

Matt opened his mouth to protest; Karen interrupted. "Matt, she's right. We owe her an explanation."

"Yes. You do," I said.

She turned to me. "I think it will help if we start at the beginning and tell you the whole story."

"I hope so. The support I needed wasn't there."

She cradled the mug in both hands, took a thoughtful sip and swallowed as though her throat hurt. "The operation started out as planned. Our backup agents arrived about a half hour before the Lupinos, got keys from the owners and sent them away with orders to keep mum, and put the No Vacancy sign in the office window. They also tacked a note for the Lupinos on the door of room twelve, ostensibly from the owners, saying they'd been called away by an emergency, and that the room was open."

"There was no note on the door when I got there," I said.

"The Lupinos removed it," Matt added.

Karen nodded. "We're getting ahead of ourselves. Agents secured both rooms as planned and plugged the toilet in room twelve with the poopy diaper."

"Who supplied the diaper?"

"My eighteen-month-old son, Colin Ray," Matthew answered, eyes alight. Good. He had a life other than the FBI.

"Whose idea was the plugged toilet?"

"It started with you, Bella," Karen said. "Remember telling us that Bootsie peed in the bushes at the airport? We figured he was incontinent, also that he had a germ fetish."

I nodded, recalling the pile of disposable wipes by his plate at that strange dinner with Margaret and Alena, also how he'd used several during the airport meeting.

"We figured he'd use the bathroom at least once during the operation," Matt added.

"A bit of a stretch," I said, "but I guess that makes sense. And his fear of germs would keep him from using the plugged toilet."

"Exactly," they said almost in unison.

Karen continued: "The backups planned to install cameras in both rooms, but there wasn't time. Margaret and Bootsie arrived early and dumped Alena in room twelve. They moved the Escalade to the back of the motel, walked through the breezeway and entered room eleven."

"Apparently they'd concluded, as we had, that the room was a good staging area," Matt added.

I pushed my mug aside. "Let me get this straight. You two parked up the road and backup agents relayed all this to you as it happened?"

Both nodded. "But, of course," Karen added, "we couldn't let you know things had changed because a transmitter is, by definition, one way. The plan had to be modified on the fly."

"Why didn't you call off the mission?"

"We discussed it, but we've been trying to nail the Lupinos for years and this was our best chance to date. We decided to go ahead because Bootsie's gun wasn't loaded."

That took a second to register. "Wait a minute! The gun wasn't loaded? Thanks for telling me."

"We considered it," Matt allowed, "but figured that, if you knew, you might take more risks than necessary."

"I see your point, though I don't agree with the logic. How did you manage to unload Bootsie's gun?"

Matt shook his head. "We have ways."

"Classified information," Karen said, effectively ending the gun discussion. "As we weighed options with the backups, you arrived. We had to go with what we had—Alena tied up in room twelve, Bootsie and Margaret waiting next door."

"Backups didn't enter room eleven until Margaret left it?"

"True," Matt said.

"When I saw Alena tied up, I knew something had gone terribly wrong. Before I could escape, Bootsie walked through the connecting door."

"That must have been tough," Karen said, covering my hand with her own, warm from the coffee mug. "But hey, you did a terrific job of getting them both to talk."

"Thanks. After the old man came in, I was worried, but not frantic. I figured the backups would enter room eleven any time. I wasn't scared until Margaret came through the door. Then I didn't know what to think." Saying this started me shivering again. Karen gave my hand another squeeze.

"We've been watching her for a while," Matt said. "As the oldest sibling, she's the presumptive heir to his organized crime empire, but now we hear there's another Lupino making moves in that direction."

"Matt, you're not supposed to talk about that," Karen chided.

I thought about what I heard at the airport. "Probably Bret, the son from his second marriage. A brother-sister rivalry between him and Margaret, perhaps."

"Could be," Matt said. "But back to today's events. After Margaret left room eleven, the two agents entered and hid in the tub behind the shower curtain."

"Cozy."

"Very," Karen said. "Long story short, he did as we hoped and went next door to use the bathroom. Our backups nabbed him and made a quick and quiet deal for him to finger Margaret for solicitation of murder and Rick Ironwood for the actual killing."

"How fatherly," I observed.

"Really," Karen said. "We then got him to fake the heart attack to draw her into our trap."

"All in a day's work," Matt added.

"Easy for you to say," I said, somewhat mollified now that I knew the full story, but still angry at the ineptitude. I could have been killed in that room.

Karen looked up from her notes. "You'll notify us immediately if you hear from your husband?"

"Absolutely," I said a bit too emphatically.

Of course there were points to clarify, notes to take, calls to be made. Mike's witness protection handbook was apparently a total loss. Still, forensics experts would try to salvage something from the ashes. I would need to make another, more formal, statement. The federal prosecutor's office and the Bureau would decide later how to handle my testimony.

I watched Karen and Matt, itching to go home and wondering when I'd be allowed to leave.I remembered Margaret's warning. "You'll get yours."

Alarm pounded in my temples. Even in jail the Lupinos could contact the rest of the family. Bret, and there must be others, uncles, cousins. "Will I be safe now that this is all over?" I asked.

Dead silence, then Karen said, "We'll make sure you're not identified."

"Can you get out of town for a while?" Matt asked.

Funny he should ask. Going to Detroit might seem foolhardy with the remnants of the Lupino family still there. But I sensed that, in this one thing, Bootsie was right. Hiding in plain sight was the smartest thing to do.

* * * * *

Sunday, May 23rd, noon

I drove home feeling, not jubilant and glad to be alive as I expected, but sullied and vaguely depressed. Today would prove to be one of those "before" and "after" times where things are never the same going forward. For the foreseeable future, I would be looking over my shoulder, as Mike must have done for years.

Would I complain about the FBI's bungling to their higher-ups? Probably not. That would embroil me in a controversy I wasn't up to after all that had happened.

I vented my frustration on the accelerator. Highway Patrol be dammed. I couldn't wait to get home to Sam and my real life.

* * * * *

For the next three days, I called in sick, turned the ringer off the house phone and let the cell accumulate messages. Parked in front of the TV or logged onto the Internet all day and almost all night, I immersed myself in stories that said essentially: "KFAX news director and *Chronicle* managing editor part of crime family. Detroit Mafia don and daughter arrested in FBI Los Lobos sewer sting operation!"

The story was the sole focus of the media world for days. So far the FBI had kept their promise and referred to me only as an unnamed participant. Apparently there'd been no leaks, no anonymous tips. For that I was grateful.

49

Wednesday, May 26th, after dinner

One of the things I love about life is how it often surprises you. I sat at my desk, Mom's address book open before me, penning notes to her friends.

For her closest pals, I enclosed a copy of the obituary I wrote in her honor, the hardest one I'd ever done. She was my mom after all. At least I felt easier in my mind. After our final evening together, I laid to rest the childish notion that my parents preferred Bea. I finally grew up the night she died. Too bad Mom didn't get a chance to know the new and improved me.

The phone rang and I jumped. "Hello?"

Silence. Telemarketer? Political pitch? Crank call?

"Hello," I repeated, cranky now.

"Bella?"

More silence. Shocked. Beyond shocked. Catatonic. "Mike?... *Mike!*" I shot from the chair, turned to Emily's portrait, shot her a thumbs up. "Is it really you? Where are you?" Tears ran down my face, dripped onto the phone.

"That's not important."

"Damn your eyes. It *is* important. Where are you" The phone was sopping wet from my tears.

"Okay, okay, I'm in New Zealand."

"Where in New Zealand? It sounds like you're in the next room." Neal Grale was right!

"Funny little place on the South Island called Te Anau." More silence, and he continued: "I...I'm so very sorry for what I had to do to you."

Sudden rage burned through me like a bonfire. "You lied to me for all the years of our marriage and now you think it's as easy as making an apology over the phone?"

"No, of course not. I read about Bootsie and Margaret online. Thank God they're behind bars."

"You lied to me about Joe Milosch, Mike. You said he was a bad cop, when in reality, as Steve Pizniak, he testified against the Mob, just as you did."

"I know, I know," he allowed. "I didn't want to, but that was the Marshal's Office cover story, and I wasn't supposed to deviate from it."

"Not even to me?"

"Especially not to you. Are you okay?"

"Of course I'm not okay, you've been gone for a month, and...and my mom died." A fresh wave of tears on my part.

"Oh, Bella, I'm sorry. Helen was a great old gal. Was it sudden?"

"Kinda. They were going to take her off chemo and call in Hospice. I think she willed her own death so as not to be any trouble to me."

"Oh God…that's tough."

"When are you coming home?"

"Not for a while. I have to go to Detroit first."

"Detroit? Why? Are you crazy? It's not safe. The place is crawling with leftover Lupinos and you're going there?" *You're going there yourself, Bella.*

"They're not all bad."

You should know. Your dead wife was one.

"Ethan, for instance," he said. "I'm glad he's been in touch with you. He's a great kid."

"That's true, Mike. How long have you known he was alive?"

"Not all that long. He called the night after we found Milosch's body."

So that call, the one that sent him out into the night as I talked with Emily, had been from Ethan. "Doesn't that seem a strange coincidence to you?"

"Like he's mixed up with the rest of the family? No way. He's a good kid. You can't imagine what I felt like when I heard his voice. It's a miracle no one can ever take away from me. And…" his voice broke, "and it almost made this worth while."

Almost being the operative word. He was right, of course, and I was thrilled for him. Perhaps the knowledge that Ethan was alive would soften some of Mike's hard edges. And now I had a stepson. Imagine that.

Mike interrupted my reverie. "I also contacted Jayne Earnhardt, his step-grandma."

"Ethan mentioned her," I said carefully. "She got him away from the Mafia influence."

"Right. She keeps tabs on the entire family from her place in Vegas."

"Why Las Vegas?"

"What better place? She has a business there, and the money and power to protect her own, and Ethan's, interests. According to her, Ethan wanted to find me for a long time and when he turned twenty-one, she made it happen."

This Jayne Earnhardt must be a powerful woman in her own right. "Change of subject, Mike. Why on earth do you have to go to Detroit? It seems like that's the number one place you should stay away from."

Silence, then, "Here's the deal…"

With Mike, there was always a deal.

"To completely clear my name I need to retrieve some papers from an old safety deposit box there."

One I didn't know about, of course. "Really? What kind of papers?" I said in an icy tone.

"Best you not know too much, Bella. Not yet," he finished, implying that sooner or later I would know everything. "I have to do this to clear my name."

"No, Mike, you don't." Silence as I pondered what I was about to say. "I have to go there anyway to settle Mom's estate. I'll be there at least a month. I'll get the papers and send them to you. Now where's the key? I already have your power of attorney."

"Um, Jayne has the key. I was going to stop in Vegas and pick it up."

Huh? "What the hell? What's that woman doing with your key?"

"It's complicated, Bella, but having her keep the key seemed like the best idea at the time."

"And is it still a good idea?" I screamed into the phone. "Are you saying I have to go to Las Vegas and pick it up?"

"Not at all. I'll call and see if she can meet you in Detroit with the key. I'll get right back to you."

*****

After the second phone call from Mike confirming that this Jayne person would meet me in Detroit with the key, I set the phone down thinking, "Can this really be happening?" And more important, was it a good idea? I had no clue, but I'd come this far. There was risk, of course, but compared to what I'd been through lately, it didn't seem like a big deal. Besides, I was curious about this woman who was so important to both Mike and his son, and who supposedly had so much power in Las Vegas. What was her business, I wondered?

I remembered my promise to contact the FBI if I heard from Mike. In fact, could they know already, having wiretapped my phone? No, that would be illegal. Which begged the question about me contacting them. No way would I give them a chance to screw this up for us. Only if Mike could completely clear his name in his own way would there be a future for us.

50

Thursday, May 27th, early morning

As I headed for the front door, the phone rang. Thinking it was Mike again, I grabbed the instrument. "Hello?"

"Bella, it's Marge from the Sheriff's Office."

"Oh hi, Marge, what can I do for you?" I wondered why she was calling me. "Is Detective Scully okay in Ireland?"

"He's just fine. Be back in a couple of weeks. Before he left, he said to call you when we got preliminary results on those bones found in your yard."

"Oh, really? So you got some. That didn't take as long as I expected."

"Well, we don't have the finals yet, they have to be sent away for further testing. But the preliminaries indicate the bones are that of a non-Caucasian, and more than a hundred years old. Detective Scully thought you'd want to know."

Hmm. "Not Caucasian, a hundred-plus years old. Thank you, Marge." I set the phone down, thinking. Old man Divina was a white man. Neal's great-great grandfather was not. Emily had a lover who died in 1893.

Another coincidence? I didn't think so. I put the thought aside temporarily. There was something more pressing I needed to address.

* * * * *

I crept through the *Chronicle's* reception area, dreading the case I needed to make with the acting managing editor, whoever that was. So intent was I on procrastination that I failed to notice the heady aroma until I passed Margaret's former office. I stopped, turned and peered through the open door.

Amy Goodheart rose from her chair and advanced toward me in all her bouffant, copper-haired, spangled T-shirt, four-inch heeled glory. She'd been fired after a reporter was murdered on a story assignment gone wrong, and now she was back.

I pulled her into a hug as though we had no past differences, then stepped aside. Something different. At last my nose told me what my brain couldn't. "You've changed your perfume."

"My Sin," she said with a lewd wink. "Like it?"

"Apropos," was the best I could manage. "What are you doing here?" I asked unnecessarily.

She rolled her eyes. "The former managing editor part of the *Mafia* for Chrissake? I'm trying to keep the shit pile this office has become from raining down on the heads of the Chicago suits."

"In other words what you've always done."

"Exactly." She reached out and again enveloped me in essence of My Sin. "Boy, am I glad to see you."

Oh dear. "Amy, I can't stay."

"What do you mean, you can't stay. I need you, Bella." She waved a hand at the staff going about their business, trying not to glance at us standing in the doorway. "You're the only straight-shooter here."

"Um, I need an extended leave."

"*What?* Tell me you're kidding," she said, managing to be wide-eyed and slack jawed at the same time. "Why?"

"How much time do you have, Amy?"

"For you? As much as it takes." She turned toward her desk and motioned over her shoulder. "Come tell Mama."

I planned to tell her everything, but seated opposite her, I changed my mind. Based on our past history, I didn't trust her. What a scoop it would be for the paper to reveal that their own obituary editor was part of a sting operation that involved the Mafia. Plus, the same obituary editor's husband had testified against said Mafia years ago, then entered, and quickly left, witness protection.

Instead, I told her about settling Mom's affairs, and concocted a story of how Mike and I had problems (if she only knew), how I'd heard he'd gone back east, how I planned to follow him there and try for a reconciliation.

"He should come to you," she said, nostrils flaring in righteous anger.

"I know, I know, but I have to start somewhere. Trust me Amy, I'm not one of those stand-by-your-man wives. I just have to find out if there's anything left of our relationship. If not, I'll walk away."

She peered at me over her rhinestone specs, nodding like she understood. (How could she?) "You're sure?"

"Absolutely."

"I'll see what I can do about the leave."

51

Thursday, June 3rd, late evening

Amy, bless her, came through in spades. How she managed to secure for me an open-ended leave I didn't know, and what's more, I didn't care. Thus began a round of frenzied leave-taking activities: booking airfare, e-mailing Mike, notifying neighbors and acquaintances, deciding what to take—and what to leave behind.

The last included Sam. Just looking at him sitting beside my study chair made my heart ache with love—and guilt for leaving him behind. "Sam," I said, "You're too big and smelly and hairy to ride in coach with me. And let's face it, the baggage compartment is not a good place for an old dog like you." *I know Bella, you've always done your best for me.* "Don't worry, my friend," I said, stroking his soft ears. "I'll think of something. I promise you." He sighed like he understood.

I'd put this decision off far too long. A kennel was not an option; he'd die of loneliness. Maybe Amy would move in and care for him. Maybe not, I didn't know where Amy stood when it came to dogs. I turned to face Emily's portrait on the wall. "Please Emily," I begged, "help me think of something for Sam while I'm gone."

Just then, the phone rang. What now? I worried about picking it up, but there was no need to. Neal Grale was on the line—with a request. Miracle of miracles, he'd heard I was leaving and wanted to rent my house while he looked for another job on the Central Coast. Dog included, of course. I gave Sam a thumbs-up and I swear he smiled.

I started to tell Neal what I suspected about his great-great grandfather and Emily, then decided to wait until I came back. It might be too overwhelming for him right now, and I was far from certain of my facts.

52

Friday, June 4th, midday

I couldn't leave without seeing Fifi Falcone and checking on Annie Milosch, who I hadn't heard from since that day at Casa de Maria. I still had her key.

As for Fifi, she had a new project. Under the family's new ownership and with her guidance, the old Mariposa Inn was now undergoing a complete renovation. I pulled the Subaru into a spot in the newly blackened parking lot, noting fresh paint on the buildings, Tuscan yellow with black trim. Very chic, very Mediterranean, a color scheme to complement the dark green shrubbery now being replanted by a bevy of gardeners.

I approached a worker on his knees constructing a brick planter. "Could you please direct me to Mrs. Falcone's office?"

He squinted up at me, using a trowel to shade his eyes. "Try the restaurant."

Fifi stood inside huddled over a blueprint with two men in hard hats. The immense room had been stripped of everything except the antique oak bar, its brass bar rail, and its signature painting of the Wandering Nun now propped against a wall.

She strode toward me, waving a greeting. "Hey you, how are things going?"

"Fine," I said, the platitude we use when we don't want to tell the whole story. "I have to go back east for a while—"

She frowned. "Business?"

"Um, sort of. My mom passed away. I need to settle her affairs."

"I'm so sorry." She laid a freckled hand on my arm.

Tears came, unbidden. Again. "Thanks. She had a good life."

"I'm sure she did, with you as a daughter."

We smiled at each other, neither of us mentioning Alena's sudden departure from KFAX in the wake of Margaret and Bootsie's arrest. When the moment because awkward, Fifi gave a discreet glance over her shoulder at the workers studying the blueprint.

"Fifi, I won't take up your time. I just wondered if you'd heard from Annie."

She laughed. "More than that. She's my new personal assistant."

Wow, that was quick. My heart soared. "That's wonderful, just wonderful. I'm sure you can use her." With her disability, this new job would be so much easier on her than being a server.

I handed her the key to Annie's house. "Will you see that she gets this? It's for her house."

She smiled. "Of course, though she's now living with me."

"Great."

"I have twenty-four hour security."

"Even better." I gazed around. "You'll need a cook or two at this new restaurant," I observed, a thought noodling in my mind.

She nodded. "We're planning a five star establishment. I've already lured an executive chef away from a competitor, but I need a sous chef and others as well. My executive chef wants staff that is relatively inexperienced, so they can be trained to follow his method. Know anyone?"

"Funny you should ask," I said reaching for my cell phone. "My nephew and his girlfriend just graduated from the Culinary Institute."

53

Saturday June 5th, early morning

I lay there, aware that my mind—as minds sometimes will—had chosen to begin this day in alternate realities: the conscious world and the dreaming one. The conscious part realized there was much to do, miles to go, hours to pass before I slept again. The dreaming world was not impressed with my schedule.

* * * * *

I stand on the crest of a hill at Escarpa el Dorado, pausing in my hike to stare at the scene before me. A lone woman perches on the cliff ahead, long skirt blowing in the wind. A parrot wearing a Joseph's Coat of colors sits on her shoulder. Surf pounds away at the rocks below, angry and insistent. The air is perfumed with salt spray and something else, a whiff of sage.

The woman appears to be studying something (or someone) on the rocks. She hears me, turns her face slightly and I see that it is Emily Divina. The parrot fidgets nervously. She turns back to the ocean, raises her arms like Moses with the Tablet and begins a high, keening wail. She leans forward, so much so that I fear that she will fall.

But she is not the one falling.

The dream shape-shifts, in the way of dreams, and I realize it is I who am falling, not swiftly, but slowly, lazily, a feather floating on a summer breeze.

I drift a bit more, and hover above Emily Divina who now stands on our mill property. She stares at a large hole gouged in the lawn. It holds a simple pine coffin. The parrot on her shoulder has morphed into a white dove. She picks up a handful of dirt and throws it on top of the coffin.

She stands there a moment longer, then, without warning, reaches up, grabs the dove, twists its neck and flings it atop the coffin. She turns and walks back up to the mill, holding her long skirt to keep it from trailing in the dust. Her eyes are on the widow's walk from which she will soon jump.

* * * * *

I sat up, gasping and sweaty. As my pulse slowed, I relived the sequence of recent events—Mike finding the bones in our yard,

Neal Grale searching for his great-great grandfather, discovering his name in the ship's log, seeing his photo among the crew of the Hesperia as they prepared for their final voyage. Marge's call from the sheriff's office with the news that the bones were that of a non-Caucasian.

At last understanding the dream's genesis, I pieced together what Emily had been trying to tell me. Somehow she was able to reclaim the body of her lover, Kawana, and bury him in the yard. She then returned to the mill, climbed the steps to the widow's walk and jumped to her own death.

She twisted the neck of the white dove, the symbol of peace, Emily's way of telling me that she had found no peace in death. Perhaps with Kawana's great-great grandson in the house, Emily would finally attain that peace.

54

Saturday June 5th, midmorning

I had just set my luggage in the front hall when I heard tires crunching on gravel. Peeking out the side window, I saw Neal Grale unloading a box from the back of his Volvo. Again I gave thanks that that the librarian had provided an answer to my prayer about Sam.

As I opened the door, the dog hovered by my side, sensing that whatever was happening did not bode well for him. I stroked his head."It's okay, Sam, Neal will take good care of you, and I'll be back before you know it." *I don't want you to go, Bella.*

Neal called a greeting in passing as he hefted the box down the hall to the spare bedroom.

"Neal, I have something to tell you," I said, as he returned to where I stood.

"What's that?" he said, a curious glint in his green eyes.

"It's complicated."

"I have time if you do."

A quick glance at my watch. "I have a few extra minutes. Here's the deal. Several weeks ago Mike found some old bones buried in the yard. The sheriff's office had a preliminary study done on them. They're over a hundred years old, and they're of a non-Caucasian. Could be a Chumash, but somehow..."

Silence while he pondered what I said. "You think?" he said, getting it quickly.

"Well, the evidence is hearsay, but some things you have to take on faith."

He nodded, murmuring, "I couldn't agree more. Go on."

"Emily Divina, the original mill owner's wife, committed suicide on New Year's Eve, a few days after the shipwreck. She had a lover according to our late local historian and I think it was Kawana. Emily's been doing her best to reveal all this in a series of dreams. Somehow she recovered his body and buried it in the yard."

"Wow," he said inadequately, "Wow." Then, "May I sit down for a moment?"

"Of course, this is your home while I'm gone. When I come back, I'll see if I can get the bones returned, they were found on our property after all. We'll have a little candle ceremony, like Hospice does for the recently departed, and bury the bones in my prayer garden. Emily also has let me know she found no peace in death, and I'm hoping that having you here, plus the reburying ceremony, will bring her that peace. Are you okay with all that?"

Eyes shining, he rose and gripped my hand. "Okay? It's more than I dared hope. More reason than ever to hang around the Central Coast." He let go of my hand and raised both of his to the heavens. "Wow. Wait until I tell Mum."

I picked up my carry-on and handbag, again glancing at my watch.

"Can I offer you a lift to the airport?" he asked, and eying my luggage by the door.

"Thanks," I said, "I called a cab. It'll be here soon."

He whistled softly. "That'll be expensive."

"I know, but it's better this way."

"If you say so." Neal scratched Sam's ears. The dog looked to me for permission to allow this familiarity.

"It's okay, Sam." Now that the time was here, my heart was breaking at the idea of leaving him with a relative stranger.

"We'll be just fine," Neal said, sensing my thoughts. He looked at Sam. "Hey, buddy, let's you and me take a walk down to the bay." He turned to me. "That way he won't see you leave."

"Good idea. Let me get the leash."

I watched the two of them walk companionably down the driveway, Sam nosing Neal's pocket for dog treats. He looked back only once.

Epilog

Saturday June 5th, noon
In the security line at the Tolosa Airport for the commuter flight to LA, I found myself behind Mom's doctor of all people. Doctor Lebovitz glanced over his shoulder as though sensing my presence. "Where are you off to?" I asked.

"New York." He pushed up his glasses. "Medical convention. You?"

"Detroit to settle my mother's estate."

"Of course. Best of luck with that. Again, my condolences." He headed for the gate.

I was the last to board the tiny jet for the twenty-eight minute flight to LAX. Heading for my assigned seat in the back of the plane, I passed the good doctor on the aisle. He patted the empty seat next to him. "Looks like no one's going to claim this. Want to join me?"

I paused, then said, "Thanks, but I've got some serious thinking to do on this flight. Lots going on."

"I understand." He shrugged. "See you around."

Unlikely, but you never know.

* * * * *

I drifted over Arizona, Mom's ashes, a ham and havarti sandwich and a chocolate chip cookie in my carry-on. I forked over five dollars for a popular beer and settled back to endure the flight. At least I had something good to eat and wouldn't have to rely on the airline's choice of a rock-hard, cold bagel. I sipped my beer, disappointed at the insipid taste.

I opened this morning's *Chronicle* and studied the lead story. Wow! An unusually low tide had uncovered a knife that law enforcement thought was the murder weapon. What about finger prints after being in the water that long, I wondered?

More to come, of course. I wondered if the Wandering Nun had anything to do with this latest bit of serendipity.

Nah, that was silly.

I put the paper aside, thoughts turning to Mike, my heart suddenly heavy with the task ahead. When it was over, would we be able to reconnect after all that had happened? The burden of earning my trust was squarely on his shoulders. Of course he'd been in terrible danger, but he'd hidden the truth of his past life for all of our marriage. There was a price to be paid for that. With a little luck and a lot of hard work I hoped we'd be able to take up our life together, not as it was before, but as it was now with everything in the open.

The plane swung north and I contemplated my newfound respect for the power that coincidence—and the happenstance of being in the right (or wrong) place at certain times—plays in our lives.

Extraordinary events, all related, had changed our lives: The Lupinos, Joe Milosch, Mike and me, finding ourselves on the Central Coast at the same time. Seeing Mike and Alena together in the Cafe Noir, and later, Alena using information from the notebook to call the witness protection program. Coming upon Detective Rick Ironwood looking for the murder weapon in the grove of the Wandering Nun. And of course, following Bootsie to the airport and eavesdropping on the meeting where they planned my demise. I shivered to think what my fate would have been I not glanced over and seen him at the traffic light, then followed him to the airport.

Why did these events play out as they did, and were they driven by a higher power? And what about dreams? I also had new regard for their ability to awaken our subconscious to ideas struggling to emerge from our brains. As for mystical figures like Emily and the Wandering Nun, they had the power to live on in our hearts and minds and, in so doing, influence our decisions for better or worse.

My mind jumped to the promise I'd made to Mom to find Bea's murderer. I never believed hers was a random killing. Where would I even begin?

As with the call from Mike, Ethan's sudden appearance in our lives, and finding Kawana's bones, I hoped luck, coincidence and something greater would all play their part.

I resolved to keep my options open. I'd entrusted my pearls to Rosa's sister, and Sam to Neal, precious treasures awaiting my return.

The End